SUCH QUIET
GIRLS

NOELLE W. IHLI

Published 2025 by Dynamite Books

www.noellewihli.com

Any references to real events, real people, or real places are used fictitiously. Names, characters, and places are products of the author's imagination.

ISBN: 979-8-9878455-9-2

First printing, April 2025

Cover design by Damonza

PRAISE FOR *SUCH QUIET GIRLS*

"This terrifying and breathtaking thriller has everything we've come to love from Noelle Ihli's novels: true-crime-inspired stories and brave, unforgettable heroines. *Such Quiet Girls* is an absolute masterclass in suspense. I loved every single page."
-Faith Gardner, author of *Like It Never Was*

"*Such Quiet Girls* ratchets up the tension so high that it will make you sweat. This is a taut, gripping, all-consuming thriller that will have your heart in your throat with every page in the best possible way. The characters are incredibly well-written and complex. Ihli keeps readers walking a tightrope of emotion while brilliantly exploring very human, visceral conflicts within the hearts and minds of each character. Stunning. Don't miss this one."
-Lisa Regan, *USA Today* and *Wall Street Journal* bestselling author of the Detective Josie Quinn series

"Say hello to your next nerve-shredding, pulse-pounding up-all-night obsession! *Such Quiet Girls* delivers all of the tension, the twists, and the emotional connection you know and love from Noelle W. Ihli's thrillers."
-Daniel, Avid Readers Club

"An emotional ride through layers of suspense and nerve-wracking tension. I was on the edge of my seat the entire time."
-Steph Nelson, author of *The Final Scene*

"Both beautiful and brutal, *Such Quiet Girls* is a testament to the enduring power of the human spirit in the face of unimaginable circumstances. It left me gasping for air along with the characters."
-Caleb Stephens, author of *If You Lie*

Content advisory: This book includes scenes involving child endangerment, kidnapping of children, and domestic abuse.

For Luke and Max.
I'd swim into the breakers for you.

1

JESSA

Soph had another nightmare ...

That was all the text message said.

The after-school daycare bus shuddered as I killed the ignition, letting out a sigh that pretty well captured how I felt: tired as hell, going nowhere.

I unbuckled my seatbelt, leaned over the aisle, and shoved my phone with more force than necessary into the cubby labeled MS. JESSA.

I knew exactly what those ellipses meant without my sister having to spell it out for me.

My daughter, Sophie, had another nightmare ... about *me*.

I blew out a breath and sat back in the driver's seat, eying the double doors of Northridge Elementary's main building. I was early for my first pickup, but just barely.

I shifted my gaze back to the four-by-four row of cubbies that had been retrofitted just inside the bus door, above the handrail. Each cubby had a little plexiglass door, labeled with a name that belonged to each of the students who would burst through the shiny blue doors of the elementary school as soon as the final bell rang.

A sign fixed to the top of the cubbies read, THIS BUS IS A NO-PHONE ZONE! in cutesy, curly purple font that arced above the Bright Beginnings Childcare Center logo: a bunch of children staring lovingly, and directly, into the sun.

"Very bright," I mumbled to myself, same as I had every day this week. The childcare center was supposed to be getting a new fleet of buses soon. Maybe they'd spring for a new logo, too.

When I'd started this job—only a week ago—I'd learned that the childcare center had a strict no-phones policy for its bus drivers *and* students. That was fine with me, but I'd been surprised by how many of the kids already had phones in elementary school. One of the first-graders. Both of the third-graders. All but one of the fourth-graders.

I side-eyed the cubbies and thought about reaching into the box labeled MS. JESSA to type back a quick reply to Lisa's text. I knew I should ask my sister how Soph was doing. Find out whether I could come by the house after my route. I could offer to bring pizza for dinner. Or just ask for details about my nine-year-old daughter's nightmare.

That was the right thing to do. The good-mom thing to do. I'd really sucked at that lately, though.

I appreciated the fact that Sophie had been able to live with Lisa instead of being funneled into the foster-care system. But it still hurt that I'd had to ask about my daughter's well-being like a game of telephone for the past three years.

So I left the phone in its cubby and shifted in the driver's seat, craning my neck to gaze in the rearview mirror so I could scrutinize my own face in the harsh, late-afternoon light. Then I forced a smile that didn't reach my eyes and wiped the beads of sweat collecting beneath the thick mop of bangs I'd cut just before moving back to Idaho three months ago.

The bangs had been yet another mistake.

I'd been trying for fresher, younger. I got neither. Combined with the "luxe mahogany" box dye I'd splurged on, the bangs made it look like I was wearing a too-bright red wig on top of my former blonde, middle-parted hair. Before the hair hack job, I'd looked every day of my thirty-eight years. Now I came across as at least mid-forties.

Maybe my hair color was the reason Soph was having nightmares, I thought hopefully. Because I looked so different from before.

I pushed the thought away before I could really latch onto it.

I knew better. That wasn't the reason.

CLANG.

"Shit." I startled at the noise—more gong than bell—that announced the end of the school day. I put the key back into the ignition, ignoring the fast thud of my heart and the fizz of anxiety that bubbled in my stomach.

"Just get through it," I whispered under my breath, trying to keep the smile on my face as I pulled the lever to open the bus doors. After a week on the job, I felt more confident that I could handle the lumbering bus and the kids. I'd nearly had a panic attack on the first day, so even a little confidence was progress.

"Hi, Ms. Jessa," a solemn little boy with auburn hair and freckles mumbled as he boarded the bus, his eyes landing on my name tag near the speedometer.

"Hi, Ked," I replied as soon as I saw which cubby he was sliding his phone into. *Ked.* Who named their kid after a shoe?

Two little girls with messy black curls dashed down the sidewalk and boarded the bus after Ked. Sage, a lanky sixth grader, and her first-grade sister—and shadow—Bonnie.

I pasted a smile onto my face then glanced away. With her long hair, freckles, and thick pink glasses, Bonnie could've been a rewound version of my Sophie. Sage, with her bob haircut and pierced ears, looked like the fast-forwarded version.

"Hi Sage, hi Bonnie," I chirped, proud of myself for remembering their names—and sounding perky.

"Just sit with Rose," Sage told her sister, ignoring me completely. Then she plopped down in the front seat and set her backpack in the space beside her.

"But I want to sit *here,*" Bonnie whined.

Sage sighed like she was being asked to donate a kidney. "I'm *saving it.*"

"Ms. Jessa said we can't save seats. That's against the rules," Bonnie said triumphantly.

Behind her on the bus steps, a little girl with a blonde bowl cut nodded vigorously. "Yeah, you *can't* save seats, Sage."

This was technically true, but I had no idea how I'd actually enforce that rule. My training hadn't covered that, and Sage had a defiant look on her face that told me she was about to argue. So I said, "Sage, put your phone in the cubby. Bonnie, why don't you just sit somewhere else today?"

Bonnie's brown eyes widened, and I knew that look. Unless something changed, she was going to start crying. "But ... I want to show her my clay person," she whispered. "We made them today in art."

I gave Sage a pleading look as she rolled her eyes and stood to slide her pink phone into the cubby with her name on it. *Come on, kid. I just want to drive the damn bus. And I don't even really want to do that.*

To my surprise, she relented.

"Fine," Sage muttered, rolling her eyes as Bonnie slid past her into the bench. "What's a clay person, anyway?"

When all of the phones in the cubbies were accounted for—minus the two students absent for the day—I checked the enormous sideview mirror and caught eyes with a random teacher standing at the curb near the bus with her line of students for parent pickup. I waved at her and smiled a little too enthusiastically. She tilted her head and waved but didn't smile back.

Shit. I shoved the bus into gear and peeled away from the curb more quickly than I'd intended. The stream of irrational thoughts kept coming like they had every time anyone gave me a funny look.

She knows you lied on your job application.

She knows what you did.

I eased my foot off the gas and pushed the panic down. *Calm down. She's a teacher, not a psychic.*

When I risked another look in the mirror, the teacher was busy helping a little boy find something in his backpack.

I forced in a deep breath and brought my eyes back to the road.

"Ms. Jessa drives like Mom," Bonnie murmured to Sage, interrupting her own speech about clay people.

"That's just how moms drive," Sage shot back matter-of-factly.

I coughed to hide the laugh that escaped my mouth and checked my speed as I turned onto the rural highway.

The Bright Beginnings after-school childcare and rec center was a good thirty-minute drive from Northridge, including a detour for my second pickup at Southridge Elementary. It was a hot afternoon, but with the air-conditioning blasting and the kids safely loaded, the ride was now almost enjoyable. I'd grown up in Idaho, but had been out of state long enough to forget how much I always loved its scrubby beauty. A lot of people complained about the "ugly" brown foothills dotted with sagebrush breaking up the cheatgrass in muted green clumps, but the landscape felt both dearly familiar and beautifully wild to me.

I sat up a little straighter in the lumpy driver's seat and glanced back at the kids, letting myself feel normal for half a second. Pretending I was just another mom with a part-time job. Pretending that my Sophie was one of the kids behind me, instead of taking a different bus home to my sister.

With each zip of the wheels on the road, I practiced the mantra I'd read online in a blog post entitled "9 Therapy Hacks You Can Try at Home."

I accept my past, understand my present, and look forward to my future.

I gave up repeating the phrase before I even reached the exit where the highway crossed the river and moved back toward Boise.

I didn't accept any of it.

Shaking my head, I shifted my attention back to the road as I made the turn off the interstate and onto the empty county highway. My second and final pickup for aftercare was at Southridge Elementary for just one student, and it meant a ten-minute detour into the boonies. I'd gotten lost the first time I drove this route, winding through the switchbacks of rural roads in a panic, too paranoid to grab my phone out of its cubby for directions. One of the kids would definitely narc.

Supposedly, Bright Beginnings was getting a new fleet of buses—complete with dashboard navigation—soon. But for now, drivers were expected to know their routes.

In the distance an orange sign sat in the middle of the road. Was there road construction? It was too far away to tell.

I gritted my teeth in frustration and nudged the bus a little faster.

At this point, my entire life was a detour. The last thing I needed was another one.

2

SAGE

But Mom said—"

I shot Bonnie the dirtiest look I knew and hunched sideways to look out the bus window, even though doing that always made me carsick.

I already knew what Mom said. Same thing she'd been saying since Bonnie was born. *"Come on, Sage. Let Bonnie tag along."* Or, *"Take care of your sister, Sage."* Or, *"Friends come and go, but sisters are for life."*

Joke was on Mom. I didn't have any friends, because ever since Grandpa's Alzheimer's had gotten worse and he couldn't watch us after school, I'd spent every day on the dumb daycare bus with Bonnie and the babies. That's what Mia said on the playground when she wanted to get me really mad. *"Bonnie and the babies."* Like it was some kind of cringey cover band you'd hear on "Kidz Bop."

I was the oldest kid on the Bright Beginnings bus by two full years. And with my long, skinny legs that came out of nowhere last summer and made me the tallest student in the sixth grade, I looked even older. Grandpa was always saying that sixth grade wasn't meant to be part of elementary school. It hadn't been like that when he was a kid. And I agreed with him. The only reason I wouldn't be going to Bright Beginnings daycare with Bonnie after school next year was because I'd finally turn twelve and go to junior high. And even Bright Beginnings knew that twelve was *way* too old for daycare.

Today was swim day, which was usually my favorite. The blue twisty slide in the indoor pool went so fast it made your swimsuit ride up your butt if you weren't careful. And best of all, the older kids—who could actually swim—got sorted out from the younger kids who had to stay in the shallow pool. But last week, Bonnie had gotten pushed down the slide by a third-grader named Kenan. So this week, Mom wanted me to stay in the baby pool with her. No slide.

I kept looking out the window and ignored the rest of what Bonnie was saying, watching the foothills turn into long rows of cherry trees as we got off the highway. There wasn't really fruit on the branches anymore. The cherry festival in Emmett happened last month, and the harvest was over. But if you pressed your nose to the crack of the bus window, you could smell the last of the ripe fruit that had missed getting picked.

"Ms. Jessa is nicer than Mr. Edward," Bonnie said abruptly, leaning so close to me that the faint, sweet smell of cherries was replaced by the peanut butter and raspberry jam sandwich she'd eaten for lunch. I could still see a little smear of red on her chin.

"How do you know if she's nice or not?" I mumbled, hunching my shoulder and pressing my nose back against the window crack. "She only said you could sit by me because you were blocking the aisle." Bonnie was right, though. Anybody was better than Mr. Edward. He'd made Rose cry at the end of last year, when she dropped the apple from her lunch box and it rolled all the way up the aisle of the bus and lodged under the brake. He'd pulled over to the side of the road and started yelling and swearing like she'd done it on purpose. *"Oh for shit's sake,"* he kept saying while he tried to pick up the pieces of the smashed apple, flinging them into the aisle. *"Fucking hell."*

I'd never heard a grownup use that combination of swears, not even Grandpa, and any other day I might have laughed, but he just sounded so mad and mean. All the kids on the bus had gone quiet, and that pretty much never happened. That was the last time anybody saw Mr. Edward, so that definitely meant he'd been fired.

Bonnie shifted on the bench beside me. To my surprise, she didn't say anything else about Mr. Edward or Ms. Jessa. Instead, she asked, "Why are we stopping?"

I sat up and leaned forward so I could see out the windshield of the bus. We were still headed toward the cherry orchards—and Southridge Elementary so we could pick up Amber Jensen. But we were slowing down. We never slowed down here.

Then I saw the big orange DETOUR sign with an arrow pointing down a dirt lane that looked like it led right through the orchard.

A little ways past the sign, parked on the shoulder of the road, was a big white van. SPEEDY SHUTTLE, it said on the side.

Something about that van seemed strange to me. I almost made a joke to Bonnie about the shuttle not being a very speedy shuttle right now, but I was still mad at her, so I kept my mouth shut.

Ms. Jessa slowed the bus to a crawl, inching closer to the detour sign, as if maybe she wanted to go around it instead of turning right, like the sign said we were supposed to. She was leaning forward, looking down the road past the sign at the parked Speedy Shuttle.

Then she sighed like the sign had been put there just to annoy her, flipped on the turn signal, and turned the bus onto the narrow dirt road into the orchard.

"Um, this isn't the right way," Ked announced, his voice monotone but loud from a few seats behind me. Ked was always piping up about something. "Ms. Jessa, this isn't the right way," he repeated.

Ms. Jessa flicked her eyes up to the big rearview mirror so she could see him without turning around in the driver's seat. "It's all right. There's just a little road construction ... or something."

Out of the corner of my eye, I saw Bonnie lean down, reach into her backpack, and pull her "clay person" out again. It was an ugly, brown squiggle that looked more like a turd than a person to me, but I knew Bonnie would cry if I said that. "Did you see how I gave him hair, Sage?" she chirped, pointing out the tiny squiggles of clay on top.

"Yeah, I saw," I said, keeping my eyes out the window as the bus finished its turn, trying to catch a glimpse of orange barrels or cones in the distance past the Speedy Shuttle. The road looked exactly the same as yesterday, though.

I shrugged and faced forward again.

It wasn't like I was in a hurry to get where we were going. I'd rather drive through the cherry orchard than babysit Bonnie in the rec center kiddie pool, anyway.

The wheels bumped down the narrow dirt road, and some of the kids laughed when we hit a deep pothole, bouncing us in our seats. I smiled, hoping the road would keep us in the orchard for a while. The smell of overripe cherries was all around us now, and it made me think of fall. I closed my eyes as that smell drifted through all the windows while the bus brushed against the leafy tree branches on both sides of the road.

Ms. Jessa hit the brakes as the road dipped then curved sharply enough that Bonnie tumbled against me, pushing my nose into the window. Someone—maybe Rose again—said "Whee!"

"Ouch!" I opened my eyes, pulled back from the window, and rubbed my nose. "Stay on your side, Bonnie!"

"What the hell?" Ms. Jessa said, loud enough for everyone to hear as the bus slowed, then stopped. I felt Bonnie stiffen next to me, no doubt remembering the apple incident with Mr. Edward.

Little gasps prickled across the bus.

At first, I thought it was because of Ms. Jessa's swearing.

Then I sat up tall and looked out the windshield. There was another vehicle completely blocking the narrow dirt road in front of us. Its hazards were on, flashing red.

Bonnie leaned into the aisle so she could see it, too. "What are they doing, Miss Jessa?" she asked.

Ms. Jessa looked over her shoulder at us and scrunched up her forehead so her eyebrows disappeared beneath her bright red bangs. She ignored Bonnie.

"It's fine. They'll move out of the way in just a sec," I told Bonnie. The words felt sticky in my throat, though. Something about the ugly gray van with its brake lights glowing orange felt wrong.

Ms. Jessa just seemed annoyed. She made a frustrated noise in the back of her throat, and her hand hovered above the horn. "Let's go," she muttered and hit the horn.

When nothing happened, she reached for the gear shift to whip the bus into reverse and drive backward, like I'd seen Mom do when we zipped right past a good parking spot at the Merc in Sunset Springs.

Then another sound rose above the low hum of kid voices.

It was coming from behind the bus. The rumble of an engine.

I shifted on the bench, swiveling my head to see out the back window of the emergency exit. A few of the other kids did, too.

The window back there was grimy, but it showed enough.

A big white van was coming up the road.

It came to a stop right behind the Bright Beginnings bus, angled a little bit so that I could just barely see the writing on its side.

Speedy Shuttle.

"Are you serious?" Ms. Jessa tilted her head into a beam of sunlight that made a strip of her hair glow neon red.

Bang, bang, bang.

Bonnie and I jumped as three hard raps came at the bus door. One of the kids shrieked in surprise.

Ms. Jessa made a noise like she'd choked on a sip of water as she stared out the glass of the bus door.

I smashed my face against the window to see for myself.

On the other side of the aisle, Ked sucked in his breath, then he said, "There's a man. He has a gun."

3

SHEENA

The door to my home office creaked open a few inches, then swung wide.

I gritted my teeth but managed to tip my frown into a smile when I scanned past the photo of Bonnie and Sage hanging by the door, reminding me to be a better human.

Dad stood in the doorway, peering at me with an expression of mild surprise. Like he hadn't fully expected to find me at my desk—even though we'd repeated this routine four times today.

He held up his arm, tapped the watch on his wrist, and grinned. "You sure I can afford this, Sheen? My pension is pretty damn good, but not this good."

I saved the spreadsheet on my computer and swiveled my chair to face him. *Give him the answer he's looking for, even if it's not quite true.*

"It looks really good on you, Dad," I told him honestly, trying to keep my voice light and neutral like his doctor had coached me. The watch was a perfect Rolex knockoff, and it did look good on him. "You worked hard your whole life. You deserve it."

That was true, too. He'd spent thirty years as a lieutenant for the Idaho State Police.

He leaned against the doorframe to my office, still holding up his wrist, where the timepiece glinted. The wry smile on his face—the same one he wore every time he asked me this question—told me he loved the expensive-looking watch to pieces. I felt guilty every time I thought about activating the GPS function. He'd know then that it wasn't actually a Rolex. But with the way things were going lately, he'd forget just as quickly.

Dad had been diagnosed with Alzheimer's two years ago, five years after he'd retired from the force. The diagnosis itself was devastating and terrifying, but also wonderful in its own way. For the first few years, I'd felt like I was finally getting to know him. Not just as my dad, but as a person. While I was growing up, he'd always been tight-lipped about his cases and the things he'd seen as a police officer. But when he moved in with us, all that changed. He opened up and told stories I'd never heard before. *"Before I forget, Sheen,"* he'd always say.

The person he was back then felt like a distant memory, though. When he first came to live with us shortly after the diagnosis, his forgetfulness felt like an inconvenience—nothing too scary.

For the first year and a half, we'd settled into a new normal that I pretended would last forever. Dad had been a huge help with Bonnie and Sage, picking the girls up after school and even pitching in to make meals—something he'd never done when I was growing up. Bonnie and Sage loved having Grandpa all to themselves while I worked.

But over the last few months, Dad's stories had gotten repetitive to the point that my stomach clenched when he'd cocked his head and say, "Sheen, I ever tell you about the time ..." I didn't mind hearing the stories again, but it was a constant reminder that the disease seemed to be progressing faster every day.

I'd stopped feeling comfortable letting him near the stove, let alone sit in the driver's seat of the car. I couldn't leave the girls alone with him anymore, which meant I'd had to send them back to after-school care—something that upset Sage so much I still felt sick when I thought about the angry tears running down her face when I first told her.

"Dad, I just need to finish up this budget before we pick up the girls from aftercare, okay? Will you check on Karen for me?"

"Where is that old gal hiding anyway?" His eyes lit up when I mentioned the cranky cat, and he turned to head back down the hall without argument. I breathed a sigh of relief and then went back to the spreadsheet, knowing I had twenty minutes at best before he made his way back to the doorway.

The realities of caring for an elderly parent—an elderly parent with Alzheimer's—had taken me by surprise in the same way caring for newborns did. I knew it would be hard. I knew it would be a lot of work. But there was no way to prepare for the gut punch of spending your day with someone who was completely dependent on you to keep them safe, fed, and cared for. And unlike newborns, it wouldn't be getting any easier with time. The disease was progressing so fast now that, even with Dad's medications, it was like I could feel his memories slipping through the cracks of a crumbling dam.

A few weeks ago, I'd put him on a waitlist for Cherished Hearts, an expensive full-time memory care facility in the foothills, twenty minutes from our house. His pension would just barely cover it. But they'd warned me not to expect an opening for at least a couple of months. Until then, I just had to hang on.

I glanced at the clock on my computer and shook my head. I'd been planning to make a real dinner tonight. Meatballs and mashed potatoes. But I hadn't even started thawing the ground beef, and pickup at Bright Beginnings was less than an hour away. I'd screeched into the parking lot at four-fifty-nine twice this week to find Bonnie and Sage the last kids there, waiting for me. I was earning bad-mom demerits left and right these days.

"Dammit," I muttered, trying to focus on my spreadsheet again. I had to finalize the file tonight. The state budget surplus was all anybody could talk about, and I was the bottleneck to finalizing the budget proposal. Cue the bad employee demerits, too.

I pawed through a stack of papers in the filing cabinet beside my desk until I found what I was looking for, the bid for new buses that would serve ten school districts in the Treasure Valley, including Northridge where Sage and Bonnie went to school. The supplier had changed the proposal twice over the last two months, which wouldn't have been such a pain in the ass except for the fact that the bid wasn't just "buses." It covered every single aspect of commissioning the new fleet of vehicles—including tires, engines, mirrors, new safety cameras, paint, and about eighty other line items.

I didn't mind numbers. Math had always been my favorite subject. But even my eyes were starting to cross when I looked at all the rows that had to be updated, checked, and rechecked. And the fleet of buses was just one of the budget allocations. The spreadsheet itself was already up to fifty tabs. Thankfully, I had only a few more fields to verify today.

I heard a happy, chirping meow from down the hall, and then, "There you are, Sunshine. How's about a few pats for my favorite girl?" I bit my cheek and focused on the numbers in front of me. The cat's name was Karen. Sunshine was the name of the cat we owned when I was Sage's age.

After fifteen more minutes of frantic scanning and tapping, my desk was a mess—but the surplus budget proposal was finally, *finally* ready for review with the committee. And, if I put the ground beef package in some cold water while I took Dad with me to pick up the girls from daycare, I could still get a real dinner on the table tonight.

"Dad? We need to pick the girls up now," I called from the kitchen, rummaging through the freezer drawer until my fingers connected with a lumpy baggie of meat. I plopped the frozen hunk into the sink and started the water. "Dad?"

When I didn't hear him respond, I shut off the faucet and walked around the couch in the living room and found Dad lying back against the pillows with Karen kneading the front of his sweater as his chest rose and fell. His gnarled hand—gold watch glinting at the wrist—rested on her orange-and-black fur. His eyes were closed, and his mouth had gone slack.

My heart twisted. The bags under his eyes, stark against the pale skin and freckles of his Irish complexion, underscored the fact that he'd had a hard time sleeping for the past few months. It was normal, Doctor Kitteridge said. Like that made it better.

For half a second, I thought about just leaving him here sleeping with the cat. Karen peered at me with slitted green eyes, purring softly, as if warning me not to remove her human pillow. Bright Beginnings *was* only fifteen minutes away.

I shook my head. Fifteen minutes was all it took for him to walk through the neighbor's back gate and start harvesting the potatoes in their garden. Or for him to try to change the oil on the lawn mower—the electric lawnmower. Or ride a bike to the gas station down the road and start a fight with the cashier because of the outrageous prices. Or empty every drawer in the house, trying to find his gun and badge.

All of those things had happened.

"Dad," I said again, picking up the cat instead of jostling his arm. He startled so easily now, especially when asleep. Last week, he'd nearly clocked Bonnie when she bounced into the living room to show him a drawing and woke him from a nap.

Dad blinked and sat up, smiling at me through tired eyes. "Sorry, Sheen. Must've lost track of time." He winked and nodded at the watch. "Useless hunk of metal."

I swallowed hard and smiled brightly. Sometimes, the moments he sounded just like my old dad hurt as much as the times he slipped away.

"Is Jacob getting home soon?" he asked as he got to his feet and rubbed the short, white stubble on his chin.

"He's working late," I lied, grabbing his hand to help him up from the couch. "It's just you, me, and the girls tonight."

It was the right answer. Reminding him that Jacob and I had gotten divorced back when Bonnie was a baby would only lead to a long conversation and upset him.

"That's okay. I didn't much like the way he was talking to you last night," he said, his mouth twisting into a frown. He put his hands on his hips and pulled back on my arm. "If you wanna know the honest truth."

I sighed, stopped trying to lead him toward the garage, and pulled him into a wordless hug.

We were going to be late for pickup for sure now.

4

JESSA

A gun. He's holding a gun.

There were maybe five feet between us, from where I sat in the driver's seat and where he stood on the dirt road, leaning up against the bus door.

If he fired that gun, he wouldn't miss. The only thing separating us right now was a flimsy piece of cracked glass that rattled when the bus drove on the highway.

Keeping the gun pointed at my head, he motioned for me to open the door.

The black box in my brain fired instructions at me before I could fully process what was happening.

Do what he wants.

Don't give him a reason to use that weapon.

Don't fuck this up.

It couldn't have been much more than a second that I hesitated with my hand on the pull-bar for the door that opened the bus door.

It felt like an eternity, though.

Behind me, the kids were making worried noises, asking what was happening. I knew I should say something to them, maybe tell them that everything would be all right. But my jaw was locked shut.

My eyes flicked to the cubbies full of cell phones—then back to the man standing at the bus door. He wiggled the gun in his hand menacingly, one finger on the trigger.

I stared at his face, still frozen.

He wore tight pantyhose pulled over his head that smashed up his nose and mouth. Like the after pictures at a theme-park roller coaster, taken right as the cars start screaming down the tracks in the wind. The opaque fabric concealed the lines of his nostrils and mouth. The afternoon sun made it sparkle a little where it was tied in a knot at the top of his head. I could just barely see the place where his eyes were supposed to be. They looked like two dark holes.

Still keeping the gun pointed at my head, he spread his feet shoulder-width in a wide stance. "Open the door, now, bitch," he barked.

Where the hell had he come from? I hadn't seen anyone get out of the van blocking the road ahead of us.

My eyes flicked to the white shuttle that had pulled up behind us as my brain spun through my options. There wasn't room on either side of the narrow orchard road to get around the gray van. Not without slamming directly into one of the trees on the sides of the road. And the shuttle was so close behind us I'd run into it the second I yanked the bus into reverse.

The smell of rotting cherries coming through the air conditioner suddenly made me want to vomit.

This is your fault.

My stomach recoiled at the thought, but it was true. I'd almost blown right past the strange DETOUR sign in the middle of the road. I couldn't see any road construction ahead. There was plenty of room for me to skirt around it and keep driving on our normal route.

Instead, I'd obediently put on my turn signal and driven left into the orchard on this bumpy, sketchy-ass dirt road. Because what if a cop saw me disobeying a traffic sign and pulled me over? What if he ran my driver's license, figured out who I was—and realized that I should absolutely not have a job driving children?

If that happened, he could report me to my parole officer back in Utah—and Bright Beginnings. Then they'd all know that I'd lied on my job application. And I'd never get Sophie back.

So I'd ignored the twinge in my gut telling me to blow past the sign. And this was where it'd landed us.

"Ms. Jessa?" one of the kids whimpered.

"Sage?" Bonnie whispered to her sister, a few feet behind me.

There was a chorus of squeaks from the cheap upholstery of the bus benches as more kids knelt on them, trying to see what was going on.

Somebody, I couldn't tell who, let out a nervous giggle. Like maybe this was a joke.

Bang, bang, bang.

The man hit the glass with the gun again, harder than before, gesturing for me to let him in. "Don't you dare touch the phones." He gestured toward the cubbies, visible to both of us along the handrail and bus entry steps.

Time seemed to slow as the thoughts whirled faster in my head.

I could reach the little cubby labeled MS. JESSA if I leaned across the aisle and snaked out my arm.

But he could shoot me long before I managed to open the cubby door and unlock my phone screen.

I turned my head ever so slightly so I could glance at the kids in my peripheral vision. I had to do *something*. But what could I do that wouldn't make this worse?

"Open it *now*," the man with the gun boomed.

My hand was sweaty on the pull-bar. I gripped it harder, wondering whether it might be too slippery to open at this point.

One of the kids started to cry, and the sound tore at my heart in a way that made it physically difficult to stop myself from turning around to murmur some kind of reassurance.

They didn't deserve this.

You do, though, I thought distantly. *Karma.*

The voice in my head sounded just like my brother-in-law Gregg. If the masked man outside the bus put a bullet between my eyes right now, he would call it good riddance. But would Sophie?

I could already imagine the sound the gun would make, a deafening crack like close-up thunder. Only this time, I'd be the one to fold in on myself, tumble backward and go still.

The man was losing his patience, but I couldn't move.

He abruptly shifted the gun away from my head and trained it toward the bus windows. "You gonna make me start shooting kids?"

That finally unfroze me. I started to pull the lever that would open the door.

The man holding the gun cocked his head, like he was pleased, and moved his weapon so it was pointed at my head again.

"Don't let them on the bus, Ms. Jessa!" a tiny, scared voice called from behind me, just as a car door slammed from behind.

"I have to," I told her firmly, hating the way the words sounded coming out of my mouth.

Keeping my hand on the lever, I flicked my eyes to the rearview mirror to see that the driver of the white van was out of his vehicle now, moving toward us, fast.

For half a second I let myself hope he was just a random driver who had followed the detour sign. Maybe he could help us. Face off with the man with the smashed-up nose and black eye sockets.

"NOW," the first man screamed.

You don't have a choice. He's going to kill us all.

My fingers felt cold and clumsy. I couldn't see this guy's eyes, but I didn't need to. I already knew from the sound of his voice that there was a deadly gleam in them. Men like him were as predictable as they were erratic.

I finally forced my hand to grip the slick lever and pull.

Do what he wants.

My head swam and my stomach sloshed. The children shrieked behind me in earnest now.

Nobody was coming to help us. And I was opening the door. That was the only choice keeping us alive right now.

Now a second eyeless, smash-faced man standing next to the first.

The door mechanism was already engaged. I didn't have to pull anymore.

My hand dropped limp to my side as the door swung fully open.

5

The pantyhose was making my face sweat like balls.

So were the latex gloves on my hands. And I was still breathing hard from shoving the heavy detour sign back into the shuttle by myself.

None of that mattered, though.

What mattered was, we'd actually done it. The hardest part was over. The lady bus driver with the fried red hair drove exactly the way we wanted and then opened up the door when Andy knocked.

Everything was going to plan, but my stomach was still spinning like a washing machine. All I could think was, *We're actually doing this. Holy shit, we are actually doing this.*

I'd imagined what today would be like in my head a thousand times. It was more real than I'd prepared myself for. The sounds the kids made were still echoing in my head. But it'd all be worth it in the end.

"I want my mom," one of the little kids was saying in a shaky voice, and that made me feel bad. But kids were like rubber bands, I reminded myself. They bounced back.

And these rubber bands were worth a shit-ton of money.

Their parents probably weren't rich: Bright Beginnings after-care was state-subsidized, so you had to be at least a little bit poor to send your kid there. That didn't matter, though. It was all part of the plan.

I snapped to attention, focusing on making sure the next steps went smoothly.

Apply yourself, Ted, I thought in my mom's snappish, Marlboro-thick voice. The one she used every time I got fired from a shitty job or left a Hot Pocket in the toaster oven longer than she liked.

She'd probably pretend she was horrified if she could see me right now. Her forehead would turn into an accordion fan of deep lines, and she'd pucker her mouth like she'd just popped a lemon. But I was pretty sure she'd also be just a teeny tiny bit impressed by how much effort me and Andy had gone to pulling this thing off. And if there was anybody who'd taught me that the law was more of a suggestion than a rule—as long as you didn't get caught—it was good old Mom.

While Andy kept his gun trained on the bus driver—Ms. Jessa, from the cutesy Velcro name tag in purple font—I brushed past him and pulled the phones out of the cubbies. I could hear him breathing loudly over the kids' whimpers while I dropped each phone into a Walmart bag with a soft thud.

Even a couple of feet away, the combo smell of Andy's BO and the spearmint hair oil he loved made my eyes water. Andy was gross. And he could be sorta dumb. But unlike me, he handled his gun like it was an extension of his hand. People always mistook him for a friendly hipster with his chubby cheeks, lazy eyes, and frizzy, shoulder-length brown hair that he rarely washed. That was a mistake. Andy could be mean as fuck.

The little girl in the seat nearest to me, a tiny kid with short black curls, was crouching with her knees on the bus bench and staring up at me with a look that made me worry my pantyhose were the see-through kind after all. I knew they weren't. I'd read the word *opaque* to myself at least a dozen times on the L'eggs packaging that promised "no rips or runs."

When I tilted my head toward her, her eyes suddenly went big and she ducked down, cowering against the tall, skinny girl beside her. Her sister, I guessed, from how much they looked alike.

"Hey," I barked, but my voice came out high and weird. Nothing like I'd practiced. I cleared my throat and tried again, aiming for deep and gruff. "*Hey,* listen up." Then I plopped the last of the phones in the bag and said the line that me and Andy had memorized. "Stand up and put your hands on the seat in front of you. If you do what we say, and keep your mouths fucking shut, nobody gets hurt."

Every head on the bus turned toward me, but nobody made a move to stand up. The sweat running down the back of my neck itched in a way that made me want to tear the pantyhose off.

I gripped my gun tighter, afraid I'd drop it if my hands started shaking the way my legs were. My body burned with adrenaline and too much gas-station coffee.

"Do what he says, *now,*" Andy screamed so loud I nearly jumped. And the kids actually listened.

They fell all over themselves getting their butts out of the seats and their hands in the air, and the ones who were crying toned it down to snuffles.

While Andy kept his gun trained on the bus driver, I reached inside the kangaroo pocket of my hoodie and grabbed one of the long, black zip ties.

"Hold out your hands," I snapped at Ms. Jessa. Her choppy bangs looked like they'd been cut with kiddie scissors. Way shorter on the right side than they were on the left. She offered me her arms without hesitation, shaking like a leaf.

I zip tied each hand separately, then together, just like me and Andy practiced.

A little girl with blonde pigtails, standing up with her hands hovering above the bench in front of her, stared in disbelief while I pulled the ties tight.

I'd been worried the bus driver would try to pull some kind of hero shit. Dive for the phones in the cubbies, throw herself on top of me or Andy like a human shield. The kind of thing that'd get you on the "Local Legend" section of KTRB.

But she seemed so eager to let me tighten those ties around her wrist, even I was a little surprised.

My phone, then Andy's phone, made three little chimes. The second alarm. Time to get moving. The bus was due to arrive at Bright Beginnings soon. When it didn't, nobody would worry too much—at least, not right away. With traffic and a busload of kids, delays happened.

That meant we had about fifteen minutes before anybody got their panties in a twist.

We'd be long gone by then.

"Hey, what's your name, bitch?" Andy kicked at the bus driver's shoe. Apparently he hadn't bothered to read the swirly cursive font. Andy was an action man—not a details man. That was me.

"Jessa," the woman whispered. Her voice sounded younger than she looked. I'd been thinking late-forties from the bad hair, but I upgraded her to early thirties.

Andy nudged me with his foot, but I'd already pulled the little notepad out of my hoodie's kangaroo pouch. No technology, we'd decided when we first started planning. The things Big Brother could see were unreal.

"Jessa what?" Andy kicked her shoe again. I wanted to tell him he didn't need to do that. She was already doing exactly what we wanted. But I wasn't about to question him in front of everybody. He hated that.

She hesitated. "Jessa … Landon."

I wrote that down.

"Walk where I tell you to walk, *Jessa,*" Andy said, making her name sound like he was still calling her a bitch as he waved the gun toward the orchard. "There's nobody out here, so if you scream, I'm the only one who's gonna hear. Do it, and I shoot you in the face. Got it?"

For a second, I imagined him actually doing it—shooting her in the face. I pushed the gory image away as fast as it came, telling myself he'd stick to the plan. He wanted the money as much as I did.

Jessa nodded and stood up, cowering away from the gun. "That's right," Andy growled. "Down the steps. March, *Jessa.*"

As Andy followed her, he turned his head toward me and nodded.

It was my turn.

I glanced at the little girl with the short black curls sitting next to her sister and wished I hadn't. Tears cut through her eyelashes like a sad doll. The way she looked at me made me think of the summer I was ten and my dad paid me two dollars for every squirrel I shot off the fence with my archery set. The squirrels ruined the giant pumpkins we were growing in the vacant field behind the trailer park. The ones we sold at The Farmstead for ten bucks each, but not if they had holes gnawed through them.

I wasn't a great shot. One little guy, I'd pinned by the tail.

The way he'd looked at me when I got close enough to see his eyes was the same look the girl was giving me right now. Eyes wide and terrified, heart beating so fast you could see it pumping in its throat.

I felt so bad about that squirrel I hid in the shed and cried until my dad came looking for me and smacked me with the flat side of an old tennis shoe. When he left us a month later, I told myself that was why.

I looked away from the little girl with the black curls. Unlike the squirrel, she'd be fine. We weren't going to hurt the kids.

With Jessa out of the way, I used the butt of my gun to smash the ancient dash camera that had recorded everything. The clunky device wasn't connected to anything, just looped over itself every day until it ran out of battery. Bright Beginnings had needed new buses for a long time, and this was one reason.

One of the kids started hollering—and kept it up—even after the last of the shattered camera had fallen into the driver's seat.

I whipped around. "Quiet!"

She turned down the volume but didn't stop. A few of the other kids were still crying quietly. I remembered what Andy had told me yesterday when we talked through everything for the hundredth time. *You gotta shut down any issues quick. If they don't think we mean business, they're gonna make problems. Scare them right off the bat.*

"Fucking hell," I muttered. Then I drew in another breath and screamed, "Shut *UP!*" in my best imitation of Andy. I moved the gun back and forth across the aisle, making sure it passed over all ten kids' heads at least once. "Dammit, shut UP. If you don't, my friend will shoot Ms. Jessa."

That did it.

Nobody even sniffled.

I pulled another handful of zip ties out of the front of my hoodie and did a quick count. There were ten kids on the bus. It would take me thirty seconds to secure each of them. Then we could get back on the road.

Hurry up, Ted.

Apply yourself.

6

With their faces all smashed up, the men with the pantyhose over their heads looked like the thing from *Jeepers Creepers*. I'd snuck downstairs to watch it one night when Grandpa fell asleep while he was babysitting me and Bonnie.

Thinking of the man as that sack-headed monster scared me so much I wanted to hide under the bus bench and cry.

They'd made the ties on our wrists so tight, the skin was burning and my fingers were starting to go numb.

I refused to cry, though. Because Bonnie—who *was* crying— kept looking at me like she needed me to be calm for her.

I wasn't calm inside. Not even a little. There was a feeling in my stomach like I was falling down a flight of stairs. Sick and spinning. But I pushed all of that down deep for my sister.

I kept looking out the window at Ms. Jessa, the way Bonnie kept looking at me, but that only made me feel worse. Because Ms. Jessa just did what they told her to do, like the bad guys were the *real* grownups in charge now and she was one of us kids.

If Mom were here, she would've done *something*. I didn't know what, but I just knew she would have. Run them over with the bus, maybe. Broken off the gearshift and smashed them over the head. Something. *Anything.* Not duck her head like a kid, follow the first guy off the bus, and just let it happen.

The scared, sick feeling crackled in my stomach like Pop Rocks.

The second guy—the one who told us he'd shoot Ms. Jessa if we didn't stay quiet—finished tying up Mindy, the girl in the last seat.

Bonnie shrank against me and whimpered as he whipped around and stomped back down the aisle to the front of the bus.

There was something familiar about him, but maybe that was just because I kept imagining the squish-faced guy from *Jeepers Creepers.* For some reason, he felt less scary than the other man. Maybe it was the way his hand holding the gun shook a little.

"You two." He pointed at me and Bonnie, then down the bus steps. "Start moving."

I'm pretty sure I know him. The spark of recognition pinged in my brain again. It wasn't just that his face looked like that creature from the movie. It was his voice, too. There was something familiar about it, like I'd heard it a long time ago. But when I tried to find the memory, the spark went out.

Maybe I was imagining it. Even so, it made the snake of fear in my stomach coil tighter, until I couldn't breathe very well.

I moved toward the bus aisle so I could walk down the steps and into the orchard, even though I didn't want to.

Bonnie made a strange little sound as I shifted away from her, and the guy tilted his head to look at her but didn't say anything. Her face was bright red from crying, and her mouth was pursed in a tight line like it was full of bees she was trying to keep inside.

Snot and tears were rolling down her face, but she wasn't going to make a sound.

She wasn't going to let them shoot nice Ms. Jessa.

I stepped back toward her and stretched out my tied hands to grab hold of her pinky finger. Just a soft touch. "Come on, Bonnie," I whispered. "It'll be okay. Come with me."

More tears poured down her cheeks, soaking the front of her purple My Little Pony T-shirt, but her mouth relaxed a little and she followed me as I moved into the aisle.

The first guy, the one who'd taken Ms. Jessa away, was waiting for us the second we set foot on the dirt. His gun was just a few feet from my head. "That way." He used his free hand to point at the open door of the gray van, maybe ten yards away. "If you try anything, Ms. Jessa eats a bullet."

Bonnie made that noise again, and a spark of anger in my stomach flared to life. *You don't need to keep saying that,* I wanted to yell. *We're doing what you say.*

I kept silent though, and for some reason that made him laugh, even though we were doing exactly what he told us to do.

"Such nice, quiet girls."

I stared right at him and noticed that there was a wet ring around his mouth, like he'd been licking his lips. That part of the pantyhose had gone more see-through, showing little bits of white when he opened his mouth. His teeth.

Bonnie heaved out a breath behind me, but kept moving past the man. I didn't turn to look, but I could hear more of the kids following behind us.

Gravel crunched under our shoes. The sun hit my cheeks. The fresh smell of dirt and grass washed over me in the tree-thick orchard as we approached the gray van. "It's okay, Bonnie," I whispered again.

I surveyed the orchard without moving my head, hoping I'd see a house somewhere, another car driving down the dirt road, anything that might mean somebody could see us. Wouldn't someone else be following that same detour sign any minute?

NOELLE W. IHLI

I couldn't hear any other cars coming down the road, though. The only thing I could hear was the sound of kids lining up behind me and Bonnie, and the man with the wet ring around his mask telling them to hurry up and keep walking to the gray van. All I could see were rows and rows of trees. The dirt road was so narrow and choked with weeds, I was starting to wonder if it was really much of a road at all. There were hardly any tire tracks.

In July, the orchard probably buzzed with activity as workers picked cherries, but the season was over now.

My eyes moved to the gray van's back doors, wide open a few feet in front of me, like the entrance to a cave. Pitch dark and full of things that might jump out at you any second.

I wanted to turn around and look at the other kids, but all I could think about was the man behind us, herding the last kids off the bus, and the other man leading us toward the gray van. Somehow I knew that if I looked at the other kids' scared faces, I'd freeze up and stop walking, and then everybody else would stop, and we'd get in trouble. So I just kept on going, like the Pied Piper, with Bonnie and the other kids following behind.

Where was Ms. Jessa? Was she inside that dark van? How were me and Bonnie supposed to get up into it with our hands tied?

Every part of me wanted to run. But I could still feel that gun trained on the back of my head.

Heavy, fast footsteps came up behind us when Bonnie and I reached the bumper. I turned my head in time to see the man with the lighter brown pantyhose jog past me to stand beside the man with the darker pantyhose.

"When I lift you up, you scoot to the back of the van real quick. Got it?" he said in that weird, too-deep voice that sort of sounded like Batman.

I nodded, but I wanted to scream when I thought about him touching me.

42

"I don't wanna get in there, Sage," Bonnie whispered, echoing my own thoughts.

"It's just a van," I told her, trying to sound like I believed my own words.

It wasn't just a van, though.

It was like every bad thing I'd ever heard about getting in a car with strangers had suddenly appeared in front of me. But none of the things I'd been taught about getting away would work. I couldn't run. I couldn't say no. I couldn't find a grownup to help.

Take care of your sister. Mom's voice.

Sisters are for life.

For the first time, Mom's words rattling around in my brain felt important instead of annoying.

I swallowed hard and braced as the man reached for me with one arm, keeping his gun pointed at Bonnie with the other.

With one quick motion, the man scooped me up and set my rear end on the back ledge of the van. "Move," he hissed, pointing at the cave-like darkness.

And I moved, suddenly realizing that after Ms. Jessa, I was the closest thing to a grownup here. And I wasn't a grownup. Not even close. For the first time, being a too-tall sixth-grader didn't feel very big at all. Sure, I could take care of Bonnie by going with her into the baby pool so Kenan didn't push her down the slide again. Yeah, I could let her tag along when I went to the park. I could help her tie her shoes when one of them came undone, or pretend to admire her clay people the way Mom would.

But none of that could help us now.

7

By the time the kids were loaded in the van, I yanked open the driver's side door of the white airport shuttle and pulled the pantyhose off my face for a breather, I was sweating buckets.

I knew today was going to be intense. I knew Andy was going to get intense. But I told myself I'd practiced every line, every step, so many times that it would be like acting out a play. No real feeling of danger.

That wasn't the case.

I made myself take three big breaths, in and out, like that guy in the jail rehab group was always telling everybody to do.

Focus on your breath. It's that simple. You'll feel calmer.

I'd thought it was sort of bullshit at the time, but turned out that shithead was onto something.

My head cleared a bit, and my heartbeat started to slow down. A breeze carried through the open window, cooling the back of my sweaty neck.

For the first time, I was glad I was the one driving the airport shuttle that stank like Andy's cologne. It was finally quiet. Nobody crying, nobody making little snuffling sounds when I pulled the zip ties tight, nobody looking at me like I was some kind of demon.

Seeing the kids freak out had messed me up a lot more than I thought it would.

I ran my fingers through my damp hair and studied the rearview mirror. My face was red and blotchy like I'd just taken a lava-hot shower, but besides that I looked fine. My dark brown hair was short enough that it never got that messy, unlike Andy's. Maybe an angry porcupine, but that was different.

Ahead of me, the daycare bus's tail lights lit up.

I watched as Andy slowly maneuvered the Bright Beginnings bus right into the orchard, through dense rows of trees. The branches were so close, they scraped the sides of the bus like nails on a chalkboard, but he pushed the bus through anyway.

The sight of it made me laugh out loud. It looked like he was off-roading in the dumbest, slowest ride ever. The sides of the faded blue-and-white bus scratched against more tree limbs, some of them making a high-pitched squealing sound as they hit the metal.

He didn't get very far before a cluster of trees blocked him good enough that he would've had to run them down.

The brake lights went on. Wasn't worth the time to get any farther into the orchard, though. After the harvest was done, this road hardly got used at all. Even if somebody did come down this way, they'd have to know exactly what they were looking for.

I watched Andy open up the bus door, run down the steps, and dash past me through the orchard. He'd taken off his pantyhose too, although his long, poofy mouse-brown hair and ratty beard didn't look that much different than usual. Andy always looked like he'd just rolled out of bed. But the intense, focused look in his eyes gave him away. Andy was dialed in.

As he jumped into the driver's seat of the gray van, I shoved the key into the ignition and started up the airport shuttle.

Part one was done. We had everybody locked and loaded—literally.

A burst of relief and adrenaline zipped through me and I let out a nervous laugh.

Before I shifted into drive and followed Andy back toward the main road, I unlatched the glovebox and set my gun inside, then carefully pulled out the piece of paper I'd tucked in there earlier.

It had thirteen names typed on it. The bus driver's at the top, then a list of the twelve kids who rode this bus regularly, along with their ages.

Jessa Landon, 38
1. Ava Johnson, 7
2. Bonnie Halverson, 7
3. Crosby Neville, 7
4. Kasia Berger, 7
5. Mindy Gamel, 7
6. Charlotte Nelson, 8
7. Evelyn Marks, 8
8. Ked Bledsoe, 8
9. Norah Katz, 8
10. Rose Carlton, 9
11. Ben Whitlock, 9
12. Sage Halverson, 12

I cross-referenced the typed list with the barely legible written list I'd just made when we boarded the bus, then drew a Sharpie through the names Kasia Berger and Norah Katz, who were lucky enough to be sick today or something.

Minus the two who were missing, that was ten kids plus the bus driver. That would make the ransom around two-hundred thousand dollars per kid. I doubted anybody cared that much about the driver to pay her ransom. As far as I could tell, she was a nobody.

I scanned over the rest of the pre-typed ransom note, feeling some of the sick churn in my stomach give way to anticipation. The note was perfect. This was going to work like we'd planned.

Then I shoved the crumpled, handwritten list into my pants pocket so I could burn it later.

I couldn't see Andy and the gray van anymore, but that was fine. I had a quick stop to make before we met up again, anyway.

Back when we'd planned everything out, I'd complained about getting stuck with this task. The idea of going into the city right after what we'd done and showing my face—well, sort of—felt like the riskiest part of the whole plan. All Andy had to do was kill time, driving around with the kids for a while until they were good and mixed up about where we were taking them.

But now, I was honestly just glad that Andy was the one stuck with the kids for a little longer.

I was already dreading unloading them.

Just focus, Ted, I told myself again. *You've got this, buddy.*

8

SHEENA

Traffic was the worst I'd ever seen it, trying to get down State Street.

Just two more blocks until we reached Bright Beginnings, but the wall of vehicles hadn't moved in at least ten minutes. There had to be some kind of accident past the next light. I could hear the sirens, but I couldn't see anything beyond the thick hedge separating a Subway parking lot from a local church.

Minute by minute, all the optimism I'd felt earlier—about finishing the budget in time, making a really good dinner for Dad and the girls—popped like soap bubbles.

Dad's fingers twitched, tapping against his knee, like he was getting ready to jump out of the car at any moment. He'd never done that before, but the past few months had been full of firsts.

"God, this takes me back," he muttered, more to himself than to me.

I glanced over, confused and impatient for traffic to start moving. "To what?"

His brow furrowed, like he was sorting through the fragments of memories. "That pileup on the 405. I ever tell you about that one?"

"Nope, tell me." This time it was true. I hadn't heard that story. I eased my grip on the ancient Subaru's steering wheel and found my patience. Surely, a teacher monitoring the pickups at the rec center could see the gridlock, which meant that maybe I wasn't going to get side-eyed if I pulled in at 5:02. *Just relax,* I told myself. *Everything is fine.*

Dad leaned forward, gesturing with his hands in my peripheral vision. "An SUV flipped on its side in the middle of the freeway. We got the call right during rush hour, of course. Bumper to bumper, just like this. We had to maneuver the squad car through all that mess, sirens blaring. People barely moved. They never do."

I nodded along, only half-listening, watching the brake lights blink ahead as Dad picked up momentum in a story about the first time he'd seen paramedics use the "Jaws of Life" to wrench open a smashed vehicle at an accident scene.

I lost the thread of his story as I watched a woman a few cars ahead of us get out of her vehicle and rush toward the intersection.

I frowned and I craned my neck but still couldn't see the intersection or the daycare center. The accident up ahead must have been a bad one.

" ... don't get me wrong, Sheen. I felt for that poor lady trapped in the car, but that machine was something to behold. You should've seen it. The thing just tore through the metal like it was nothing. A couple of squeezes, and *bam,* we've got the door off, and she's in there, wide-eyed, breathing heavy, but not a scratch on her. Can you believe that?"

I flashed him a smile despite the anxiety dripping through my veins. "That's a lucky break."

"Luckiest I've ever seen," he said, shaking his head, his eyes distant but still twinkling. "You should've seen her face when we pulled her out. She just kept saying, 'Thank you, thank you,' over and over again. The paramedics checked her out, and she was fine.

Just shaken up. Those were the best calls, you know?" His voice faltered a little. "Ones where we got there in time. Did the right thing. Got to be real-life heroes, for just a minute."

"You helped a lot of people, Dad," I said softly, knowing his memories had turned to the calls that still haunted him. He shrugged and looked out the window. The irony of Alzheimer's was that it affected his short-term memory the most. The things he wanted to forget were the ones with the deepest hooks.

I drew in a steadying breath as the car in front of me crawled forward a few inches then hit the brakes for what felt like the hundredth time.

When I glanced down at my cell phone, ready to call Bright Beginnings to tell them I was definitely going to be late because of the traffic, I saw that I'd already missed a call from them.

Frowning, I turned the ringer off Silent mode.

Usually, the high-school-age staffers called only when I really took pickup down to the wire—five p.m. exactly. I still had a good six minutes.

Shit. Had one of the girls gotten hurt? Had Bonnie been pushed down the slide again? I gritted my teeth. If Sage sent her off into the kiddie pool by herself …

"It's just traffic, Sheen," Dad said for the eighth time and patted me on the shoulder. "No sense rushing. We'll get there when …"

He trailed off and looked out the window, and for a moment I envied the fog in his brain that had likely made him forget where we were going in the first place.

"Thanks, Dad," I said, trying to keep my voice light. Then I tapped on the missed call.

Instead of a receptionist, I got an annoying busy signal.

I drew in another breath, reminding myself that a new phone system was part of the budget for the local elementary schools and their aftercare satellites. The idea that anybody still used landlines, especially an institution that cared for half of Ada County's kids, felt extra ludicrous today.

Another siren wailed closer, and a chill worked its way down my neck. What if something bad had happened at the rec center?

I gripped the steering wheel tighter as I thought about school shootings and gas leaks and car accidents.

The light turned green for the dozenth time, and we inched forward. Just far enough that I could see the daycare entrance.

"Oh, Lord. Sheen, something's really going on up there." Dad craned his neck to see. "Didn't the girls go to that daycare once upon a time?"

I didn't answer him.

Instead, I slowly put the car into Park where it sat in the center of the road. My legs had turned into cold, limp noodles.

There wasn't an accident ahead.

The Bright Beginnings parking lot was filled with flashing red-and-blue lights.

Police cars. At least twenty.

The rest of the parking lot was filled with staff and parents. I couldn't breathe. This looked like the scene of every school shooting I'd seen covered on the news.

This couldn't be happening.

Without saying a word to Dad, I yanked open the car door and started running toward them.

My stomach seized like it had the time Sage slipped out of sight in IKEA, while I took too long staring at a display of drawer organizers. So much adrenaline and panic it felt like I was going to vomit or pass out.

Only this time, it was worse. This time, something bad, something awful, had really happened.

I darted around a car with its hazards on, stopped at the front of the intersection. Like me, that parent must have arrived for pickup and seen the chaos in the parking lot.

No, no, no, no.

The crosswalk showed a red STOP hand, but I ran across the road anyway.

There weren't any cars speeding past. Traffic was completely stalled.

Farther down the road in all directions, people were leaning out their windows. A few even laid on their horns. But in the gridlock at the intersection right beside the daycare, all eyes were fixed on the parking lot.

I charged into the crowd and angled toward a tall teenage girl wearing a teal polo shirt with the Bright Beginnings logo. Her name tag read SHELLY.

"What's going on?" I choked out, shoving my way forward, heart pounding out of my chest. "Where are my kids?"

Shelly glanced at me and held her arms out at her sides in a helpless gesture. "We're doing everything we can."

"Doing everything you can?" My heart clogged my throat. I wanted to throttle her. "What are you talking about? Where the hell are my kids?"

Another woman with messy platinum hair pushed past me, already in tears. "Tell us now!"

Shelly glanced between us, her eyes wide. "We're getting text alerts set up so we can—"

"So you can *what?*" I shrieked. "Just tell us what's happening!"

"The bus is missing."

The woman with the platinum hair recoiled like she'd been slapped. She was breathing so fast, her nostrils flared with each inhale.

I could barely get the words out when I gasped, "What does that *mean*? You can't just *lose* a whole bus."

The other woman was talking too, both of us at once. "What … why … can't you fucking track it? Doesn't the driver have a cell phone? Why the hell haven't you found them yet?"

You can't just lose a whole bus.

For just a moment, a bubble of hope burst through the sludge of panic in my gut that at least there wasn't an active shooter. At least nobody was dead.

The bus was missing. And my kids weren't here, which meant there was a possibility that nothing bad had even happened.

Thoughts spun through my head like desperate lifelines.

Maybe the parents and police in this parking lot are panicking for nothing.

Maybe the bus had a flat tire.

Maybe one of the kids threw up, and they had to stop.

Maybe—

"I'm really sorry," Shelly said, sounding near tears herself. "We've retraced the bus route twice now, but … there's nothing. The bus driver isn't answering her phone." She glanced behind her. A police officer was moving toward us through the parking lot. "The police are taking over. They want to talk to everybody. I'm just … I'm sorry." Her voice broke on the last word.

Without saying another word, the woman beside me let out a wordless howl and rushed away, in the direction of the police officer.

Shelly and I stared at each other.

It was painfully obvious that neither of us knew what to do.

Behind me, I realized someone was shouting.

A new warning prickled in my brain.

I knew that voice.

I turned my head in time to see Dad bring his fist down on the hood of a truck. "Simmer down and stop honking. Somebody should've paddled your ass when you were a kid," he boomed, his deep voice cutting through the melee of panicked voices, a smattering of honks, more sirens in the distance.

Dad faced a souped-up, too-tall truck at the front of the gridlocked intersection. It had monster tires and a bro-flag trailing off the back. There was a college-aged kid with a mullet leaning out the driver's side window.

No. This couldn't be happening.

With a strangled yelp, I rushed back the way I'd come through the parking lot, back into the crosswalk, and yanked on Dad's wrist.

Harder than I needed to, but I didn't have the presence of mind to be calm. To tell him the girls were in trouble. So I grabbed him.

Face red with anger, Dad spun to look at me and snatched his arm back. The kid with the mullet laughed, like this was some kind of skit in a reality TV show.

"Dad, stop!" I cried, trying to hold on.

My fingers slid down, catching on his watch.

Before I could blink, the clasp popped, and the watch landed hard on the asphalt at our feet.

Dad went completely still and touched his wrist, face bright red, eyes flashing at me, honking truck forgotten.

In my peripheral vision, I could see a police officer heading our way.

"What the hell are you doing, Sheen," Dad said, chin quivering with rage, both of us still facing each other in the middle of the road.

I could barely hear him, but his words still hit like darts. Because I didn't have a clue.

9

SAGE

With every second that went by, the inside of the gray van felt more like an oven. I tried not to imagine all of us being cooked alive, but I couldn't help it.

The bare floor was uneven and bumpy, with some metal parts poking out, like maybe there used to be seats back here.

A couple of the kids had started screaming once the man slammed the back doors and the hot, sticky van went dark.

Bonnie was one of them.

"Shh," I told her, hearing the man's footsteps run around to the driver's side. "He'll get mad and come back."

A little window between the driver's seat and the back of the van cracked open a few inches.

I just knew the guy was going to yell at us. Tell us again how he was going to shoot Ms. Jessa—who sat hunched in the very back part of the van, her hands *and* her arms fastened together behind her back.

Instead, Ms. Jessa was the one who yelled.

"Be quiet, *now,*" she barked.

Her voice was so harsh, Bonnie didn't even finish her wail.

The other kids went dead silent, too.

The driver slammed the window shut without another word.

I scooted closer to Bonnie, afraid to say anything else and suddenly hating Ms. Jessa a little bit. Not as much as I hated the men with the pantyhose over their faces, but enough to make me glare at her. When kids cried, you were supposed to tell them everything would be okay. You didn't yell.

I wanted to tell her that. I wasn't afraid of talking back to grownups—that's what the note in my report card from Ms. Butler said last year—but then the van lurched forward, nearly toppling me over onto Bonnie.

Where were the men taking us? What were they going to do? One time, a babysitter let me and Bonnie watch a *Dateline* episode about a girl who got kidnapped on her way home from school. Her face was all over giant billboards and posters in the city where she lived, even though she'd been missing for ten years.

"That's so sad. Her poor family. They can't even have a funeral," the babysitter—who was three years older than me but two inches shorter—had said.

Because she's for sure dead, I knew.

Would me and Bonnie be on a billboard like that, too? The men said they wouldn't hurt us if we did what they told us, but I bet the person who kidnapped that other girl told her the same thing.

I squeezed my eyes shut.

The van made an abrupt left turn, pitching all of us to the side. I planted my feet against something metal sticking up from the floor and braced so I wouldn't fall over.

Bonnie pressed her body tighter against me and whimpered but didn't scream again.

Thud, thud, thud. Other kids gasped as they lost their balance and hit the sides of the van.

Ked's voice, tiny and scared, announced, "I get carsick."

Someone else, maybe Ava or Mindy, whispered, "I do too."

I didn't get carsick too easily. I read my book the whole way to McCall last summer, when we went to the lake with Mom and Grandpa. But even my stomach had started churning in the hot, dark van that kept making tight left turns. Almost like we were circling.

A single, dull pinprick of light came through one of the painted-black windows behind my head, but it didn't make any difference. It looked like a dead star in the darkness.

"I have to go to the bathroom," Rose said in a tear-thick voice. "I held it after school, so I wouldn't miss the bus."

"Me too," Bonnie choked.

Me too, I thought, but kept it to myself.

Ms. Jessa didn't say anything for a few minutes. Why wasn't she helping? Instead, she just sat there like a lump on a log.

"Just hold on. We'll be there soon," I said in my loudest, strongest voice. Somebody needed to say it. Somebody needed to comfort these kids.

Blechhh.

Before I even realized what had happened, the rotten-sweet smell of vomit hit my nose.

"I'm sorry," Ked whispered. He was crying now, too.

* * *

For a while, I tried to keep track of the ways the bus turned.

Left, left.

Right, right, right, hard left.

Left, left, left, hard right. The turns kept coming quick and fast, and I had the thought again that we were going in circles. Were they trying to mix us up? Make it impossible to tell where we were going or how far away?

At least it was something to think about besides the smell of hot throw up and how my own bladder felt like a balloon ready to burst.

Before long, I gave up keeping track of the turns and just started praying that we'd stop soon. There wasn't any way to tell how much time had gone by, but it felt both shorter and longer than the drive to McCall.

My throat was full of cotton and my body felt like it had the day Bonnie and I stayed in the rec center hot tub too long. Hot and itchy and a little bit woozy at the same time.

After Ked, I heard two more kids throw up. Rose and Charlotte. I knew because they both said sorry afterward.

The smell made me want to do the same, but I held it in. The road had finally straightened out, which helped my stomach feel better. But it didn't do anything to help with how bad I had to pee. I braced so tight my teeth hurt from clenching.

Bonnie's sticky body felt like a half-baked cookie melted against me. She'd gone quiet for a little while. But I could feel her shaking now, long shudders that lasted longer every time.

"Sage, I can't hold it," she said so quietly I almost missed what she said. I could hear the horror and shame hot in her whisper.

"It's okay, Bonnie," I whispered back.

"No it's not," she rasped, voice hitching as her body started to shake again. "I'm not a *baby*."

I swallowed the hard lump in my throat and screwed my eyes shut again. Then I leaned over and whispered, "I know you're not. I have to pee, too. It's not a big deal."

And before I could think about it too hard, I stopped clenching and let go of my bladder.

It felt awful and relieving at the same time. The hot liquid soaked through my jeans and made my cheeks burn harder. I'd never peed my pants before. Bonnie had done it last year though, in kindergarten. The teacher sent her home with a note that she'd have to wear pull-ups to class if it happened again. Bonnie was so embarrassed to go back that she made herself sick and got to stay home from school the next day.

Bonnie went silent and let out a little "Oh."

I could still hear her snuffling, but then she stopped shaking and whispered, "Thanks, Sage." Then she did the same as me.

10

JESSA

Jessa Landon deserves to rot in hell.

That's what my ex-brother-in-law said when he'd testified at my court hearing a little more than three years ago. Looked right at me and spat it, like he hadn't asked me whether I wanted cheese on my burger at backyard barbecues over the years. Like he hadn't silently side-eyed the scratches on my arms and the purple-and-yellow bruise on my thigh, where his brother had slammed me into the wall.

His words ran through my mind on a loop now. *Jessa Landon deserves to rot in hell.*

Because here I was, rotting in hell.

I'd lost track of how many kids had vomited and peed themselves. The dark, boiling interior of the airless van smelled so bad I couldn't tell anymore whether I was more afraid of breathing or not breathing.

Some of the kids were still crying.

I wanted to hug them, comfort them, but my arms and hands were zip tied so tight, I couldn't feel my fingers or toes anymore. I kept opening my mouth to tell them it would be okay. I could've done that, at least. My mouth wasn't taped shut. I could've said something nice, instead of just yelling at them to shut up when one of the little girls first started screaming.

I wasn't going to tell them everything would be okay, though. I'd been down that road before.

"It's all right, Soph. I'm sorry the yelling woke you up. It was just the TV ... Daddy and I had it on too loud. Everything is fine. Go back to sleep, baby."

Sophie rubbed her eyes and lay back down in bed. "Okay, Mama."

She believed me. And there was a relief in that, even a sort of righteousness, that made everything waiting for me outside her bedroom slightly more tolerable.

"When will they let us out of here?" one of the kids asked, and the words hung in the cave-like darkness of the cargo area unanswered. None of the other children responded. The question was clearly meant for me.

I kept my lips shut and put my head on my knees.

I lingered on the edge of Soph's bed a few seconds longer until her breathing deepened and her rosebud lips went slack in sleep. I lay my hand, smarting from where he'd dug in his fingers, on Soph's perfect, tiny arm. I gently brushed her smooth dark hair, still feeling the sting of my own scalp where he'd grabbed my hair as I tried to pull away from his vise-grip. He'd wanted me to "look him in the eyes" instead of "being a shame-faced bitch" by walking away from him.

Soph loved her daddy. So did I.

When the argument started downstairs, he'd been making us late-night grilled cheese sandwiches, wearing the Godzilla boxers that made me laugh.

That was the real Matt. The Matt who carried spiders outside the house instead of smashing them. The Matt who wrote me a love letter every birthday, every Valentine's Day, every Christmas. The Matt who made me late-afternoon alphabet soup while I was pregnant with Soph because it was the only thing I could eat without vomiting.

The van took a corner fast, knocking all of us to the right.

"Ms. Jessa? Our moms and dads will come find us, won't they?" one of the little boys asked.

I swallowed the lump in my throat, thick with all the comfort—and lies—I wanted to reassure him with.

"Just hang on a little longer, okay?" was all I could manage.

And really, that was the best any of us could do now. Accept the shitstorm, curl up in a ball, and take it until it was over. Like I had so many nights when Matt was drunk and angry.

You didn't poke the bear. You didn't fight back.

When I tiptoed back into the hall and closed Soph's door, the downstairs was quiet. I thought maybe Matt had gone to sleep.

That was good. Sleep usually reset the bad nights.

He wasn't asleep, though. He was waiting for me at the bottom of the stairs, ready to take up where he'd left off when Soph had started crying.

"That guy on the Ring camera? I saw his face when you answered the door, Jessa. Don't tell me that's the first time he's been to the house. You know him. Are you fucking him?"

I shook my head, hoping he could see the tears brimming in my eyes. Sometimes that snapped him out of it. Not this time, though. "And why do you need a gym membership so bad? Who are you meeting there? Don't you dare lie to me, Jessa ..."

The driver of the van hit the brakes hard, jolting me out of one nightmare and into the next.

The engine cut off.

My head felt like a lead balloon, empty and so heavy I could barely hold it up.

Were we finally stopping? What was next? Who were these psychopaths?

They're bears. And they'll tear you apart unless you play dead, my brain shot back.

"Ms. Jessa," Ked moaned, his monotone voice one of the few I recognized.

"Just do what the men say," I snapped at him, fear slamming the words out harsher than I meant to.

Everything and everyone was quiet for half a second.

Then I heard a noise. *Thud, shuffle, thud.*

The movement was coming from the other side of the van. Was one of the kids getting up?

I blinked in the darkness and whipped my head around, trying and failing to see who was moving around. Someone *had* stood up. "Stay sitting down," I hissed, panic making my chest tingle with dread.

The pinprick of dim light, the only thing cutting through the darkness in the back of the van, suddenly blinked out.

Then came a scratching sound.

The pinprick of light got bigger.

One of the kids, I couldn't see who, had gotten up and was picking at the black paint on the window.

No, no, no, no.

The men were going to walk back here and open up the van doors any second now.

And that kind of defiance was exactly how things spiraled from bad to worse.

11

From the orchard, I drove the Speedy Shuttle two miles toward Boise, along one of the single-lane ranch exits.

"Slow and steady," I told myself every time I was tempted to inch the shuttle over the speed limit. There weren't any other cars around. And Bus 315 wasn't even due to arrive at Bright Beginnings for another ten minutes, so nobody knew the kids were missing. But there was no point taking chances.

The shuttle had air conditioning, but I opened the window just a crack, because the smell of Andy's BO and that stupid spearmint hair oil was pretty strong in here. I felt bad for the passengers he would be taking to the airport later this evening—which was the whole reason he had the airport shuttle van today. The cash tip from the lady he'd taken to the airport earlier was still sitting in the cupholder up front—along with a used tissue.

"Gross, dude," I mumbled, as I flicked the tissue onto the floor. We'd debated who would drive which vehicle, just like we'd argued through every other detail of the plan about a hundred times over the past two months. The white airport shuttle was Andy's work car, but it was an automatic. The gray Craigslist van was a stick shift, and that's what it came down to. I could've learned to drive a stick—or at least I told myself I probably could have—but I just knew I'd stall it when the pressure was on.

As I approached the next turn, I checked the sideview mirror and scanned the horizon. This side of the Treasure Valley was mostly foothills, dotted with tiny towns that barely deserved their own gas station. So even during "rush hour" the roads were mostly empty.

When the coast stayed clear, I slowed to a crawl, rolled down the driver's side window, and tossed the Walmart bag of cell phones into the murky water of a weedy ditch.

"Bye, bitches," I murmured, glad to be rid of the little tracking time bombs, a few of which had pinged with text messages while I was driving for the past fifteen minutes.

The police would find the phones, eventually. Maybe they'd even be able to trace the history of cell tower signals back to where we'd left the bus in the orchard, once the investigation really got rolling.

But all that would take time.

And it'd lead them to jack shit.

I let out a big breath and hit the accelerator, careful not to push the van past sixty-five as I headed for the Sunset Springs exit.

The bougie community was smack in the middle of the hills between Boise and the rest of rural Idaho. Half of it was McMansions, built during a real-estate boom over the past three years. The other half were more normal-looking houses, tucked into the foothills on land that was cheap ten years ago. A long line of big, billboard-type signs right before the entry road to the community shouted bullshit like RURAL LUXURY, A CITY IN THE HILLS, and COUNTRY LIFE, CITY PERKS.

Sunset Springs was almost finished building its own—fancy—elementary school. But for now, all of the kids still had to be bussed ten miles to shitty Northridge, in the boonies. There'd been a big fight about it.

The city of Boise had made one change, though, in response to the bitching from the Sunset Springs McMansion moms. Bright Beginnings, in Boise, had been added to the list of state-subsidized after-school care programs. So now the Northridge kids could go there for after-school care, too.

It was the kind of shit I never would've paid any attention to before. "Sunset Swings"—that was what people from Boise called it, with its Stepford vibe and rumors of swingers—didn't mean anything to me.

People like me, who lived out in *real* Idaho near Northridge, mostly referred to the planned community as "the good gas station," with its sparkling new Chevron. It even had one of those vending machines that could spit out an Oreo shake in two minutes. I took a girl there once, after I got out of jail. Right before Andy got me the job at the quarry.

The girl ended up being a loser, but she was the reason I'd set foot inside a cutesy little pizza parlor on the edge of town—Speedwagon's. The tiny restaurant was separated from the new developments that'd popped up like stucco flowers over the past three years. It'd been there since before the McMansions, but had gotten a facelift.

And that's where I was headed now.

"Jesus Christ," I said to myself as I pulled the shuttle onto the shoulder of the road next to Speedwagon's. A twee little letterboard facing the road read, YOU WANNA PIZZA ME? The place was ridiculous, but still, even outside the smell of grease and cheese made my stomach growl.

I wasn't here for pizza, though.

I peeled off my gloves, then shut my door with my hip and glanced around, trying not to look obvious about it.

"Keep your shit together, Ted," I whispered. "It's all good."

I looked behind me at Highway 55. A couple of cars blazed past.

I looked to the left, then the right. A posh sign shouting SUN-SET SPRINGS, ugly brown hills, and a cheesy "orchard" where the bougie residents could pick apples in the fall.

In front of me, Speedwagon's new stucco siding and neon sign blinked a welcome. The parking lot was empty, thank Jesus. Dinner rush wasn't on yet.

I already knew the place didn't have security cameras. Not as of last week, anyway. Still, I moved my eyes back and forth across the front entrance for any sign of surveillance.

Nothing.

The door jingled when I walked inside.

A skinny, high-school-aged girl with an underbite and huge brown eyes jumped up from where she'd been leaning on the counter with her phone. "Oh, hi. Welcome to—" She stared at me, clearly panicked.

My mouth went dry, and I wished I had the pantyhose back over my head. Did she recognize me from last week? Did this girl have a photographic memory or something? Why the open mouth, though? I'd been in and out in five minutes tops, to case the place—and pick up a goddamn pizza because honestly, they were pretty damn good.

"Welcome to *Speedwagon's*," she blurted triumphantly, and her face relaxed.

I forced out a laugh. She didn't recognize me. She was just stupid. She'd forgotten the name of the place she worked at.

"What can I get ya?" she asked, making her voice all high and weird, like she was trying to flirt or something.

I smiled back, kept my face totally neutral. *Get in, get out, be unmemorable.* "My friend just had a baby," I said, impressed by how good the story sounded coming out of my mouth. "I wanted to send her dinner tonight. She lives just a few blocks that way, but I don't wanna bother her. Can you guys deliver it?"

The girl made a little "Aww," sound, then nodded vigorously. Her short brown hair, slicked in a tight ponytail, didn't move. "That's so nice of you. Yeah, for sure. What do you want? We have a special. Two medium two-toppings for twenty bucks."

I pretended to look at the menu. "Um, just a large pepperoni."

She nodded again. "Okay, cool. What's the address?"

My throat was so dry, I could barely swallow. I reached into the kangaroo pouch of my hoodie and removed the envelope I'd brought with me. "Address is right here. Can I actually tape this note to the box? My friend, she's been having a rough time. You know, new mom. Just leave the pizza on the doorstep for her, okay? In case, like, the baby is sleeping. I already told her I was sending dinner."

The girl bobbed her head up and down like she really did know how hard it was to be a new mom, even though she'd probably never even kissed a dude. Her eyes went all big and shiny. "Aww, for sure. Lemme grab some tape for your note."

Three minutes later, I was making a beeline back to the shuttle van.

I kept my hands shoved in the pouch of my jacket, resisting the urge to pump my fist in the air. We'd done pretty good work for a couple of functional deadbeats.

That's what my mom called me and Andy. "Functional deadbeats." Like it was some kind of disease diagnosis. Like she thought I was every bit as dumb and useless as he was. Like she was any better than me, wearing a hairnet and serving up sloppy joes at the old folk's home in Emmett, then getting high as a kite and sitting in front of the TV with beer and a bag of chips until she passed out.

Andy had graduated high school, at least. Not me. I'd actually gotten good grades. Some A's, even. But then I spent the last two weeks of my senior year in the hospital, then sixty days in jail.

Trespassing.

Unlawful use of a motor vehicle.

Driving under the influence.

Drug possession.

Criminal vandalism.

Five charges, all because I was over eighteen. By two weeks. And ... because the dirt bike I was riding, trying to jump the gap at Canyon Creek Park was "borrowed."

Andy said his buddy knew he was taking the bike. But when it got wrecked—and me with it—the "buddy" pressed charges. Against me, specifically. Since I was the one who wrapped the bike around a tree at the bottom of the gully, and got caught with an eighth of pot in my back pocket I didn't even want. Andy had given it to me for my birthday.

So, yeah. *Deadbeat* was sort of in the cards after that. No matter how much my mom nagged me about getting my GED or "applying myself," it wasn't going to lead anywhere.

Nobody wanted to hire someone with a record. Or date someone with a record. The shitty job at the quarry with Andy was the biggest win of my adult life.

I'd been fucked straight out of the gate.

Look at me now, though.

I was on my way to pulling off the best and biggest heist in Idaho.

And I was gonna get away with it, too.

12

The coating of paint over the van window was thick. And it was hard to reach with my hands tied behind my back. But when I turned around backward, stood on my tippy toes, and pried at the paint with my thumb fingernail, it gave a little.

"Sit down, stop doing that!"

I ignored Ms. Jessa and kept reaching and scratching, making the pinhole the size of a quarter—big enough that I could see out of it when I turned around to inspect my work.

"Sage," Ms. Jessa hissed, when the light coming through the paint splashed onto me like a mini spotlight.

I ignored her, the same way I ignored the recess monitor when she told me I wasn't allowed to sit on top of the monkey bars, even though there was no rule about it. Mom and Grandpa had been reading us *Harriet the Spy* at home, and sometimes I asked myself what Harriet would do in a particular situation.

Harriet would stay on the monkey bars. And she'd take the chance to look outside this van.

The paint didn't come off in big chunks like I'd hoped, and my hands were so numb from the plastic ties that I couldn't move my fingers very fast—but it was working. When I turned around again to peer out the hole I'd created, I could see outside the van just a little bit.

A few feet away from the window, there was a reddish-gray rock wall. It went up as far as I could see. Like we were at the bottom of a cliff, in a big pit.

To the left of the wall, toward the front of the van, was some kind of big pile. Chunks of concrete, dirt, broken bits of plastic and metal. It looked kind of like a dump, where we'd gone on a field trip to learn about why it was important to recycle.

I had no idea where we were. Nothing looked familiar. Were we actually at the dump? At the bottom of a cliff? How long were we in the van? It felt like hours, but that might've been because it was so awful in there. My breath came faster, and I accidentally kicked one of the other kids when I shifted my foot. Behind me, Bonnie started to cry again.

The van shook, and I froze. Up front, came the sound of a car door opening then closing.

I tensed, ready to sit back down. I didn't hear a second door open or shut. That meant just one man was getting out of the van. I was pretty sure the other one had driven the white shuttle. Was he here now, too?

I pressed my eye closer to the tiny hole I'd scratched into the window. I could see him, but he didn't look in my direction.

My stomach tensed, and my body felt shaky. I stayed where I was, though.

"Sage!" Ms. Jessa sounded like she was going to throw up now, too. She shifted a little, but there wasn't much she could do to stop me with her hands and feet tied.

Footsteps thudded, and the man came into view. He was looking over at the junk pit.

I studied him like my eyes were lasers. He had long, puffy brown hair that was frizzy and greasy at the same time. He was a big guy, with sweat stains under the arms of his brown T-shirt and baggy cargo shorts.

"He's just standing there," I whispered, my tongue thick in my mouth. I could taste the vomit in the boiling-hot air. "He doesn't have the pantyhose on his head anymore. He's holding it in his hand." I looked all around, trying to make sense of what I saw. "I don't know where we are." My voice shook a little. "There's … a rock wall. A lot of dirt. A bunch of junk."

The other kids stayed quiet.

Ms. Jessa didn't tell me to sit down again. Instead, she made her voice low and sharp and said, "Sage, the second he starts walking again, you sit down. And then all of you, do exactly what the men ask when they open up the van. No arguing."

I nodded impatiently and kept looking.

He kicked at a rock on the ground and said something under his breath.

Then he turned around.

The first thought that popped into my head was that he looked like Jesus, but mean. And chubby. The sun was hitting his greasy, shoulder-length brown hair just right, so it glowed a little bit. He had a beard the same length as his hair. His lips were chapped, like he'd been licking them. There was a big, angry crease between his stringy eyebrows, and his eyes were all squinty since he was facing the sun.

I opened my mouth to tell Ms. Jessa and the other kids what he looked like. I wasn't sure how it would help, but it was the only thing I could think to do. "He has long, brown hair—"

"Don't tell us what he looks like," she snapped back in a whisper. "There's a reason they don't want us to see their faces."

I swallowed but didn't say anything else. Was she right about that? Or did she just want me to sit down and shut up?

Those questions made my stomach twist up tighter. It was the same feeling I got when Grandpa asked me a question again and again or called me "Sheena" or asked what book we were reading at bedtime, even though it was the same one as the night before. *Harriet the Spy.* Like I needed to be careful with the grownup I was talking to. I didn't know why Ms. Jessa was being so mean, but it made my eyes blur and my throat close up.

Thinking of Grandpa and reading at bedtime just made the feeling worse.

We weren't going to be home for bedtime tonight. The sun was already most of the way down the sky.

Would we ever be home for bedtime?

Greasy Hair moved a few more steps toward the back of the van, and I tensed, ready to sit my butt down and pretend I hadn't just seen him.

Ms. Jessa heard the footsteps too and made a gasping noise. "Soph," she hissed, then corrected herself. "*Sage,* sit down."

I bristled. And a line from *Harriet the Spy* popped into my mind. *Keep your head when all about you are losing theirs and blaming it on you.*

One of the other girls had started crying again.

"What are they going to do with us?" came Ked's solemn, scared voice.

"Are we going to die?" a shrill voice, Rose's maybe, asked loud enough that I jumped.

"No," Ms. Jessa said. "If we just stay calm and don't make them mad …"

Greasy Hair cut his eyes toward the van.

I jerked back from the peephole and tried to step toward where I'd been sitting before. Somebody had moved their leg, though, and I tripped.

I gasped and fell backward, landing hard on the metal floor—and somebody's lap—with a thud.

Something slammed against the side of the van from the outside.

A few kids shrieked. One of them was Bonnie.

"Quiet! I told you not to fucking move in there," Greasy Hair barked.

I lay frozen where I was, heart pounding, even though my hip was hurting, pressed against something sharp on the van floor.

Terrified, I waited for Greasy Hair to yank open the van doors and pull me out. When he didn't, I slowly wiggled away from the lap I'd fallen onto so I was sitting.

"Sage?" Bonnie whispered in a tiny voice through the silence. It set off another wave of whimpers through the van.

Inch by inch, I scooted my way back to her through sticky, sweaty bodies until we were side by side again. With the little hole of light coming into the van, I could just make out the expressions on the nearest kids' faces.

Bonnie, like the other kids, had her eyes open wide and her mouth squeezed shut like she was afraid of what might burst out. Her bangs stuck to her forehead, sweaty and damp as if we'd just gotten out of the swimming pool at Bright Beginnings.

I turned my head to look at Ms. Jessa, in the back corner of the bus. She'd pulled her knees up to her chin and tucked her head so that her bright red hair covered her face.

The seconds dragged by.

Then the minutes. What was Greasy Hair doing out there?

More footsteps crunched on the gravel. Every time they moved away, I got scared that maybe he was just going to leave us cooking in here and never let us out. But when the sound moved toward us, I got scared he was going to open the doors and shoot somebody with that gun.

The other kids must've been thinking the same, because after a minute, everybody was breathing fast, like there wasn't enough air for all of us.

Maybe there wasn't.

I squeezed my eyes shut and tried to think. *Keep your head.*

I didn't know what Greasy Hair was waiting for, but I knew that all these kids couldn't keep it together much longer.

So I grabbed the first idea that hit my mind. "Bonnie," I whisper-blurted, "I'm going on vacation and I'm bringing ... a tomato."

The fast-breathing whimpers in the van got quieter.

Bonnie made a little sound that could've been a laugh or a cry. I held my breath. It was her favorite game. And Mom's. The two of them always wanted to play it while we drove in the car. I was terrible at the game, so I usually looked out the window and rolled my eyes.

"I'm going on vacation and I'm bringing a tomato and an apple," Bonnie said finally, hesitantly.

"Then you can come," I told her.

Bonnie scoffed. "That was too easy."

"Why can she go on vacation?" Ked asked.

"They're both red things," Bonnie told him, sounding almost like her normal self. "Tomato, and apple. You have to try to guess the pattern."

Someone made an "Ohh" sound. Then Charlotte's voice piped up. "I'm going on vacation and I'm bringing a bike."

"Can I come if I bring a bike and a car?" Ben said.

"Nope," Charlotte said proudly.

"How about a bike and a bumblebee?" Ava asked, pronouncing it "bubbobee" like her nose was all stuffed up. It was the first time I'd heard her say anything at all.

"You can come," Charlotte replied excitedly.

In the back corner of the van, Ms. Jessa lifted up her head. I still couldn't see her eyes, and she didn't make a sound, but her shoulders were rocking up and down, so I was sure she was crying.

We kept playing the dumb game for maybe fifteen minutes until we heard the sound of tires in the distance, rolling through the dirt toward the van. Then the low hum of an engine.

I swallowed the sticky spit in my throat.

Greasy Hair took a few fast steps toward the sound.

The tires stopped rolling right behind us, and the engine hum died.

A door creaked open.

All of us went quiet enough to hear Greasy Hair say, "Fucking *finally.*"

I wanted so bad to stand up again and look through the hole in the window, but I already knew I couldn't see outside the back of the van. And the shaky, scared feeling in my stomach warned me not to move a muscle.

Something was about to happen.

13

When the quarry's dirt road finally opened up to narrow switch-backs, I'd had to slow the shuttle to a crawl so I wouldn't ding up the underside. I hooked a left and headed for The Pit, a closed section of the quarry that had been relegated to a seldom-used dumping site for random junk, bigger equipment parts, and industrial waste. After half a mile, I brought the shuttle to a stop, pushed my hair back from my forehead, and forced the tight, dark-brown pantyhose over my head. Then I checked in the rearview mirror, just to be sure my face was covered.

"Holy shit," I breathed, still taken aback by my own appear-ance. You couldn't see my eyes at all. Just two faint, circular shad-ows on either side of my nose, which was smashed down flat like the ogre in *Shrek*. My eyelashes scraped against the stretched-tight fabric when I tried to blink, and my nose was already starting to hurt again. I probably could've got a bigger size pantyhose, or a better mask, but I would've had to go searching for it. And that meant leaving a trail of evidence.

As I maneuvered the shuttle down the final stretch of the nar-row switchback, the gray van came into view at the edge of The Pit.

Then I saw Andy—barefaced and grinning at me like a monkey as he came around the side of the van.

Panic, then rage, burst like flares in my brain.

"Hey, Teddy Bear," he said as I skidded to a stop in front of him and banged open the door.

"Dude, put your pantyhose back on," I snapped the second I got out of the shuttle. This wasn't what we'd agreed to. And he knew I hated that nickname. For one, it made me feel like we were still in high school and I was still a skinny, acne-covered teenager with an unironic mullet. For another, he never used it when he was really joking around. There was acid behind it that meant he wanted to put me in my place.

Not for the first time, a worm of doubt wriggled at the back of my mind. Andy wasn't exactly my first pick for accomplices, and this was why. When he got mad, or annoyed, he could be a loose cannon.

It wasn't like I had another option, though. Andy *was* my option. And he knew it.

As if to prove my point, Andy lifted his middle finger defiantly and cocked his head, staying where he was behind the van. "It's fucking *hot* out here. They can't see through the paint," he said, nodding at the blacked-out windows. "What took you so long?"

"I took the exact right amount of time," I shot back, not backing down like I usually would. And I had. I drove the speed limit, right to the digit. Took back roads off the highway, like we'd talked about. "Everything is good," I said, lowering my voice so the kids in the van couldn't hear me.

Andy lowered his middle finger and shrugged. "Fine, Teddy Bear. But we gotta hurry." He pointed at the shuttle van behind me. "My next pickup's in half an hour. We gotta get the cargo stowed." He pointed a thumb at the van, then reached into his back pocket for his wadded-up pantyhose and pulled it over his head.

I gritted my teeth. He didn't have to call them "the cargo," but it was time to smooth things over. Fighting was only going to make him more stubborn.

He took a few seconds to wrestle his hair beneath the tight fabric, finally succeeding in smashing it flat against his scalp and against his face.

"You look like a dumbass." I forced a laugh, relieved he had the disguise back in place. We could take the pantyhose off once we had the kids safely stashed. Until then, it was better to be careful. If they saw us, this perfect plan was going to veer into territory I had no interest in touching with a ten-foot pole.

I listened for the sound of cars crawling along the dirt road, but all I heard was silence. There was almost zero chance of anybody coming down here over the weekend. The Pit was no-man's land. And even the working sections of the quarry shut down at four o'clock sharp, Monday through Friday. Shifts started at the buttcrack of dawn during the summer and early fall, and Andy's dad—who owned the quarry—wasn't about to pay anybody overtime.

We had the place to ourselves until Monday.

But what was the point of all our—my—careful planning if we were going to cut corners?

"Come on, help me move the slab," Andy said, walking toward a sheet of metal at the edge of The Pit.

He pointed to a warped yellow metal sheet lying in the dirt. This particular metal sheet was a panel from a long-dead excavator, about the size of a door.

I glanced at the back of the gray van as I hurried to catch up with Andy. None of the kids had made a peep since I'd showed up. Were they okay? It was pretty hot, and a ransom wouldn't work if the kids were dead. The Pit was mostly shaded, and the sun was already setting past the steep rock face rising above us at the edge of The Pit, but the air hadn't cooled down even a little yet. The airless van, with its blacked-out windows, had to be boiling inside.

I pushed the thoughts away. They'd only be inside a little longer. Kids were rubber bands, I told myself for the hundredth time. They bounced back from shit like this. I thought of what Andy had told me when I started getting cold feet a few days ago: *If anything, this'll give the little snowflakes something to make them feel extra special once they're back home.*

I squatted down on one side of the warped yellow metal sheet, careful not to touch the jagged edges gleaming silver. Andy hunched on the other side. "One, two, three, go," he said, then we both grunted and heaved the heavy sheet a few feet to the right, just enough to expose what was underneath.

With the metal sheet out of the way, the smell of damp dirt and a subtle whoosh of cooler air rose up to meet us. It wafted up from a dark, yawning hole leading down into the earth and felt good on my hot skin.

Good. It wouldn't be a total oven, at least. Kids might even be glad to go down there, after baking in the van.

"Damn, this is so good," Andy gushed, craning his neck to look down at what we'd built.

I felt a tiny rush of pride, too. It was absolutely perfect. We'd been working on "The Bunker" almost since I'd begun working at Northside Quarry with Andy a year ago.

It'd all started when we'd been tasked with widening the dump pit to make room for a discarded shipping container.

"Dude, this thing is HUGE," Andy had said, when the flatbed dumped it at the edge of the pile and we got our first look at it.

The words BODO TRANSFER COMPANY were painted in worn, scratched-up letters on the side of the enormous shipping container, tipped onto its side. Andy was right. It *was* huge. The dimensions were listed right on the side. Twenty feet long, eight feet wide, twelve feet high. *"Jesus Fucking Christ,"* I'd replied, *"This is half the size of my house."*

I'd felt heat rise in my cheeks the second I said it. Because of course it was nearly the size of my house. I still lived in my mom's shitty double-wide. Which basically *was* a shipping container.

Andy had ignored me though, stepping closer to the cracked, roll-up side door that had come open when the shipping container landed in the dirt. *"You know, people make like, doomsday bunkers out of these things,"* he said. *"Bury them in the ground, stock them with food and guns."*

I'd nodded, not really thinking much of it. *"That'd be dope."*

He'd looked at the dozer and excavator we'd been working all week, widening the edge of The Pit to make room for the shipping container so it wouldn't block the road. Then he glanced around at the piles of fresh dirt we'd mounded up. *"We could bury it,"* he'd said, raking a hand through that wild, fork-in-a-socket hair.

And so we did.

At first, we'd just planned on making it a bunker fort. Somewhere we could slip away and smoke pot on the clock. Or where Andy could, anyway. I didn't like the way the closed-in space made my brain feel slow and stupid.

We kept the fort a secret. Easy enough, since we were the pissants in charge of hauling waste and broken equipment to The Pit.

It took forever, but by the time we were finished, the bunker was a masterpiece.

We dug a hole deep enough that the top of the shipping container was four feet beneath the earth, lying on its side with its roll-up door facing up. Then we built a four-foot shaft made of plywood around that roll-up door and backfilled dirt over the rest of the shipping container. The only thing visible after that was the opening to that narrow, square plywood shaft.

As a finishing touch, we sent two ladders down the shaft: a long one that went all the way down to the bottom of the shipping container, and a shorter one that let us shimmy down the shaft. Then we covered the opening in the dirt with that heavy yellow excavator panel, which hid everything.

To the casual observer, the only thing visible was the old excavator door. It looked just like all the rest of the crap lying around the perimeter of the junk pile.

It was the perfect hiding place.

Too perfect to waste on stolen minutes at work, smoking pot. It got the wheels turning in my head.

When I finally told Andy about the plan—because I needed a second guy, and because he knew about the bunker—he got so excited he looked like he'd just taken a hit of something.

I shook my head, pushing the memory away so I could focus.

"You ready?" Andy asked, breathing hard and striding back toward the van. "'Cause it's go-time again, motherfucker."

I gave him a dumb half-salute and wished I hadn't. I hated that I was always pandering to Andy. He wasn't very smart. He wasn't even very nice most days. Maybe it was just because he was one of the few people who didn't treat me like a total disease when I got out of jail.

I tugged the pantyhose down, even though it was so tight around my face I could barely breathe through my nose. "Yeah, let's do this."

14

The van doors flung open.

Before I could even gulp in a breath of fresh air, Greasy Hair was barking at us in a cranky, impatient voice. "Get out! Single file. *Move*," he demanded, even though he'd barely opened the door half a second earlier.

I could tell it was him, even with his face all squished by the pantyhose again. The other man, who I'd decided to call Jeepers in my head, held up a gun. He really did look like the thing from *Jeepers Creepers* with the particular way his face smashed flat under the sand-colored pantyhose.

I didn't let myself glance at the side window of the van where I'd spied on Greasy Hair earlier. With the light coming in through the open doors, it wouldn't be too noticeable. At least, that's what I hoped.

Don't look at the hole I made in the paint, I told him with my mind, like I was a Jedi from *Star Wars*. And, like a weak-minded Storm Trooper, he obeyed.

The temperature outside was cooler than the boiling van, and I swallowed air like I'd been suffocating. I wanted so bad to be able to wipe the sweat dripping down my neck, into the collar of my shirt and down my back. I was so hot and thirsty.

"No, not you," Greasy Hair snapped when Ms. Jessa shifted at the back of the van and tried to get up. "You're last, bus driver."

Ms. Jessa froze the second he spoke to her.

I darted my eyes around, seeing more of the same alien land-scape I'd glimpsed through the pinhole in the window paint. Dirt, broken machine parts, heaps of junk, jagged cement, rocks. The cliff wall rose up so high, it looked like we were at the bottom of the earth. The white shuttle van was parked a few feet behind us.

Jeepers stood beside it, crouched a little, like he thought we might run the second Greasy Hair opened the van doors, and he was gonna catch us. Or shoot us.

Greasy Hair cleared his throat and took a step back from the van. His smashed-up expression beneath the murky pantyhose didn't change, but I knew he was disgusted from the tone of his voice. "God, it stinks in there," he called to Jeepers, putting his hand in front of his face. "We were driving for what, an hour? Guess the ba-bies needed diapers." He laughed, like he'd made a really funny joke.

Jeepers grunted but didn't laugh.

I leaned closer to Bonnie and whispered as quiet as I could, "We're *not* babies. They're … buttheads."

"Shut up, no talking," Greasy Hair snapped, but I felt Bonnie's body relax a little against me. Mom never let us say the word "butthead," but I just knew she'd be okay with it right now.

The thought of her and Grandpa made me want to cry again.

Take care of your sister.

I blinked back the tears and snuck a look at Ms. Jessa. She had her head ducked, staring at the floor of the van like she wasn't even here.

"You, let's go," Jeepers piped up in a weird, too-deep voice, stepping forward so he was next to Greasy Hair and pointing at Ked. "Line up right over there." He flicked the gun he held, pointing at somewhere past the van. Once again, I got the feeling Jeepers was trying to disguise his voice, but it still pinged somewhere in my memory.

I couldn't decide if that idea made me more or less scared.

Ked hesitated, then scooted closer to the edge of the van.

"He said let's *go*." Greasy Hair grabbed him by the arm and dragged him the last few inches on the van floor. Ked yelped, his brown eyes huge and his brown hair slicked to his head with sweat. When his feet hit the dirt, he hurried alongside Jeepers, who led him away from the van.

Rose, then Crosby, then Mindy scooted off the edge to follow Ked and Jeepers, while Greasy Hair dragged more kids out of the van and pointed them somewhere past the white shuttle.

Once the kids moved beyond the van's open doors, I couldn't see them anymore. But after a few seconds, I heard Ked, then other kids, gasp—like whatever they saw over there was even scarier than the two guys with guns.

My stomach hurt like I was going to throw up, and my legs burned, sticky where I'd peed my pants.

"Move, move, move," Greasy Hair kept barking, rushing us faster and faster even though it wasn't easy to scoot along the van floor with our hands tied.

Before I knew it, I was the one swinging my legs until I hit the dirt, Bonnie right behind me. She was breathing fast the way she did when Mom dropped her off for the first day of kindergarten.

So was I.

Bonnie, then Ava, then Ben, scooted off the back of the van close behind me like scared ducklings following the leader.

"Move," Greasy Hair told me, like it was the only word he knew.

I stared back at him defiantly, thinking of Ms. Jessa with her head bowed behind me.

Even without being able to see the whites of his eyes, I knew he was staring right at me.

He didn't know I'd scratched the paint in the window.

He couldn't read my mind. He couldn't make me duck my head—give up—like Ms. Jessa. And I wouldn't let him make any of us feel bad for wetting our pants.

A little fizzle of courage popped like soda bubbles through the sloshing fear in my stomach.

It lasted until I walked around the van toward Jeepers and the rest of the kids.

I could now understand why Ked had gasped.

He was at the front of the line of kids, standing at the edge of a big hole in the dirt, next to a giant yellow sheet of metal.

The hole in the ground looked like a mouth, waiting to swallow all of us kids.

The top part of a ladder poked out of the hole. Jeepers was standing next to it, holding a pair of scissors in his hand.

He was cutting Ked's ties.

All my courage-bubbles popped, and I knew that if I hadn't already peed my pants on the van ride here, I'd have done it now from pure terror.

They were cutting our hands free so we could climb down the ladder.

They were sending us all into that hole.

Bonnie's breathing went from fast to lightning-speed, like she was an out-of-control wind-up toy that'd been twisted too far.

The other kids, who had realized what was about to happen too, were starting to panic right along with her.

When Jeepers cut Mindy's ties, she drew in a gasp of air and suddenly darted forward so fast I barely realized what was happening.

She was making a run for it.

Some of the other kids gasped, and I could feel them wondering if we should all try to run. My legs tensed, even though my hands were still tied.

Then, with two quick strides, before anyone else could move, Jeepers caught Mindy by the shirt.

She landed hard on her arm in the dirt in a way that made my own arm hurt, then she started to cry.

Jeepers stared at her, breathing hard, then turned to look at the rest of us. "Don't do that," he growled angrily.

My eyes moved to Greasy Hair, a few feet away, who hadn't even bothered to move. His gun was still pointed at the open van doors, at Ms. Jessa. He burst out laughing over the sound of Mindy's crying. "It's like they want me to shoot their bus driver," he called over. "When you get your hands free, you stay *quiet,* you go down the ladder *fast.* Got it? And I don't wanna hear any more bitching or crying," he added loudly.

He cocked the gun, like we needed any more reason to be afraid.

I craned my neck, trying to get a glimpse of Ms. Jessa. She wasn't the grownup I would've chosen if I had my pick, but I still wanted to see her, to know she was here with us.

Greasy Hair tilted his head. I still couldn't see his eyes, but I just knew those dark sockets behind the pantyhose had landed on me. "And if that doesn't light a fire under your asses, we'll pick off the oldest kids first."

15

The police officer who had dragged Dad away from fighting with the guys in the truck took my statement. It lasted maybe fifteen minutes.

Dad interrupted twice, blustering, "You can't detain us without a warrant. Let me see your badge. I'd outrank you in my day, don't you know that? What in the Sam Hill is this about?"

The officer was patient and kind to him but didn't re-explain what he'd already told us both. There was no sign of the children. Or the bus. None of the kids or the bus driver were answering their phones.

I knew that much already. Sage's phone just rang and rang and went to voicemail.

The FBI was already working alongside the police.

Ten children, vanished into thin air.

Two of them, mine.

I could barely choke out half-coherent answers to the questions the police officer asked, clenching and unclenching my hands uselessly until he gave me his cell number and told me to go home.

There was nothing I could do to help my girls from the Bright Beginnings parking lot.

The police were already doing everything possible to locate the bus, the phones, the kids.

I took Dad's arm and walked through the churning sea of parents. Some had red eyes, or clenched jaws, like they were trying not to scream. Others were fighting with each other and the police, voices raised shrill and sharp. Then there were the ones, like me, who looked like they'd been holding onto an electric fence without letting go. Wide-eyed and shaking, waiting for the surge of awfulness to stop.

"What in the Sam Hill is going on?" Dad repeated yet again, looking around furtively then back at me. "Sheen, what happened?" he blustered.

I stopped walking and stared back at him. His tear-stained cheeks were still wet from the initial five minutes his mind had taken in the horror of what the officer told us both.

Sage was gone. Bonnie was gone.

For a second, I almost wished I could trade places with him. Purge everything I'd seen and heard. But I could tell from the way his arm shook that his body hadn't forgotten what he'd learned. Just his mind.

"It'll be okay, Dad," I told him, but I knew my performance wasn't convincing. "Come on, our car is over there." I pointed down a side street where an officer had reparked the car we'd left in the intersection. It had taken half an hour, but officers had finally managed to break up the gridlock, coaxing keys from distraught parents until cars could continue through the jammed intersection. But with the growing number of red-and-blue lights flashing all across the parking lot, traffic stayed at a slow crawl from rubberneckers anyway.

The curious onlookers wanted the same thing the parents and police did: To find out what the hell was going on.

As Dad and I got into the car, I felt something jingle in my pocket. Dad's Rolex. The clasp was completely broken. He'd raged at me about it for a few seconds—then forgotten as soon as the officer started talking. Even so, I watched as he absently rubbed his wrist.

The street swam in front of my eyes, and I wondered if I should be driving at all. I knew I could call someone. A coworker. A neighbor. They'd be eager to help.

No. I could already imagine their horrified pity and barely concealed curiosity. Just like the people driving by in a slow stream past the Bright Beginnings rec center.

What I needed was a friend, but I'd lost most of those during my divorce five years ago. My world had bloomed when I first married Jacob. His friends were my friends. It was love at first sight—a *"whirlwind romance,"* Dad had said when we got married just nine months after meeting.

It wasn't until we got divorced that I realized how small my share of our world really was. And how "our" friends were really Jacob's friends all along. They all quietly disappeared, practically overnight, even though he'd been the one to leave me for his office manager Jenny, who he'd been "in love with for years"—and was pregnant with twin boys.

I got the house in Sunset Springs, and the girls—who were two and six at the time. He moved to the East Coast with his mistress to start over.

The last time I'd tried to text him a couple of years ago, I'd gotten a message saying that the text couldn't be delivered. He'd erased us.

I blinked back the tears and gripped the steering wheel like it could anchor me in my body.

Dad and I drove in merciful silence through the neighborhoods until we reached the onramp to the highway that would take us back to Sunset Springs.

Then Dad suddenly shifted in the passenger seat to face me. He cleared his throat. "I ever tell you about that hiker, Sheen? Mindy Falcrest?"

The words pinged through my numb brain. This was one of the higher profile cases he'd worked on while I was growing up. The story had been in the local and some national news for almost a week —and it hadn't ended well. I knew it was one of those stories that haunted him, but I had no idea what made him think of it now. Maybe that same growing dread, that same helplessness from all those years ago mirrored what he felt now and had churned the memory up. He'd never told me the story firsthand. I'd only read the old articles. And as much as I didn't want to shut him down, I couldn't handle it right now.

"No, Dad," I said more angrily than I'd planned.

He went quiet. When I glanced at him in the corner of my eye, I was horrified to see that his jaw was clamped down and trembling. Like he was trying not to cry.

"I'm sorry," I muttered, tilting my head so he wouldn't see the tears leaking down my own cheeks.

He was silent for so long, I thought he'd given up on the story. But from the tentative smile he flashed me as he repeated, "Sheen, I ever tell you about that hiker, Mindy Falcrest?" I realized that what he'd forgotten was my angry outburst.

"Tell me," I whispered, eyes on the road.

He sat back in the passenger seat and sighed heavily. "A woman went missing—a thirty-year-old with a young family. Mindy Falcrest went hiking out by Prairie, Idaho in the boonies. We weren't that worried at first. She was one of those ultra-outdoorsy types. There was still plenty of daylight. Good visibility for searchers, plenty warm outside. Her husband found her car at the trailhead when he drove out there that afternoon." He sighed again. "Mindy was only meant to be gone for a couple of hours when she left that morning."

Despite myself, my mind latched onto the thread of his story, desperate for a moment's respite from the nonstop, churning-sick despair in my gut.

"I was the one in charge of the search and rescue. The hiker's daughter—an itty bitty eight-year-old girl who was missing her front tooth—kept insisting her mama took 'the hot springs trail,' a few miles south in middle-of-nowhere Featherville. It didn't make sense. Mindy's car was at the Prairie trailhead, right where her husband thought it'd be. The husband said ... he said the little girl was just upset and confused. That his daughter had gone on the hot springs hike with her mama the year before—that's why she remembered the place." He cleared his throat and waited a second before continuing. "We searched for three days. Brought out horses, a helicopter. No sign of that woman. Had us all racking our brains. Finally, because I didn't know what else to do, I sent a couple of guys over to Featherville."

He waited so long to keep talking, I almost thought he'd decided not to continue. But finally, he said, "We found Mindy in Featherville, collapsed in the brush just twenty yards past the trailhead. She'd been dead for about a day."

My stomach lurched. I realized I no longer wanted to hear the rest of the story. But when I opened my mouth to ask him to stop, I couldn't get the words out past the hard lump in my throat.

Dad kept going. "Thought at first she'd had a heart attack. But the autopsy—which the husband didn't want—showed kidney failure as the cause of death. Turns out, he'd added antifreeze to her energy drink that morning. Husband found her unconscious on the trail when he 'went looking for her.' Pushed her into the brush and moved her car to the Prairie trailhead."

The churning sick in my stomach roiled harder. How could he remember all of that so well, when he couldn't remember what we'd just learned about Sage and Bonnie?

Dad blew out a breath. "He didn't realize his daughter knew Mindy was really going to Featherville. If I'd listened to that little girl—hell, if I'd listened to that nagging in my gut—there's a pretty good chance we would've found her mom. Probably even saved her life. But 'kids are unreliable.' That's what my partner reminded me."

"Oh," was all I could manage. I slowed the car, debating whether I needed to pull over onto the shoulder so I could be sick.

"Kids know more than you give them credit for," he said sadly. "After that, I promised I'd listen to the kids, take more time to listen to my gut."

The highway swam in front of my eyes, and tears wet my cheeks, but I was glad he seemed done with that story. I realized I'd missed the first turnoff for Sunset Springs. I needed to calm down my breathing or else I was going to crash this car.

Then Dad spoke again, his voice suddenly irritated and harsh. "I got something to say, and I know you don't wanna hear it."

I really didn't. I couldn't listen to anything more about the Mindy Falcrest case. I bit my lip to keep from saying so. *Just get through this. It's easier than telling him to stop talking.*

"You've gotta knock it the hell off," he said abruptly in the voice I remembered from when I was a teenager and he found a joint I'd hidden in the garage.

I cocked my head in shock. His tone of voice was beyond annoyed.

He doesn't know what's happening. Just get home, I told myself, digging as deep as I could for patience. "Okay, Dad," I managed in a strangled voice, hoping it would pacify him. I wiped at my cheeks as my mind pinballed from one thought to the next, desperate for some action to take, someone to call, anything that would get me my girls back. Was I really just supposed to go home and wait for more information?

I'd overheard some of the parents talking about driving back and forth along the highway and side roads. Bright Beginnings and the police were doing the very same thing. Nobody had found a single thing yet.

The FBI was working on tracing the location of every phone on that bus.

What else could I do?

Nothing.

"Don't 'okay, Dad' me," he huffed, turning to face me. "I know you don't want to be coddled right now. But maybe what you need is some tough love."

I gritted my teeth, stayed silent, and kept my eyes straight ahead. I had no idea what he was talking about anymore, but the gruff words landed like salt in a wound just the same.

"Marriage is sacred. Not somethin' you rush into after a few months to play house. But you're an adult and God help me for trying to talk sense into you. What's done is done. My mother raised me all by herself. You'll be all right, too."

I gripped the steering wheel so hard my fingers went numb.

I couldn't do this right now. I was going to explode. He thought I was crying about my divorce. About Jacob leaving me—years ago.

"Stop, just *stop*," I snapped, my patience long gone. "No more." My voice hitched, and this time I couldn't hold back the tears from rushing down my cheeks. I swiped at them furiously and kept driving into the hills, ignoring his sullen silence. Fifteen more minutes, and we'd be back home.

My empty, silent home.

A police cruiser, lights off, passed me on the left.

Please find them, I begged whoever sat behind the tinted windows. *Find the bus driver. Find my girls. Turn on your lights, your sirens. Find them now, goddammit.*

Dad huffed and shifted in his seat, and I bit down on the inside of my cheek. He wasn't ready to back down.

"That's the problem with your generation," he muttered. "Can't handle the hard truths. Self-care and 'put yourself first.' I'll tell you what, Sheen. Sometimes you gotta put yourself *last.* If you were a teenager, I'd tell you to cry all you want. But you're a mother. So pull yourself together and snap out of it. Your babies come first. Bonnie and Sage need you right now."

It was all I could do not to howl.

16

I was the last one left in the putrid-smelling van, its floor smeared with vomit and some puddles of urine. From where I sat in the back of the cargo area, I couldn't hear the kids anymore, their snuffling noises or panicked breathing.

All I could see was a man with a gun, silhouetted between the van doors. He had his smashed-up, masked face turned away from me slightly, his attention focused on the direction he'd sent the kids. But I felt certain that if I moved a muscle, he'd snap his attention back to me.

What would happen next? All I knew was we had to be very, *very* careful.

Just do what the men say. Don't cry. Don't talk back, I begged the kids silently, picturing the defiant gleam I'd seen in Sage's eyes when the van doors opened.

I felt sick when I thought of the way she'd ignored me after I told her to sit back down.

Defiance won't accomplish anything. It's not worth the risk.

Sage was too young to understand that.

I'd been the same way once.

The two men clearly hadn't noticed the scratched-off paint—yet. But I knew all too well that it was the little things, the small subversions, that could suddenly send you and everyone you loved spiraling headlong into danger. If they thought we'd seen their faces, any hope of getting out of here alive was gone.

I tried to squeeze my bound hands into fists, but my numb fingers barely obeyed. *Just do what they say, Sage,* I wanted to scream so loud she'd hear me, wherever they were taking her and the other kids. *Don't do anything stupid.*

Instead, I kept my mouth shut tight and did exactly what I was supposed to do.

Nothing.

Because I had to get out of here alive.

Because I had to get back to Soph. The silly, sweet, baby-faced, just-started-kindergarten, front-toothless child I'd lost three years ago—now the shy, quiet nine-year-old living with my sister who wouldn't call me "Mom" anymore.

I'd thought about her every day like a lifeline during my pretrial hearing to keep myself calm and quiet—when what I really wanted to do was tear my hair out by the roots. And every day for three years when I woke up staring at a cage door until my parole was finally granted.

At least then, I thought I'd get back to her—even if it took a long time.

Now, I wasn't so sure. And that thought scared me as much as the idea of dying.

"Hurry it up," the man pointing his gun at me muttered under his breath, and I scooted toward him, thinking he was talking to me. He was the one who'd told the kids, *"You do what I tell you. Otherwise, we shoot your bus driver."*

But the second I started moving, he waved the gun. "Not you, bitch. You stay still."

I froze, confused. Then I realized he had one foot turned slightly away from me and his head tilted, like he was keeping one eye on something happening in the distance. Where the kids had gone. I tried to take advantage of the breeze blowing in through the open van doors, dispersing some of the stench in the van. But my gag reflex rose again as the smell of vomit and urine mingled with the scent of him. Like rotten mint and dried sweat.

I swallowed the bile and kept quiet, daring to really study him for the first time. He was tall, maybe six foot. Lanky and thick-set. He stood with his feet wide apart, and his knees bent a little, ready to move. He kept clenching and unclenching his free hand, making the muscles in his forearm pop up and down.

My stomach lurched yet again. Maybe I was starting to lose it from the heat and the terror and the zip ties cutting off the blood flow to my arms below the elbow, but I could've sworn he was wearing the same kind of minty cologne Matt had loved—and I secretly disliked.

Instinctively, I looked at the man's neck, bare beneath the jagged line of pantyhose. There it was, right beneath his jaw. The carotid artery, I knew from watching *Grey's Anatomy*. It was almost invisible when a person was calm, just a soft thrum of a pulse. But if you riled them up, that artery thumped so hard you could see their neck beating in time with their heart.

It was the first thing I looked for when Matt came into any room.

His face could look so calm, his expression so docile. Those soft brown eyes almost sleepy, his bee-stung lips parted in a half-grin.

It was the face everybody saw. His executives and managers and employees at TSuites, the startup he'd co-founded with his brother that was poised to sell for $340 million. The business partners and customers who commented on his LinkedIn and Forbes articles about TSuites' "innovative, employee-first" company culture never failed to say how Matt was, "Such a good human being," "One of the good guys," and "Damn, I wish he was my boss."

It was the face Sophie saw, too. When he read her *Little House on the Prairie* before bed, made cinnamon waffles for us on Sundays, and rented actual ponies for Sophie's fifth birthday so all the kids in her kindergarten class could ride in our sprawling front yard.

The only person who *didn't* see that face all the time was me. And the only warning I ever got that he was about to rage—or pin me to the bed until I promised I wasn't cheating—was that thrumming pulse going wild at his neck beneath his chin.

"Okay, your turn. Move, now."

I startled but stayed frozen a moment longer. Matt's face loomed so large in my mind, I could've sworn it was his voice coming through the thin fabric.

I blinked, zooming back into the stifling hell of the van.

The man holding the gun didn't have to ask me twice. I was already scooting my butt across the van floor so fast, I heard the back of my jeans rip on the pocket where it caught on something sharp.

He laughed in surprise. "Glad somebody knows how to hustle."

When I got to the edge of the van, I wanted to crane my neck to see the kids. I could hear distant whimpering again, but it sounded so far away. Where had they taken them? Where were they taking me?

Instead, I kept my eyes lowered obediently.

He grunted. "You want me to remove those zip ties on your legs?"

The smell of his deodorant was making me sick. I wanted to retch again.

I just nodded, though.

He snickered again. "And you know what'll happen to the kids if you run?"

When I nodded again, he reached his free hand into his pocket and pulled out a Swiss Army knife. "Good girl. A+ student."

When he finished cutting the ties on my legs, he grabbed my arm, motioning for me to let him cut the ties on my wrists, too. My numb fingers tingled as the blood rushed mercifully back.

I shuddered in relief but didn't bother celebrating the freedom. As long as he had that gun, I might as well have been his marionette.

He snapped his fingers and flicked the barrel of the revolver, motioning for me to walk away from the van. When I looked up, I saw the second man maybe twenty yards away. He was standing at the edge of a junk pile.

I walked toward him with quick, measured steps. Not so fast that he'd think I was running, but not so slow he'd think I was dawdling. I resisted the temptation to look around me.

It wasn't until I stopped walking, a few feet away from the second man, that I saw the gaping hole in the earth in front of me. It came out of nowhere, just a black pit in the dirt at our feet. Like an enormous snake had made its home there. What the hell was this?

I felt so dizzy I nearly crumpled.

There was no sign of the children. But there was a ladder poking out the top of the hole in the ground.

Then it hit me. I was going down there. That's why they'd cut my ties.

The kids were already down there.

My ex-brother-in-law's words found their way to the front of my mind again. *Jessa Landon deserves to rot in hell.*

Those words felt more real than ever now as the second man flicked his gun toward me and I forced my hands to grab the first rung of the ladder.

I stifled the panicked voice in my head begging me to do what Sage had done earlier: disobey, resist, refuse to go down into that hole.

I ignored that useless voice and kept my head bowed as I moved down another ladder rung. That wasn't the way out. The way out was doing whatever they told us to do. They were the ones with the guns.

No, no, no, no, my mind screamed with each inch I descended.

Small spaces terrified me. When I was a little girl, I'd wedged myself inside a neighbor's shed during a game of hide-and-seek. The latch had engaged from the outside, trapping me inside for maybe all of five minutes until the other kids heard me screaming. Something big, with prickly legs skittered over my arm.

I'd had nightmares about it until I was in college.

It doesn't matter. Just do what they say and there's a chance we'll all survive.

I tried to keep my body from shaking, but it was no use.

"Chill out, lady," the man said in a scratchy whisper. "You're gonna fall."

He leaned closer and pressed his gun against the back of my head, like if I moved a muscle he'd blow my brains out. The hard, narrow barrel dug painfully into my skin as if he were trying to push it into my skull. But then the man mumbled, "It's not that bad down there. Just hang tight, okay?"

17

SAGE

I thought the other kids would cry, or refuse to go down the ladder into the hole.

I thought I'd probably cry or pass out, too.

However, it turned out, when there were enough bad things all around you, the only choice was to move to the least bad thing.

And that meant moving away from the man with the gun and hurrying down the ladder, into the hole in the ground, with Bonnie right behind me and Evelyn Marks right behind her—we were the last kids down.

One rung.

Two rungs.

Three rungs.

I counted until twenty before the number scared me so much I quit counting. I felt like the ladder was floating in space because I couldn't see the bottom of the pit. I knew that was dumb. It had to go somewhere. Ladders didn't go forever. But that didn't stop me imagining it.

Each time I stepped lower, I looked up at Bonnie above me, her tiny frame silhouetted dark against the opening of the hole. The sky was turning that rich, cloudless shade of blue Mom loved. *Cerulean,* she'd said, like that big beautiful word itself was part of why she loved it.

"It's okay, Bonnie, we're almost down," I said in a shaky voice, even though I had no idea. It was getting darker by the second. All I could think about was, were those two men with guns going to cover up the hole, like this was a grave?

Bonnie clung to the ladder like a baby monkey, gasping whenever she took a breath. The air wasn't nearly as cool as I'd thought it might be down here. The smell of dry earth mixed with the scent I remembered from when Mom took me and Bonnie thrift shopping. Old clothes. Other people's laundry detergent. A hint of musty body odor.

My hands felt sticky and hot on the rickety ladder rungs.

I tried to notice everything, taking pictures in my mind like I'd done when the van stopped and I scratched away the paint in the window. I didn't know how it would help us, but it was the only thing I could do besides give up and let the pit swallow me and Bonnie whole.

At the top of the pit, where the sky showed through, the hole was square and narrow, like a chimney. Just large enough for a person to crawl down the ladder like Santa Claus.

The four walls of the chimney weren't dirt. Instead, they were some kind of cheap, scratchy-looking wood. The wood walls bowed in a little.

At the bottom of the chimney, where we were, the pit opened up into a big, dark room or cave. I blinked my eyes open and shut, trying to see anything.

There was just darkness, and some shuffling and whimpering sounds beneath me that I hoped was the other kids.

Above me, Bonnie sucked her breath in so fast I thought she was falling for a second. But she kept quiet, and I knew she was just trying as hard as she could not to cry.

When I put my foot down next, expecting another rung, it finally hit something springy and soft. A mattress, I realized. "Oh," I gasped, then stepped back and ran right into another kid—Rose, I recognized from the squeak she made.

In the dim light coming from above, I could just see the glimmer of Bonnie's wide eyes when she let go of the ladder and tumbled into me, with Evelyn right behind her.

The three of us looked back up the ladder, at that little faraway glimpse of pale blue sky.

All I wanted to do was scramble back up all the ladder rungs and then run as fast as I could, as far as I could, until I found a grownup who could actually help us.

Instead, I watched as the opening was suddenly blocked.

For a second I thought Jeepers or Greasy Hair were coming down here with us.

That made me clamp my teeth down on my cheek so hard I nearly bit part of it off. Bonnie grabbed hold of my arm and dug in her fingers.

"It's Ms. Jessa," I whispered after a second, relieved despite myself. Ms. Jessa wasn't exactly great at being a grownup, but she was a mile better than Greasy Hair and Jeepers.

Another shape moved into the sky above Ms. Jessa as she climbed down from the chimney and into the big open space.

I could tell from the lumpy, weird shape of the body and head that it was Jeepers.

"There's some water in jugs along the wall," he said in that same weird voice he'd used earlier. Almost silly, and too deep. "And a couple flashlights. Some toilet paper. I ... I built you a toilet in one corner. It's just a bucket and a piece of plywood with a hole cut in it, so be careful when you sit on it. Otherwise you'll get splinters."

Another voice—Greasy Hair's—growled something I couldn't understand.

"Oh, for shit's sake," Jeepers muttered under his breath so soft I almost couldn't hear it. Then, to us, he said, "And there's some peanut butter sandwiches. There's not that much. But ... we'll bring you more when it runs out."

"Come on, they'll figure it out." Greasy Hair was standing next to Jeepers now, at the top of the hole. He grabbed the top of the ladder, grunted, and shook it so hard it wobbled and creaked. "Come on, lady. Let's go. *Move.*"

Ms. Jessa moved faster, reaching the bottom of the ladder just in time as both men started hauling it up and out of the pit. When the bottom of the ladder went past the ceiling of the room, they set the legs down on the narrow ledge with a *thunk* and fussed with something that made the top of the ladder slide downward in a loud set of clanks, turning it from a tall ladder into a short one.

From where I stood looking upward, it looked like the ladder was suspended in midair above us, but that couldn't be true. *It's resting on the roof of this little room,* I realized, tucking that thought away even though the information seemed useless. The top of the room—or whatever this place was—was so high up there was no way any of us could reach it without that ladder. But noticing it was what Harriet the Spy would do. So I did, too.

Ms. Jessa stumbled around on the squeaky mattress for a second, getting her balance beside me. I could hear her breathing, raspy and hard like she'd just finished running a race. She looked up at Jeepers and Greasy Hair. Then, in a voice like she was apologizing for opening her mouth at all, she said, "Wait, hold on, please? You can't just leave us down here—"

Greasy Hair laughed, cutting her off and waving away what she said. "You'll be fine. We left you water." He gestured down into the hole. "We thought of everything," he said, like he was pretty proud of himself. Then he waved to Jeepers. "Come on, help me with the roof. Let's close it."

I watched in terror as Jeepers nodded, then grabbed hold of the ladder and lowered himself down into the chimney.

Close them in.

That was when Mindy lost it. Not just crying or whimpering, but *lost it.* "No, no, no, no, NO," she started screaming, so fast I could barely tell where one *no* stopped and another began.

Her panic was contagious, like yawns. Ben's voice, then Rose's, then Bonnie's joined in, begging the men not to shut us in.

I swallowed my screams back, afraid of what it would feel like to let the terror fully into my lungs.

"Quiet," Jeepers thundered when he tucked his chin and looked down at us, and even Mindy Gamel forced her screams back into little whimpers. "You've got everything you need down there," he snapped. "Nobody can hear you. So when you scream, you're just making us mad. Don't try anything stupid, and you'll be out of here soon. If you're good and quiet, you get out. If you're bad, bad things will happen."

Saying something under his breath, he moved down a few more ladder rungs until he reached the spot where the wooden chimney ended, at least ten feet above our heads. Then he stepped to the side.

"We won't have enough air," Ms. Jessa said, her voice trembling in the sudden silence. "Our carbon dioxide—"

"There's a couple of air tubes in the shaft," Jeepers muttered, not looking at her but pointing up at the top of the hole.

I tried to swallow, but my sticky, dry throat barely obeyed.

A loud, echoing scrape filled the dark room as he started dragging something heavy across the opening to the chimney.

The ceiling of the little room groaned and squealed, like a hurt animal.

My view of the ladder, Greasy Hair's smashed-up face looking down at us, and the dim light at the top of the pit started to disappear. A few trickles of dirt fell down onto my cheeks, but I didn't even brush them away.

Bonnie gripped my arm harder.

I realized I'd grabbed onto Ms. Jessa's hand without meaning to. I didn't pull it away, though.

In a few more seconds, we'd be completely sealed underground.

18

By the time I finished positioning the thick slab of plywood over the hole in the roof of the shipping container, and lugging the heavy excavator battery on top of that, I was sweating so bad that my whole head was soaked through the pantyhose.

We probably didn't need the extra layer of security. The kids were twelve feet beneath the ceiling of the bunker. It wasn't like they could fly. But why risk it?

I blew out a breath and tried to ignore the churning in my gut.

Getting the kids into the van had been bad, but this was a thousand times worse. It felt like kicking puppies. I'd tried not to look in their eyes while we led them to the hole in the earth, but there were so fucking many of them I couldn't help it.

They'll be fine. They'll bounce back. They'll have a crazy story to tell when they're older, I reminded myself for the hundredth time. Other people had it way worse. Their parents cared enough about them to send them to after-school care instead of leaving them to fend for themselves in a trailer park every day, like mine had. On good days, Mom left the double-wide's door open so I could come inside and watch TV. On bad days, she locked it and refused to wake up.

So yeah, I'd never been shoved into a dirty van, or kidnapped for ransom, or forced into a hole in the ground, but these kids would be down there for a couple days, max. I'd survived my shit, and so would they. And if I could, I'd trade my crappy memories of growing up for that experience in a heartbeat.

"For shit's sake," I mumbled, bracing my hands against the excavator battery and managing to nudge it a few more inches. It wasn't quite in the middle of the thick plywood slab, but I figured it didn't matter. The battery was plenty heavy, and the effort of moving it around in this confined space had me breathing hard. It was almost impossible to lift. Getting that battery positioned at the edge of the shaft a few days ago had been one of the hardest parts of the whole setup.

I hadn't weighed the battery, but I could tell from how hard it was to lift that it weighed nearly a hundred pounds. Besides, the ladder was pulled up. And even if the kids—or the bus driver—could somehow get to the plywood, twelve feet above them, without a ladder, they wouldn't be able to push that battery away from the opening.

I kicked at it, just for good measure … and because I wanted to kick something.

It didn't budge, but the shipping container made another groaning sound and shifted slightly beneath my feet. I froze. The shipping container was solid, reinforced by metal rods running along the sides, but the pressure from all the dirt was more intense than I'd expected. The metal kept making that pained creaking sound. The plywood sheets we'd used to reinforce the shaft were buckling in a little, but no worse than when I'd checked them yesterday.

They would hold for a few days.

They had to hold.

"Dude, hurry the fuck up. My boss is going to rip me a new one," Andy whined. "I'm already late. He just texted. My pickups are wondering where the hell I am."

I gritted my teeth and finally gave in to the urge to tear the pantyhose off my head. The kids couldn't see either of us now. "Almost done," I growled. What I wanted to say was that he'd given me the worst jobs, but I knew he couldn't wait any longer to get to his shuttle pickup.

Working quickly, I double-checked to make sure the air hoses tucked against one side of the plywood were in place—and not smashed up too much. They snaked upward, through the shaft, poking out a few inches aboveground near the hole entrance.

Andy insisted we didn't need the air tubes. *'There's a ton of air down there, Teddy Bear,'* he'd said, as if it barely mattered. *'And they don't need food. Just water. People can go weeks without food. We aren't trying to build a daycare down there.'*

"Let's gooooo," Andy snapped, peering down at me. He was getting mad now, but he had to wait a few more minutes. I could get out of the shaft by myself, using the ladder. But the metal excavator door was heavy enough, it needed two people to lift back into place to cover the hole in the earth.

I finished inspecting the battery's position on top of the plywood, hurried up the ladder and out of the hole, and dusted off my hands.

Part two of the plan had gone off without a hitch.

The kids were secure. They weren't happy down there, but they were safe. And nobody had any idea where they were—or who we were. If they did, the quarry would be swarming with police by now.

I grinned at Andy as we hefted the yellow excavator door to cover the hole, but he just glared. He looked like a drowned rat with his greasy hair plastered to his head. I wanted to make a joke about it, try to lighten the mood. I knew better than to say anything, though. Most days, his personality matched his looks. Dopey stoner hippie. But he had a dark side that came out when he was stressed or pissed, and I'd learned to give him space until he chilled out.

The second we set down the heavy metal door, Andy swore under his breath and held out his hand. "Keys," was all he said.

When he'd snatched them away from me, he jogged toward the white shuttle van, opened the back passenger door, and hefted the detour sign onto the dirt without a word. Then he dusted off his pants, jogged back to the driver's side, and drove away down the narrow dirt path in a cloud of dust.

I lifted a hand to wave at the back tires. A late airport pickup was nothing compared to what we'd just pulled off. He was planning to quit that shitty side job the second we got the ransom money, anyway.

He'd calm down when he got back.

I opened the driver's side door of the gray van and checked inside the groove of the door to grab my burner phone that I'd tucked there earlier. Then I pressed the ON button until the pixelated, gray screen lit up.

I scanned the news alerts from the local station I'd turned on notifications for earlier that morning.

The story about the missing kids and bus driver had hit the news fast and furious. I read the headlines, then the articles, nodding when it became clear that it was all panicked fluff.

They had no idea where those kids were or what had happened to them.

I tucked the phone in my pocket for later then lugged the detour sign through the dirt and opened the back doors to the gray van. I shoved it inside the stripped cargo area, holding my breath so I wouldn't smell the vomit and the urine.

We'd have time to hose down the van later.

I closed the doors again and sat down on the bumper until I couldn't hear the crunch of the airport shuttle's tires anymore.

I made myself take a big, deep breath.

Without the noise of sniffling kids and Andy barking orders, the quarry had gone completely silent. Peaceful, almost.

Big, stacked-up clouds were gathering above the steep quarry wall rising above my head. A faint ray of light from the sun, sinking down on the other side, cut through the clouds like an Easter postcard. *"Get-yourself-right-with-Jesus clouds,"* Mom always said when that happened. I felt the tiniest twinge of guilt when I imagined the look on His face if he slid down that beam of light and saw what me and Andy had done with those kids.

Then I flicked it away along with a mosquito trying to suck my arm.

I'd promised myself I'd do some good stuff with my share of the money. Maybe even help some kids. I'd rebalance the karma.

Andy and I hadn't told each other what we planned on doing with our shares of the money or where we planned on going when the ransom came through. I told him it was smarter that way, so we wouldn't be able to rat each other out if everything went tits up and one of us got caught.

Really though, it was because I didn't want him tagging along with me.

Andy was an okay dude. He was the only one who didn't judge me when I got out of jail. He'd gotten me this job, and he'd done his part helping me dig out the bunker for the kids. But I was the one who'd planned out the real logistics, thought through everything that could go wrong, insisted we practice timing and run drills on every possible scenario.

I'd done the same with my own escape plan.

Living in my mom's shitty double-wide for the past year hadn't been all that bad when I could dream about my new life as a millionaire.

I wasn't stupid, I knew a million dollars wasn't *that* much anymore. Inflation and cost of living and whatever. Some of the houses in Sunset Springs cost that much.

But a million was plenty in Cuba—just a ten-hour trip on a cruise boat away from Miami. My cellmate Daniel was the one who gave me the idea, once he warmed up to me. When I first got to jail, he glared at me like I was a skid mark on a pair of jeans. But when I stayed quiet, didn't pick fights, and stayed the hell away from his side of the cell, he decided he liked me. And after a few days, he started opening up.

His family was originally from Merida, Mexico—across the water from Cuba. His family had moved to California, then Idaho, when he was a kid. There was no work in Merida, but there were oranges to be harvested and potatoes to be dug for cash under the table.

However, when Daniel was a teenager, two of his cousins had gotten into bad trouble back in Merida. Some deal went south, so they made a run for Cuba.

The Mexican government tried to get them back, but the Cubans wouldn't lift a finger.

And they *definitely* wouldn't lift a finger for Uncle Sam.

One day, some meth-head named Corey tried to accuse Daniel of stealing his Twix. I was the one who saw the sharpened toothbrush handle snake out of his pocket. I was the one who hip-checked Corey just in time to keep the homemade shiv from making contact with the back of Daniel's neck.

Corey got sent to solitary. And later that night, Daniel told me he was still in touch with his cousins. They'd promised to set him up if he ever got in a tight spot again.

All he had to do was get to Little Haiti in Miami with five thousand dollars in his pocket, and they'd do the rest. Fake passport. Fake ID. Fake birth certificate. They'd already done it for his brothers.

They'd do it for me, too. No questions asked.

So that was where I was headed as soon as I got my share of the ransom money.

Besides Mom and Andy, there was nothing keeping me in Idaho. It wasn't totally accurate to say that my life had gone to shit since jail. It had *started out* as shit. The stink just piled on over the last two years. Sometimes I was the one shoveling it, but not always.

So I was plenty happy to leave it all behind.

Mom's ears must've been burning enough for her to wake up from her latest bender, because my phone pinged right then. *Bring home something good for dinner.*

I punched out a reply before I could feel bad that I hadn't stocked the fridge for her yesterday. *There's some leftover spaghetti.*

I wasn't great at cooking, but I was better than Mom. She was so skinny when I saw her again after jail, it hurt to look at her. Half of her hair had fallen out, and her clothes hung so loose on her limp body I barely recognized her. When she got high, she forgot to eat unless somebody put food in front of her. And she was high most of the time.

"Meth diet, huh?" Andy had joked when he came by to pick me up for work one time and Mom made a rare appearance at the door.

I'd laughed, but he was right. When Mom wasn't high and manic, she was asleep. And when she wasn't asleep, she was high and manic. She ate when I cooked. It'd been that way since my dad moved out five years ago.

I ignored the second ping of my phone, probably something about how the spaghetti was old so she just wouldn't eat.

"Take your own advice and apply *yourself,* Mom," I mumbled, kicking the tire of the gray van and wishing Andy would hurry and get back from the airport.

19

When Dad and I finally pulled into the driveway and I hit the garage remote, my bleary eyes nearly scanned right past the pizza box sitting on the porch. If it hadn't been for the curvy red *Speedwagon's* logo on the side of the pale gray box that blended in with the long shadows on the cement, I would have.

Dread and gratitude yanked a tug-of-war in my chest. I hadn't ordered pizza, which meant that somebody had sent it to us. Was it a wrong address? Or had someone heard about what happened at Bright Beginnings and sent a mercy dinner? Who, though?

I wasn't sure my coworkers even realized I had kids. I certainly didn't know anything about their families. The job had been fully remote since the pandemic, which meant that aside from the occasional Zoom meeting, we didn't know much about each other. For the most part, I was just their middle-aged coworker named Sheena who knew how to wrangle Excel spreadsheets and kept her microphone on mute and used a Hawaii-themed video background that blocked out the mess in her office. Sometimes, I didn't even have that. Dad wandered in so often, his confused expression suddenly parting the palm trees on my Zoom background, that I'd started turning my video camera off most of the time, too.

The instant I parked the car in the garage, Dad hefted himself out of the passenger seat, slammed the car door, and stomped into the house without a backward glance.

His abrupt lecture about my divorce had withered into stony silence, either because I wasn't playing along or because he'd lost the thread of it. But there was no doubt he was still at a boiling point, even if he didn't know why.

I slumped back in my seat in a daze.

A ping on my phone jolted me back to attention. A new voicemail.

I scrambled to grab it from the car holster. Was it the police? The daycare center? How had I missed a call? My hands shook so badly I nearly dropped the phone twice as I tried to navigate to the voicemail.

The garage door growled shut, plunging me into darkness while I sat shaking in the driver's seat, waiting for the message from an unknown number to begin playing.

"Hi, Sheena, this is Debbie from Cherished Hearts Memory Care—"

I slowly set the phone down without listening to the rest of the message, then stared at the barely visible outlines of seldom used lawn equipment and dried-up paint buckets on the shelf in front of me.

For a few seconds, I refused to draw in a new breath, just exhaled and exhaled and exhaled until it felt like my lungs might collapse into the jagged hole in my chest.

Part of my brain still stubbornly refused to accept the situation with the girls or Dad. This couldn't be happening. I couldn't do this. My head buzzed like it was filled with trapped bees, angry and desperate for a way out.

Like every parent I knew, I was familiar with the dizzy head-rush of losing a child for a few minutes on the playground or at a grocery store. That intense, blind panic you could barely tolerate. The terror. The feeling of time standing still. The dread that something truly awful had happened in the five seconds you turned your back.

That combination of feelings hurt so bad you didn't think you could endure it without collapsing under the pressure. I'd never tried to imagine what it would be like if I was forced to live in that state for longer than a few seconds.

It was worse than I could've dreamed.

A banging sound from inside the house cut through the buzzing bees in my brain.

I couldn't leave Dad alone in there. I couldn't shut down, no matter how badly I wanted to.

Before I opened the driver's side door and went inside the house, I reached behind me and grabbed the two tangled sweatshirts lying on the backseat.

One was Bonnie's, a stained pink My Little Pony fleece with too-long sleeves. The other was Sage's, a plain red hoodie. For all the times they insisted they wouldn't get cold at the park, then shivered.

I hugged Bonnie's pilled fleece hard against my face, pressing it against my mouth. Then I screamed.

When I ran out of air, I drew in a shuddering breath. I didn't feel better, but it made the frantic bees settle down just enough that I could get myself out of the car and inside the house.

Karen the cat met me at the door, chirping a greeting and winding through my legs with delighted meows.

"Dad, are you hungry? There's pizza," I called robotically, walking the few steps to the front door to retrieve the box. My stomach recoiled at the idea of food even as it rumbled at the same time. I would try to eat, even if I didn't want to. I'd half-assed lunch, trying to finish the surplus budget in time before pickup, and Dad had skipped it altogether. His anti-psychotics, which he took in the mornings, meant he wasn't hungry until evening most days. We were both running on fumes by then.

"Dad?" I called again as Karen flung herself onto the floor and purred harder, wriggling with her white-tipped paws in the air.

I opened the front door and bent to pick up the pizza box, peeking inside. The pepperoni pizza was still warm, but the cheese was starting to cool on top, grease congealing into tiny hard puddles instead of glossy drips.

When I shut the box, I noticed that there was an envelope taped to the top, right in the center. I tore it off as I carried the pizza to the kitchen table, hoping the note would tell me who I could thank for our dinner.

"Dad, come eat, please?" I called down the hall. "It's pepperoni. Someone sent it to us."

There were two sheets of paper inside the envelope. Typed. A long note.

The bees still circling in my head went silent, stunned, as soon as I read the greeting.

Sheena Halverson, this will be your only warning: Do NOT contact the police. Do NOT contact the FBI. Your every movement is being watched.

Read this note and its instructions very carefully. Bonnie and Sage are depending on it.

My phone pinged. I ignored it. It pinged again. I forced my eyes to focus back on the instructions on the note and read every word.

If you do what we ask, your girls will come home to you. So will the other kids. They are alive and well—for now. But their fate is in YOUR hands. Any attempts to contact police or deviate from our demands will result in swift and merciless consequences.

Don't play games with us. And we won't play games with you. If you want to see your daughters again, you will withdraw a total of $50,000 in cash, in separate transactions from five banks in the Treasure Valley. These withdrawals will be made from the Boise City bond funds. If questioned, you will respond that this money is for a down payment on the new buses for Northridge Elementary. Exact amounts and bank names are listed below on page 2.

You will bring the cash, in a backpack, to the Bull Creek trailhead at Little Eddy campground at exactly 7:00 p.m. on Saturday, August 27. You will come alone.

I stopped reading to stare at the page. That was tomorrow.

Leave the backpack under the trailhead sign. Don't talk to ANYONE. Don't hang around the campground.

Then drive away. We will not retrieve the money until you leave.

After the cash drop-off, you will return home and transfer the remaining bond funds—two million dollars—into a Bitcoin wallet using the steps listed on page 2. Wait for instructions. We will be watching. Once we have confirmed the Bitcoin transfer, we will release the children to you.

Do not attempt to trace this communication. Do NOT contact authorities. Do NOT speak with other parents. Do not tell ANYONE about this note.

Follow these instructions TO THE LETTER.

We sincerely hope you succeed.

I let the first page of the note fall to the floor. As promised, the second page was a list of detailed instructions for which banks to visit, which amounts of cash to withdraw, even where to park at the trailhead.

My heart drummed so hard, the words on the white paper swam in front of my eyes like static on an old TV. This couldn't be happening. None of it.

I'd barely finished scanning it when a commotion from the front of the house made my head snap up.

Someone was screaming.

20

SHEENA

It wasn't just *someone* screaming.

I knew that voice. Dad.

Letting the second page of the note fall beside the first on the kitchen floor, I ran down the hall and out the front door in time to see Dad charge into the neighbor's door. "Help," he bellowed, "I need help, somebody help, please!" He tore through the hedge beside the Forneys' walkway and started banging on their front door.

He sounded so distraught that for just a second, I looked around wildly and shrank back to the porch. The words in my head from the typed ransom note blared like a foghorn above the sound of Dad's hollering. *Your every movement is being watched.* Had Dad seen something? Was there someone watching us right now?

"Dad!" I called, jogging after him onto the sidewalk. "Dad, please come back, it's all right."

Lies. Nothing was all right. The lives of ten children, two of them mine, were suddenly in my hands. I'd thought nothing could get worse than hearing that they were missing. But this was worse.

Ignoring me, he gave up pounding on the Forneys' door and moved with shocking speed toward the Andersons' house.

The street was empty, except for a silver sedan driving toward us. It pulled over and I recognized Mr. Heller from two houses down when he jumped out of the car. He shot me a sympathetic look beneath his bushy gray brows and jogged toward Dad, who had nearly tripped on a garden hose in the Andersons' yard as he darted toward their front door. "Ron, hey! It's me, Chez Heller. What's going on?"

"I need help, need backup," Dad gasped, turning around and stumbling toward him with his hands above his head, like he was surrendering.

Chez turned to look at me, pity written all over his face.

Movement in my peripheral vision caught my eye, and I realized it was the Andersons' blinds. Someone, probably terrified, was peeking out at us. Shame and sadness and panic and desperation swelled so big in my chest, I thought I might pass out in the neat-cut grass.

But what Dad had said to me in the car earlier pounded in my head on repeat. Wrong crisis, right words.

I didn't get to fall apart right now. Sage and Bonnie needed me. Dad needed me. I couldn't let them down, even if I had no earthly idea what the hell I was supposed to do.

"I'm here to help, it's all right," Chez was saying. "Look, Sheena is right over there." Chez pointed at me, and Dad whipped around to verify.

Dad's pale face, freckles popping dark, sagged with confusion and a hint of relief. He lowered his hands and looked from me to Chez.

"What in the Sam Hill ..."

I hurried toward him, seizing the break in the chaos. "Thanks, Chez. We're okay, aren't we, Dad? Today's been a tough day."

Chez opened his mouth like he wanted to say more. Like maybe he'd heard about what had happened and remembered I had two little girls. Surely the kidnapping must have hit the news by now.

The police officer in the parking lot had said there were eight other kids on that daycare bus, with Sage and Bonnie. There were other families reeling tonight in Sunset Springs, all of us hit at once like shrapnel from an explosion.

"I'm sorry," Chez said gently, those furry gray eyebrows bunched together in a deep furrow. "Do you need anything ..." I could feel him searching for my name.

"Sheena," I choked out, mind zipping back to the ransom note on my kitchen floor. *Do not speak to ANYONE.*

I had to get Dad back inside the house now. Then I had to figure out what to do next. "Thanks for your help, Chez," I said brusquely. "Come on, Dad, let's go inside."

To my relief, Dad let me take him by the arm and we walked back to the house without another word.

The two sheets of printer paper lay on the ground where they'd fallen.

The pizza box sat open on the kitchen counter.

Karen mewled in delight and trotted toward Dad. "I'm not hungry yet," he mumbled, scooping her up and heading for the den. "I'm gonna take a nap with the cat."

"Okay, Dad," I choked out gratefully as he walked away.

When I heard the bed springs creak in the other room, I knelt and picked up the note, using my sleeve this time.

I already knew I wouldn't go to the police. Not yet. I wasn't going to be stupid about potential evidence either, though.

I could already imagine the outrage from neighbors—even other parents of the missing children—calling me stupid, reckless, selfish. But I couldn't stop imagining what Dad's expression would look like if he read that note. He wouldn't rush to call the police—even though he'd proudly worn that blue uniform for more than thirty years.

People think that if you're in uniform, you've got all the answers. They need to believe that, makes them feel safe—but that doesn't always make it true. Trust your gut, Sheen, he'd say, if his mind was sharp.

And right now, my gut told me that if I ignored that note, I did so at Sage and Bonnie's peril.

I wanted so badly to call someone, anyone, who could help me figure out what to do. Even Jacob—if I knew how to contact him. Bonnie and Sage were still his daughters. Surely he'd want to help me if he knew what was going on.

Do not speak to ANYONE.

No. I couldn't even call Jacob. I blinked hard, sick with fear, and tried to think. *Move. Do something. You're the only one who can help them. They're counting on you. They're terrified. What if they're hurt? Hurry, for the love of God, hurry.*

Moving on pure adrenaline, keeping one ear tuned to the bedroom for any indication that Dad was on the move again, I tucked the envelope and pages of the note into a gallon freezer bag and put it in the mostly useless tiny cabinet above my stove range where I kept Dad's medication.

Then I stared at the pizza box, unsure what to do with it. I couldn't throw it away. What if there were fingerprints or evidence there? Yeah, it had come from Speedwagon's delivery, but I had no idea who else might have touched it. Could you get fingerprints from a box?

I frowned. I couldn't keep it in the house. Not with Dad around.

My heart squeezed painfully.

I suddenly knew what I had to do.

Shoving aside random containers in the refrigerator to make plenty of room, I carefully slid the box onto the bottom shelf for safekeeping.

Then, moving faster, I pulled my phone out of my pocket and stood in the far corner of the living room where the blinds were closed, ignoring the flurry of texts that had come through for a few minutes longer.

I sank down against the wall and listened to the full message Debbie from Cherished Hearts had left me. Then I redialed the number.

When her cheerful voice picked up on the second ring, "Cherished Hearts Memory Care, this is Debbie," I squeezed my eyes shut and got the words out as fast as I could before they were choked out by tears.

"Hi, Debbie. It's Sheena Halverson calling you back." My voice broke, but I pushed to say what I needed to say. "I know it's late, but you said you had an opening. And I really need somewhere to take my dad tonight."

21

TEN MINUTES BURIED

I'd heard the expression "So dark you can't see your hand in front of your face."

I thought I knew what that might be like. Thought I could imagine a blackness so complete it swallowed you whole.

I was wrong.

For a few minutes after the last shreds of light disappeared overhead, the shipping container—at least that's what I assumed this thing was—erupted into chaos. Crying kids, sharp inhales and exhales, shuffling and running into each other, begging the man with the pantyhose over his head to open the hole back up.

Beneath it all was the squealing chorus of squeaky springs from the old mattresses lining the bottom of the bunker. They shuddered and shifted as ten pairs of feet moved back and forth, finding the walls.

In a daze, I shuffled backward until my back hit the wall of the container. It was bowing inward, like it could barely contain the weight of the earth pressing in against it.

Little gray dots danced in the darkness as I blinked my eyes faster, imagining all those thousands of pounds of dirt suddenly breaking through the straining walls of the bunker, covering our heads and eyes and noses.

How much air was down here? Even more importantly, how quickly would our own carbon dioxide start to poison us? I forced my lungs to fill, then release the breath, but all I could think about was suffocating down here in the dark.

"I think I found a jug of water," one of the boys cried after a few seconds.

The exclamation was followed by a brief silence, where I could hear the faint sound of footsteps crunching above our heads.

The other kids heard it too.

"Help, help, help!" one little girl screamed, the sound filling up the impossibly dark room.

That snapped me out of my stupor. I stumbled toward her voice, my shoulders bumping against other small bodies as I moved.

It was all I could do not to shake the little girl—Evelyn I realized. "Shh, Evelyn," I hissed, making my voice loud enough that the other kids could hear me. We couldn't panic. We couldn't lose our heads. That only ever ended badly. "That's the bad men up there," I told her, grabbing her arm in a way I hoped wasn't hurting. "We just need to be quiet and we'll stay safe, okay?" I bit back the most terrifying thoughts spinning through my head. What if they decided we were too loud—and blocked off the air hose?

No. The kidnapper had said there was an air tube that was bringing in at least some fresh oxygen. That was more evidence they actually wanted to keep us alive—not hurt us. We just had to stay calm and hunker down until the men got what they wanted.

I forced my breathing to turn steady and pushed the disturbing thoughts far away. "Who found water?" I asked. We were all thirsty. We needed to ration it, make sure it doesn't get spilled in the dark.

"I did." This time, I recognized Ked's voice. "And there's some cups. And I can smell food, too."

Excited murmurs rose from the other kids in response.

"That's great, Ked," I said, moving toward the sound of his voice, thankful for the distraction. I drew another steadying breath. The kidnapper had been telling the truth about leaving us some food and water. Maybe that meant he was telling the truth about letting us go once they got the ransom. But it also meant they were likely planning on leaving us down here for a while.

"Jessa Landon deserves to rot in hell." My ex-brother-in-law's words singsonged in my head for the umpteenth time.

This isn't hell, I told myself firmly. Hell didn't have food and water. "Let's all sit on a mattress and have a drink, okay?" I called into the darkness.

I could do that. I could take charge in this small thing. The thought of making some kind of order out of this chaos was comforting.

"I think there's a toilet over here," another voice piped up from behind me. Sage's voice. "I saw it before the light went away. It's just a bucket with a piece of wood over the top, but ..."

"That's great, Sage—"

"Ms. Jessa, you could probably lift me. If you stand on it and help me up, I bet I could reach the ceiling," Sage burst out in a rushed whisper, before I could finish. "I could try to—"

More excited murmurs from the other kids.

I whirled toward the sound of her voice, panic turning my already dry mouth to cotton. "No," I barked, louder than I'd intended.

"But—"

"No," I said again, quieter, peering around the darkness for a faint green or red light that might indicate we were being watched down here. I didn't see one. "We are going to do exactly what the men said, and then we are going to get out of here. Do you understand, Sage?"

She didn't respond this time.

"Come toward the sound of my voice. I'll pour everyone a little water," I rasped. I shoved the guilty feeling down and felt for the plastic cups stacked beside a row of water gallons. I hated to squash that precocious hope. Hated to imagine the crestfallen look on her face. The same one I'd glimpsed in the dim light of the gray van, when I'd demanded she sit down after she'd scratched that little hole in the van's window paint.

But encouraging her now would be worse.

Encouraging her might get us all killed.

The kids stumbled around each other to form a haphazard line along the mattresses nearest the water jug. As I felt my way down the line, pushing cups into little hands, I made each of the kids tell me their names and their favorite animal. I didn't know how long we were going to be down here, but from the number of water gallons—ten I'd counted—it might be days.

That thought filled me with dread. And maybe I imagined it, but each breath felt a little harder to pull in than the last.

I shoved the terror away. It wouldn't help.

We needed to settle in.

"Ben, Australian Shepherd."

"Mindy, unicorn."

"Ava, I like all animals."

"Bonnie, kitties."

I oohed and ahhed over each animal. *Yes, I love kitties, too. Australian Shepherds are so smart! I wish I could pet a unicorn.*

I reached for the next pair of hands but found hunched shoulders and tangled curls instead. "Sage, what's your favorite animal," I asked.

She didn't answer for a few seconds. Her shoulders shuddered like she was trying and failing to hold in a silent sob.

"Sage?" Before I could tell myself it was a terrible idea, I knelt in the dirt at the edge of the mattress and grabbed her hand.

I expected her to yank her hand away. Instead, she squeezed back for just a moment, then pulled her hand back gently, drawing in a big breath like it would keep her from deflating again.

My daughter Sophie had done the same thing when she fell, while she was learning to walk.

The small gesture made my heart ache so badly I could barely swallow.

I'll keep you safe, I promised Sage silently, the way I'd promised Soph so many years ago.

No matter how angry you are, I will keep you safe.

I was about to move on to the next kid, come back to Sage in a minute, but then she cleared her throat. "Sage, badger."

That made me smile. "Badgers are fierce," I said. "They were my college mascot, too."

"They're the best diggers," she said quietly. "A badger wouldn't be afraid down here. She'd just dig us out."

She'd be afraid when she found those men with guns waiting for her at the top, I thought to myself, but I bit the words back.

22

THIRTY MINUTES BURIED

Whoever made the peanut butter sandwiches and tucked them into a Styrofoam cooler in baggies knew how to do it right.

The peanut butter was spread evenly on both sides of the bread, thick enough to cover the slices in a smooth layer. A good layer of jam that didn't quite reach the bread edges oozed between them, so the crusts didn't get soggy.

I hadn't expected the pantyhose men to know how to make a good sandwich. When I finished the chunk Ms. Jessa gave me—after making me swear on my life I didn't have a peanut allergy—I wished I had another one.

"It's good, isn't it?" I whispered to Bonnie.

"Yeah," she said, her voice small. Then, "I wish there was a light. It's really scary down here."

"It's just dark," I told her, like I had at bedtime when she got scared and came into my room. "Dark can't hurt us. It's okay."

I could tell that some of the other kids were listening to us, from the way the chewing sounds got quieter. A few of the kids sighed, like they needed to hear that about the dark, too.

I wanted to talk about my idea again. Jeepers was still up above us, at the top of the hole. At least, I was pretty sure it was him. I'd listened hard after they'd closed up the hole and Greasy Hair had said something about needing to pick somebody up. Then a car had started up and tires had growled away.

For a while, Jeepers went away. When he came back, he took big steps above our heads, back and forth, like he was circling around. I could just barely hear his footsteps when they crunched on the ground. I was glad Greasy Hair was gone for now. Maybe Jeepers would leave soon, too.

As the minutes went by, I licked my lips and tried to think. If Ms. Jessa helped me, I could reach the ceiling, where the hole was covered. Maybe I could find a way to push off whatever they'd covered the hole with and get into the wooden chimney.

We had to at least try.

Ms. Jessa wouldn't help, though. I screwed up my face in a frown, staring in the direction where I could hear her handing out more food and water. She thought the men would keep their promise. And maybe, if it was just Jeepers, there was a tiny chance he would. I just knew he was the one who'd made the sandwiches.

Greasy Hair, though? I got the feeling he lied a lot. Told you one thing and then did something else. The way Dad did that first summer he left. Promised he'd come and visit me and Bonnie all the time even though him and Mom were getting a divorce. Bonnie was still a baby then. She didn't understand what he was saying. I did, though.

I took a last sip of water from the cup I was sharing with Bonnie. There were only six plastic cups, so we had to share. Then I squinted up at the ceiling and tried to see anything.

I didn't think I'd be able to. It was too dark. But after a few seconds, I could make out a fuzzy, dark gray ring of light overhead, in the ceiling of the shipping container room. It was so faint that when I blinked, it took a second for my eyes to find that gray circle again. It was there. And if I could just reach it, I could try to get through it.

My legs itched to move, to try. But I couldn't get up there alone.

I sat there in the dark on the stinky mattress and thought for a while, since that was the only thing there was to do.

Then I had an idea.

"Hey, Bonnie? You remember that game, Telephone, we played with Mom and Grandpa?" I asked her.

"Yeah," she said quickly. Telephone was one of her favorites. It always made both of us laugh when the sentences got all messed up and silly.

I took a big breath and leaned close to her ear. "Okay, we're going to do that. Only don't mess up the words, all right? Repeat this to the next kid, and tell them to pass it on: Sage has a plan. We gotta help her."

I felt silly the second I drew back, but Bonnie didn't ask questions. She was whispering to Rose Carlton. My heart pitter-pattered when Rose let out a murmured "Ooh" of hope.

I didn't really have a plan. Just a 'hair-brained' idea, as Grandpa would say. But another line from *Harriet the Spy* had been rolling around in my head since Ms. Jessa told me to stop talking about escape: *"Life is a struggle, and a good spy goes in there and fights."*

The feeling pressing at the back of my stomach told me Harriet was right.

I decided that Ms. Jessa was like Cook—Harriet's cook—who was nice enough but thought Harriet was out of control. Always saying things like, *You think you're a spy, but you're still just a little girl. You need to find something better to do than sticking your nose where it doesn't belong.*

I had to be like Harriet, not Cook. I didn't just have to sit here because I was a kid. I didn't have to listen to the only grownup down here.

I could do something.

I strained my ears and heard the kids passing my words down the line of mattresses. Just a few more kids, and everyone would've heard it—as long as the message didn't get too mucked up.

I'd been trying to convince Mom I was a big kid—not a baby —for the past year. That I didn't need to ride the bus to Bright Beginnings with Bonnie anymore because I was too grown up. That I wasn't afraid to be home by myself if Mom had to run errands after work.

"Why?" I'd asked her, so many times. *"I'm grown up enough."*

"Because you're not ready and because I'm your mom" was what it always came down to.

That was true. I never had a response to that last part.

But I was starting to think that maybe Mom wanted me riding the bus with Bonnie to Bright Beginnings not because she thought I was a baby or because I wasn't ready. It was because *she* was a grownup. And grownups got to be in charge.

Just like Ms. Jessa wanted me to sit still and be quiet. Not because she really knew what was best. It was because she was a grownup, and grownups got to be in charge.

The same thing was true for the men in the masks.

They were grownups—with guns. So they *really* got to be in charge.

I listened hard past the sound of Ms. Jessa's voice. She'd finished getting everybody a drink of water and was coming back down the line to collect the empty plastic cups.

On the other side of the dark room that smelled like dirt and old clothes and hot peanut butter breath, someone was whispering. I heard my name in the middle. Sage.

I felt along the bottom of the mattress, doing the math in my head. I wasn't sure my idea would work yet, but it was taking shape faster now that I was giving it room to breathe.

After a while, Jeepers' footsteps crunched overhead again, going away from us. Then tires rolled along the gravel, getting closer this time. I guessed even though I couldn't be sure, that it was Greasy Hair, back from wherever he'd gone.

"Sage, what are you gonna do?" Bonnie whispered, her sweaty hand feeling for mine again as she leaned close. "What's your plan?"

I didn't answer, just squeezed her hand because I still needed to think a little longer. "I'll tell you soon, okay?"

The only thing I knew for sure was that I was done listening to grownups. Done pretending that they knew what was best.

I was going to be like Harriet.

I was going to fight.

23

After I hung up with Debbie from Cherished Hearts, I set the phone down and stared at my hands, splayed on my knees.

I'd be driving Dad to the memory care facility. Not in a week, like Debbie had first proposed—but tonight. I told myself it wasn't a firm commitment. Just a safe place to take him for a couple of nights.

I had less than twenty-four hours until I was supposed to take the ransom money to Little Eddy campground. I could already tell it was going to be a race against time to do what the kidnappers had asked. Some of their specific requests might even be impossible, from what I knew about withdrawal limits. I needed to be certain that Dad was safe while I did what I had to do tomorrow, even if he hated me for it.

My breath came in rapid gasps that I tried to make as quiet as possible. If I sobbed out loud, Dad would wake up. And I wanted to let him sleep for a few more minutes before I got him up to make the drive to Cherished Hearts. It wasn't far—maybe twenty minutes, out in the foothills near the old quarry.

My phone pinged again and I finally read the texts that had been coming through since I'd found the ransom note on the pizza

box. All of them were from a number I'd gotten texts from previous-
ly, when Bright Beginnings relayed information about pickup proce-
dures and field trips.

These texts were nothing like the ones I'd gotten before.

*PARENT UPDATE: Police have located the children's phones.
We are unable to give more information at this time to protect evidence in this active investigation.*

My stomach rolled. *Evidence. Active investigation.* Those were
words from CSI and Forensic Files. Not my children's aftercare
provider. They hadn't said the word "kidnapping" yet. Did they
know? I glanced at the half-open blinds in my living room, then back
to the note. My eyes scanned faster, desperate for more information,
for a text that read "We've now found the children safe."

The second, third, and fourth texts were mostly useless. Dupli-
cate info about police contacts and repeated reassurances that,
"Bright Beginnings is doing everything possible to aid and cooperate
with police and FBI."

There was a plea for parents to come forward with any information they hadn't already disclosed that might help officials find
the bus and the children.

My jaw clenched as I pictured the pizza box I'd carefully
stored in my refrigerator. There was probably evidence on that box.
On the ransom note. Maybe there were cameras at Speedwagon's
that the police could use.

I was intentionally withholding information in a crime investigation. One that directly involved my two children and eight others.

My phone creaked, and I realized it was because I was clenching it so hard.

I couldn't come forward.

Any attempts to contact police or deviate from our demands will result in swift and merciless consequences.

I could only imagine what the kidnappers meant by that. If they were degenerate enough to plan and execute something so heinous against elementary school children, I had to believe that their threats weren't empty. If I didn't do exactly what they asked, and something happened to my girls, and those children, it was *my* fault.

That thought burned through the guilt. All that mattered was keeping them safe, keeping them alive.

My phone pinged again.

PARENT UPDATE: Police and FBI have located the missing bus.

My heart leapt, then crashed as I read the rest of the update.

Detectives are still working diligently to locate the children and bus driver at this time. All public statements will be relayed via KTRB. We are unable to give additional information in order to protect evidence in this active investigation.

They'd found the bus, but not the children.

I braced against the helpless feeling that pressed so hard in my lungs it was nearly impossible to breathe. From the bedroom down the hall, Dad's mattress creaked.

I'd never considered the idea that the police might find the bus, but not the children. How? How had the kidnappers managed to make eleven people disappear into thin air?

Dad's footsteps thudded down the hall, slow and uneven. "Sheen? I had a doozy of a dream. Just awful. It was the Schneider case all over again, but instead of that little boy it was Sage and

Bonnie who went missing. I've got an awful headache, where's the Tylenol?"

The Schneider boy. My blood ran cold. Micah Schneider had been abducted from a busy McCall beach on the Fourth of July, right before Dad retired. A few hours later, the mother got a call from an unknown number. By that time, the family had already called the police. When she realized the kidnapper was on the phone, she thrust her cell into the hands of an officer standing beside her.

The caller hung up and didn't call back. The police traced the call to a burner phone. Micah Schneider was found dead ten days later.

The story struck me with fresh horror now.

Dad blinked at me. "Sheen, you all right? It's been a stressful day, hasn't it?"

I forced Micah Schneider from my mind. And for the briefest moment, I told myself I could handle this. I didn't have to take Dad to Cherished Hearts tonight. He was confused, sure, but his demeanor was settled now, not frantic. Maybe the chaos that had happened with Chez in the street was just the shock of what he'd learned in the rec center parking lot that had sent him into such a bad spell.

Dad shuffled his feet at the end of the hall, looking rumpled and red-eyed from his cat nap. Then he frowned. "Is Jacob still at work? That man needs to prioritize his family," he mumbled, brows furrowing as he looked at me, then tilted his head toward the stairs that led to Sage and Bonnie's rooms. He lowered his voice. "Can't let the girls see you like this, Sheen. Wipe those eyes and get your chin up. Marriage isn't easy."

My heart sank. "Dad, I need you to come on a drive with me, okay? I … I ruined dinner, so we're going to stop at Big Judd's, okay? And then …" I swallowed, not wanting to lie to him but not sure how to do anything else. Dad loved the burgers at Big Judd's. It was enough to perk up his appetite even when he turned down everything else.

He shrugged but went for the shoe rack to put on his sneakers.

I wiped my eyes and stood up from the couch. When he'd gotten his shoes on, I grabbed his hand. "There's an emergency at work, and I need you to stay at … somewhere else tonight, okay? Do you remember the place we talked about? Cherished Hearts? It's really wonderful, the foothills are beautiful out there, and I just talked to Debbie who says they could take you tonight as a sort of—"

Dad yanked his hand away and stared at me like I was speaking French. "What emergency? If you need to go somewhere, I'm fine right here," he said incredulously. Karen leaped up onto the counter and made a plaintive meow, angling herself toward Dad's arm a few inches away. He reached to pet her. "You'll leave the cat home alone, but not me? I'm perfectly capable of taking care of myself, Sheena Renae. I was a goddamn lieutenant." He looked back toward the stairs. "Where are the girls, anyway? Where is Jacob?" His voice rose to a thundering boom with each word, and I could see him getting agitated again.

"Dad, please," I begged, tears spilling over before I could stop them. "I've been divorced from Jacob for years. The girls are gone, and I'm at the end of my rope. Please, Dad. Get in the car."

I strode across the kitchen and reached into the cupboard above the microwave, careful not to let my hand come in contact with the ransom note again. My fingers curled around the first pill bottle I found, and I pushed it toward Dad so he could see his name on the label. "I can't leave you alone. You have Alzheimer's. I'm afraid you'll hurt yourself while I'm gone. Please, just listen to me and get in the car!"

The last part came out like the snap of a belt, harsher and louder than I'd intended.

His eyes flicked from the prescription bottle then back to me. I watched the clouds part long enough for him to purse his lips and duck his head. "Okay, Sheen," he said softly, all the fire gone out of him just like that.

I wanted to wrap him in a hug, tell him I was sorry, tell him about the ransom note and ask him whether I was doing the right thing. Instead, I rushed down the hall to his room and grabbed his pajamas, some clothes, and anything else I could cram into the duffel bag in the closet in sixty seconds.

I knew all too well by now that I might only have a few minutes before the pathways that had become tangled and unruly in his mind crossed and we had to have this conversation yet again.

Debbie had told me he'd have everything he needed for tonight if I could just bring his medications and some clothing for him, and I had to take her at her word.

"I love you, Dad," I choked out. "I promise I'll get you anything else you need soon. Just give me one day, okay?"

He nodded slowly and rubbed his wrist. "Where's my Rolex?"

I swallowed hard. The broken watch was still lying in the cup holder of the car where I'd left it. "It's getting fixed right now. We'll have it back in a couple of days. Won't be long. I promise. I love you, Dad," I tried again, desperate for him to say it back.

Instead, he glanced up the stairs one more time, then shook his head and headed to the garage.

24

"Teddy Bear, my man! Beer me."

I rolled my eyes, but I was glad Andy was back. I was also glad his mood seemed to be so much better, now that his shuttle drop-off was done. I glanced at my burner phone to check the time: 6:42 p.m. His next drop-off wasn't until 1:00 a.m.

He slammed the driver's side door behind him and held out his hand toward me, making a "gimme" motion.

"Okay, but just one. Your boss is gonna kill you if you bring the shuttle back late again," I warned, because I knew how fast Andy could chug a six-pack, and the last thing we needed was his boss trying to track down the shuttle if he passed out or got too drunk to drive.

"Thanks, Mom." Andy snorted at my back as I headed for the rickety shelter a few feet away. Andy and I had built it ourselves, same as we'd rigged up the shipping container. The doorless sheet-metal and plywood shack was an eyesore, but it fit right in with the junk and dirt piled up as far as the eye could see in this section of the quarry. Both side walls were warped, making it look like the whole thing might collapse if you kicked at it. But it'd held up plenty well, offering shade and a place to sit on top of the big Coleman cooler we kept inside.

I'd added a fresh bag of ice on top of the cheap beer we'd bought at the gas station yesterday evening, when I came by to check on the bunker one last time. And to add the peanut butter and jam sandwiches. I knew it was stupid. I knew Andy would've made fun of me for that last check. But I wanted the sandwiches to be fresh. This wasn't one of those *Lifetime* episodes where some creep chained up his victims and made them eat dog food or garbage like that. This was a civil kidnapping.

Just a transaction.

I tucked four beers into the pouch of my hoodie then headed back to the spot I knew Andy would already be sitting, on a couple of flat tires we'd dragged away from the edge of the dump pile. Close enough to the bunker shaft that we'd have eyes on it. Far enough away that the kids wouldn't be able to hear us talking.

The less they heard my voice, the better.

It had been a year and a half since I'd worked at Bright Beginnings as a bus driver. Right before I landed myself in jail. I was there for just ten days, right after I'd turned eighteen. It was my first job that felt like a step beyond the teenage after-school jobs I'd had since I was fourteen, frying tots and assembling burgers at a drive-in, or breaking down pallets at the shipping yard.

The kids on the bus could be annoying as hell, but I'd actually liked the job. Especially because my then-girlfriend Kiersten was one of the "Counselors in Training" at the rec center. She told me that if I did a good job with the bus route, she'd put in a good word for me at the rec center. Some people got paid just to keep the basketballs lined up in the gym, wipe down equipment, check out rackets and balls to the kids and adults who had memberships.

I didn't do a good job, though.

My job as bus driver and my title of "Mr. Edward"—my legal first name—lasted for exactly a week and a half, when that little girl's damn apple rolled all the way down the aisle and got caught under the brake pedal and I panicked. Ran my mouth a little. But to be fair, I thought we were all gonna die. I calmed down afterward and even said I was sorry, although I wasn't. The dumb girl with the apple should've apologized to me, really.

I didn't think it would be that big of a deal. Maybe a slap on the wrist or a lecture from my boss at the rec center. Kids heard swearing all the time at school, and anyone who thought their little angels didn't drop an F-bomb or two had their head up their own asshole.

The next morning though, I got a text telling me that, effective immediately, I was no longer employed by Bright Beginnings for violating their "Zero tolerance" policy on "Driver conduct."

I thought my girlfriend Kiersten would be on my side. Might even help me get a second chance, but she said there were three write-ups in the system about my "Verbal outburst," and there was no coming back from that. It took some doing, but she finally logged into the system and read them to me.

Three parents had called Bright Beginnings to complain about my "unprofessional, violent language." One of them even threatened to withdraw her child from the program if I stayed on as a bus driver.

"For shit's sake," I'd muttered, and Kiersten had given me a look like, *Are you serious? How could you be so stupid?*

We broke up that night, because that was the exact same look my mom gave me when I burned the bottom of the frozen pizza or woke her up from a nap in the middle of the afternoon or got my pay docked because money was missing from the register, even though I swore it wasn't me who'd taken it.

So I'd just called Andy and we got drunk and he dared me to jump his "buddy's" motorbike.

And, like a drunk idiot, I had.

Later, while I was lying in the hospital bed—right before I went to jail—I couldn't help remembering how when Kiersten had logged in to the Bright Beginnings system, her username and password looked like the same ones she used for everything else.

Username: KierstenK. Password: K1erst3nK.

I wasn't trying to be a creep. But after getting fired and banged up and pushed into jail, I did briefly fantasize about logging into the system and fucking some stuff up with scheduling or something. Kiersten worked at the reception desk, so she had access to pretty much every part of Bright Beginnings' back-end system. I wouldn't do enough to get her fired or anything. Just enough to make a couple of people give her the same look she'd given me. *Are you serious? How could you be so stupid?*

By the time I got out of jail, that particular destructive impulse had passed. Not all the "Take responsibility for your actions" lectures and group counseling sessions went over my head.

Still, out of curiosity, I tried logging into the Bright Beginnings system the week I was released from jail. The week I turned nineteen.

To my surprise, Kiersten's login info worked. Maybe I shouldn't have been surprised. It had only been six months that I actually spent locked up, but it felt like forever.

So that's what I did at night, all that first week I was back in Mom's double-wide. During the day, I tried to find another job, tried to get her to eat, tried to wrangle my life back into some sort of control. And at night, I logged into the Bright Beginnings system and read write-up after write-up, internal memo after internal memo.

Some of it was boring. But some of it made me feel better about getting fired. People got written up for the dumbest shit. Even perfect little Kiersten had gotten dinged for not answering the phone with the proper greeting too many times.

One of the all-employee memos from management read, *"Many of you have noticed an uptick in write-ups for policy infractions. This is not intended to embarrass or single out any individual employee. Rather, at Bright Beginnings, we must all take responsibility for the image we project to our community. With the bond vote coming up next week, our relationship with and service to our community must be above reproach. The budget surplus will, pending a vote from parents and citizens in the school district, provide much-needed renovations and resources to our aftercare program."*

I didn't know about the budget surplus until then. I figured it was small potatoes, since Bright Beginnings wasn't a big, fancy rec center.

I was wrong.

My mouth nearly dropped to my chest when I saw the number—in a memo for upper management.

Two million dollars. That's how much the budget surplus was.

"Fucking hell," I whispered when I saw that number, counting the zeroes twice.

A few weeks later, when I was really starting to sweat about the idea of ever getting a job again now that I was a legit felon, Andy sent me a text and asked if I wanted to work with him at the quarry. He'd vouch for me to his dad. If I did the work and didn't mind sweating it out in the junk pile section of the quarry, it wouldn't matter that I was an ex-con.

Maybe he did it because he felt guilty for the fact that I took the heat for the stolen bike. Or maybe he was grateful I'd never snitched on him. Either way, I took the job and stopped spending so much time snooping on Kiersten's login to Bright Beginnings.

However, after a month or so of working with Andy, I told him about the budget surplus.

That was right around the time we were supposed to dump the broken shipping container in The Pit.

When I told him about the budget surplus, Andy's eyes went wide and he screwed up his face in concentration like I'd just given him a free wish from a genie's lamp. That look on his face while he stared at the shipping container made the hair on my arms stand up, like this moment was going to mean something.

I'd never gotten a sign from the universe. Mostly just "fuck yous." But when I thought back on all that serendipity, it sorta felt like a sign.

When Andy started asking more questions about the bus route, where the kids put their phones, whether there were cameras on the bus, I went along with it. Why not?

When Andy asked to see the roster—and we realized that two of the kids attending Bright Beginnings belonged to Sheena Halverson, City Council Treasurer—that clinched it. She had access to the money, and two of the kids belonged to her. She'd be the perfect target for the ransom note, and maybe we could even scare her into not involving the police.

We were going to give Bright Beginnings the ultimate finger—and pull off the perfect kidnapping for ransom, too.

"Cheers, dude." Andy held up the beer I'd just retrieved for him, sloshing a little onto the dirt outside the airport shuttle. "We're fucking geniuses, you know that?"

I held up my cold can to his and leaned back against the van. "Yeah, dude. Cheers."

Andy motioned to the covered hole in the ground, a short distance from where he'd parked the shuttle. "I still can't believe some of them peed themselves." He snickered. "They weren't even in the van for that long. Good thing you made them a toilet down there, I guess."

They were just scared. I bit back the reply on the tip of my tongue and grunted, not wanting to talk about the kids anymore.

Relax, I told myself, trying to get the muscles in my arms and legs to uncoil. The past three hours had been organized chaos. Now, all we had to do was wait—and not fuck anything up—until it was time to meet Sheena Halverson at Little Eddy to collect the ransom money.

Andy still had his 1:00 a.m. airport pickup, but that would be cake. Nothing to do with the kidnapping.

I took a long pull of watery beer. The quarry was peaceful now. Silent and still warm enough to make you feel lazy and relaxed.

I forced myself not to look at the ridged metal sheet, a stone's throw away.

They're fine, I told myself, repeating the phrase again and again until the beer started to make my head just a little fuzzy and the words started to ring true in my brain.

25

FOUR HOURS BURIED

I stayed quiet for a long time, waiting until I was pretty sure Ms. Jessa had fallen asleep—and until I didn't hear anymore crunching footsteps or tires above my head. By the time that happened, most of the other kids had fallen asleep, too. Bonnie's fast breathing and sniffles had turned into heavy breathing. She'd curled her warm, sticky body into a ball and laid her head in my lap.

Careful not to move too quickly, I nudged her, and she made a soft, squeaky sound and sat up.

I whispered into her ear before she could say anything. "If we stack the mattresses on top of each other, we'll be able to get a lot closer to the top of the hole," I said in a whisper that suddenly felt loud in the dark room.

She nodded against my ear, so I kept going.

"Then we can at least try to listen when they talk. Maybe we could even reach the top of the hole," I said, forcing my brain to remember the details of what it felt like climbing down the ladder. If each rung was about as thick as the mattresses were wide ...

"Hush, Sage," Ms. Jessa hissed, and I jumped. She was still awake. "You need to stop—"

"You can't make me stop," I hissed back, standing as tall as my skinny frame would go. Ms. Jessa couldn't see me right now, but I hoped she remembered that I was almost a foot taller than she was—even if I was skinnier. She could probably wrestle me to the ground if she really tried, but I was smart enough to know that scrappier beat bigger any day of the week.

Karen, our calico cat, was at least twice the size of the stray, skinny tomcat that sometimes came into our garage, and she backed down every time that tomcat arched its back and skulked over to eat her food.

I waited for Ms. Jessa to protest, to grab my arm, to tell me I was being reckless and putting everybody in danger, same as she had before. To my surprise, though, she didn't say anything else.

Her breathing, no longer quiet and even, sounded like she'd just run up the stairs.

I was breathing hard, too. I told myself it was just because I was afraid, but I was also worried there wasn't quite enough oxygen in the stinking, dark room.

I knew from what Jeepers said that there was an air hose at the top of the bunker somewhere, bringing in new oxygen. But how much air could a little hose really bring down here? Was it enough to keep up with eleven people breathing in and out, in and out, all this time? I shoved the scary thought away and locked it up tight, telling myself there was no way we'd actually suffocate. The men wouldn't let that happen. After all, they couldn't get any ransom money for us if we were dead, could they? The air felt thick and sour, though. Each breath felt a little harder to pull into my lungs.

"Grownups think that kids always have to do what they say," I whispered, not talking to Ms. Jessa anymore, but to Evelyn, and Mindy, and Ben, who were stirring awake. "Because they think *they're* the smart ones. And we're just a bunch of dumb kids. *Babies.*"

A wordless murmur rippled through the darkness.

Ms. Jessa still didn't say anything in response.

Her breathing had gone a little quieter, though. Not calm, just quiet.

I could feel her hating what I was doing, but she didn't try to make me shut up again or tell me to sit back down.

Maybe she was still shocked that I flat-out refused to listen to her. Maybe she could hear the claws in my voice that said I wasn't going to sit down and shut up unless she actually tackled me and pinned my arms and legs—and even then, I'd holler and bite her like the tomcat would.

Or maybe she was just afraid of what would happen if the men heard the ruckus down here. And that was the one thing the men were going to come investigate: a ruckus.

Either way, I kept talking, sensing that more kids who had fallen asleep on the dirty mattresses were pricking up their ears to listen. "Both men are still up there right now—but not close to the hole. If we can get a little closer to the surface, maybe we can hear what they're saying to each other. Plus, it'll be easier to hear when they get in the vans and drive away. Then we can try to find a way to get out of here." I gulped down another swallow of air. "We need to know what they're going to do next. And if they're … if they're telling the truth about not hurting us."

Someone made a tiny whimper that I felt deep in my stomach. Because what if we found out they *were* planning to hurt us, what could we even do about it?

Rose's voice popped from the darkness from a few feet away. Scared and tiny but eager, too. "How do you know what's happening up there?" she asked. Not in a mean way, but like she actually wanted to know.

My heart thumped and my skin prickled. I wasn't the only one who couldn't stand just sitting down here, doing nothing.

"I've been listening really hard for clues," I said. It wasn't easy to hear what was going on all the way down at the bottom of the bunker. The ceiling was at least eight feet high. You had to really pay attention to the sounds coming from beyond the hole and the wooden chimney. And even then, it was tricky to hear much.

Ked piped up. "If Sage can't hear them very well, that means they can't hear us very well, either. We don't have to be that quiet."

"Yeah, exactly," I rushed. "They won't get mad at us for stacking the mattresses, because they won't know we did it. We can knock them down if we hear them opening up the hole."

My mind rewound all the information I'd gathered so far, trying to remember if I'd said everything I wanted, waiting for Ms. Jessa to start blustering any moment.

She didn't.

So I kept talking.

"Are they right above us?" Bonnie asked, sitting up.

"No," I said, hoping I was right. In the short minutes between getting out of the gray van and being forced down into the dark earth, I had seen that this hole in the ground was on the edge of a huge junk pile. It wasn't really close to anything else except all that trash and dirt. So unless the kidnappers were going to sleep right in the dirt, on chunks of broken rock and metal, they weren't directly above us. "I'm pretty sure the men are over by the vans."

"Where are the vans?" Ms. Jessa asked, her deeper grownup whisper louder than anybody else's.

I blinked in surprise and turned toward her voice. "They're on the dirt road with the gravel," I said. "Not that far away, but far enough. That spot where they first let us out."

"And how do you know that?" she pushed, like this was a test.

"Because there's sharp stuff all over the dirt out here." I remembered the feeling of my sneakers slipping over loose gravel, shards of plastic, and big pieces of trash. "Stuff that could pop a damn van tire," I added, throwing in the swear like I'd heard Grandpa do when he forgot me and Bonnie were in the room.

Swearing in front of a grownup made my face flush hot, but I didn't want to take it back, either.

"And you think both men are up there right now?" Ms. Jessa asked. Only this time, it didn't sound quite as much like she was hoping I'd give the wrong answer. This time, it sounded like she might actually want to know the answer.

"Yeah, I'm positive," I said.

After I'd heard the sound of approaching tires crunching on the gravel above us, there was the slam of a car door, then two faint sets of footsteps crunching around for a few minutes. Then mostly quiet. The last thing I'd heard was the faint sound of Greasy Hair's laugh from the direction of the dirt road.

The sound of his laugh was sharp and quiet at the same time. It made me think of the ugly, raspy noise the dried corn stalks made in the wind at a Halloween carnival called The Thicket that Mom took us to in Declo last year and was way too scary for Bonnie.

I hadn't heard any more tires crunching since then, and I'd been listening as hard as I could.

While I talked, I was getting more and more sure about a new thought knocking around my brain: The men were going to leave us alone at some point.

It was the only thing that made sense. They'd gone to a lot of effort to put us down in this hole. They seemed so pleased with themselves that they'd made such a good trap. They weren't worried about us escaping, at all.

They left us lots of food and water and even a bathroom, which meant they didn't plan to check down here any time soon.

They'd told us to shut up again and again, tying up our hands while we were locked in that van. But when they sent us down here, into the ground, they just smiled like my teacher Mr. Heller did when he caught you red-handed, trying to sneak a peek at your phone during class. *Gotcha. Now you're mine.*

Those two guys didn't want to sit out here all day and all night. They just wanted to leave us down here. Maybe they'd even drive away at some point, just for a little while. To eat, to sleep, or see their families.

And when they did leave, I was going to be ready. Not sit down here like a dope.

"But there's only four mattresses," Crosby Neville said, breaking into my thoughts in a grumbly voice, sounding just like he did anytime he got on the bus and saw somebody sitting in his usual seat.

"We can fold them in half and make them twice as thick," I said, making sure my voice wasn't getting too loud. What had started as a scared whisper was getting stronger.

Crosby made a satisfied "Mmm hmm" noise.

"Oh, yeah, good idea, Sage," Rose added, almost sounding excited.

"Can you all help me move the mattresses?" I asked nobody in particular.

There were scuffling noises as other kids stood up, started to shove the mattresses around, whispering back to me.

"Yeah, where?"

"We've got one of them folded up, Sage!"

Ms. Jessa kept quiet and stayed where she was. She didn't help. She didn't try to stop us though, either.

26

The dark house was overwhelmingly, excruciatingly quiet.

For the first time in more than a decade, I was alone. Utterly, and completely alone.

I couldn't bear to look at the girls' bedrooms, or Dad's. Or the kitchen, where I'd left the note and pizza box. So I locked myself in my bedroom with my laptop, eyes glued to the bright screen as the minutes and hours ticked past, reading everything I could find online about the missing children, memorizing the information, and combing through Reddit discussions.

By the time I looked at the clock, it was 12:30 a.m.

What I really needed was sleep. But sleep was impossible, my mind churning through every awful thing that had—and might—happen. And what I needed more than sleep was for my girls to be home safe. But they were gone, and anything but safe.

My throat ached so much I could barely swallow, and my head felt so full of tears and terror that I imagined the toxic floodwaters slowly drowning me from the inside out.

I kept pulling up the photos that had been posted on KTRB and read the articles one more time, even though the words and images were seared into my mind.

There were three main articles on the site. The first headline was, "ABDUCTED: Ten Northridge Elementary Students and Bus Driver, Missing."

They'd included a photo that I recognized right beneath it. Sage, Bonnie, and three other kids playing foosball in the rec room at Bright Beginnings. I'd seen it in the monthly newsletter just a few days ago. I could hardly stand to look at their smiles. Lanky Sage was facing the camera and smiling with her mouth but not her eyes. She stood more than a foot taller than the other kids, with her curly black hair in a ponytail I'd wrangled and re-wrangled that morning. Bonnie wasn't looking at the camera. She was looking at Sage, her identical black curls swept over one brow so you could see the adoring expression on her face.

The article beneath the photo was sparse, repeating information I already knew from the police. Careful, un-inflammatory words that didn't say much at all. *Police and FBI are working with Bright Beginnings and Northridge. Panicked parents left cars stopped in traffic to pour into the rec center parking lot, looking for answers. The children, ages seven to twelve years old ...*

The comments section, on the other hand, was anything but sparse. It swelled and blazed like a dumpster fire, ranging from white-hot sympathy that tore me up to flippant emojis and LOLs that hollowed me out.

I CANNOT imagine what those poor mamas are going through. Hold your babies close, everybody. PRAYERS.

Are you fkin serious a FKIN BUS GOES MISSING. Fake news??

Popo here are dummmmmmmbasses.

There's gotta be so much they aren't telling us. There's gotta be a ransom note. They aren't just gonna take a bunch of kids for shits and giggles. Hope they don't botch it like they did in that one movie.

When I read that last comment, I had to run to the bathroom and dry heave.

There *was* a ransom note. And I already knew I was going to botch it.

I was alone, way past my breaking point, and if something went wrong it would be all my fault. But if I went against the kidnappers' explicit instructions—and something went wrong—it would be my fault, too.

Dad's often-repeated words echoed louder than ever. *Trust your gut.* If he were here—and himself—he'd be reminding me about Mindy Falcrest and all the other cases where things had gone sideways after following "protocol."

I dug my fingers into the palms of my hand. My gut was screaming that the people who'd written that ransom note meant what they said.

I closed the first article and opened the second. This headline, posted on KTRB thirty minutes after the first, read, "UPDATE: Missing Northridge Students' Phones Located."

There was no photo this time. The article went on to explain that the police had located the students' and bus driver's phones on the side of Highway 55, out of sight down a crumbling embankment.

Most likely, the kidnappers had dumped the phones there right after the abduction. The police and FBI were holding the phones, searching for any clues. But, as the article speculated, it was pretty clear that the kidnappers were fully aware that the phones could be used to track their location. And they weren't going to allow that to happen.

The third article was the one that made my stomach clench hardest.

The headline read, "UPDATE: Northridge Elementary Bus Found, Abducted Students Still Missing."

From the timestamp on this last article, police had located the bus right about the time I was opening up the ransom note attached to the pizza box.

I couldn't stop staring at the photo—a distant glimpse of the bus itself, nestled among the trees of what appeared to be a cherry orchard. The last rays of sunlight glinted off its white paint and turned the shadows coming from the gnarled cherry trees into long, dark arms reaching across its sides. Like the bus itself was being held captive against its will.

The number of unanswered questions spinning in my mind were mounting: Why was the bus in the cherry orchard? The narrow dirt lane that led deep into the orchard wasn't on the bus route. Why had the driver turned that way in the first place? How had the kidnappers forced the bus to go there? Why hadn't any of the kids been able to get to their phones to call for help?

This last article showed a photo of the phone-cubby system at the front of the bus. I recognized it from a brochure from Bright Beginnings I'd seen back when I signed Bonnie and Sage up for aftercare. "Student and driver safety is our priority!" the brochure read. "Phones are stowed and inaccessible at all times during transit."

The irony dug its claws into my chest.

I shut the web browser only to open my Maps app and retrace the route I'd need to follow in the morning.

Five banks, five different counties in the Treasure Valley, five withdrawals of $10,000 each.

About three hours' drive time, if traffic was good. Plus time to wait in line at each lobby, fill out the appropriate paperwork, chat with the tellers like I wasn't fighting for my life. If I got to the first bank the moment it opened at 9:00 a.m., I would be finished collecting money around 3:45 p.m.

I blinked away the blur in my eyes that was turning the phone's light into a dancing halo in the dark room.

Whoever had made this plan had clearly researched withdrawal limits—but not enough. In general, it was true that $10,000 was the trigger-limit that would alert the federal government, and that this amount could technically be withdrawn from several banks without hitting the Feds' tripwire. Especially if the withdrawals came from different counties. However, I knew from past experience that multiple withdrawals of even numbers would trigger the tripwire more quickly. Trying to withdraw exactly $50,000 was way too risky.

I would need to bring evidence of city expenditures for each withdrawal—which I'd be able to do, given the surplus bond funds and the upcoming expenses with the new bus fleet.

Not $50,000 in one day, though.

I could *maybe* stretch it to $40,000 if I was really ballsy. But even that was asking for trouble when I really thought about it.

And if I drew attention to myself with reckless withdrawals, that would mean a fast-track to scrutiny from the government—and police. Probably the FBI, since they were already involved with the case.

If the police started scrutinizing my behavior, and the kidnappers were watching like they said they would be, they would quickly realize I had screwed this whole thing up.

So I *couldn't* screw this up.

I had to assume the writers of the ransom note would be angrier if I drew police attention than if I withdrew slightly less money than they'd asked for in cash.

Follow these instructions TO THE LETTER.

My stomach lurched again and I swallowed back the bile.

Basically, they'd be angry no matter what I did. *You're going to fuck this up, one way or another,* my mind wailed.

Despair fizzed through the fear, making my stomach turn over again and again.

I sat up and switched on the lamp sitting on my nightstand, finally admitting that sleep would not be happening tonight. Then I pulled the Maps app up yet again, calculating the drive time to Little Eddy campground this time. Two hours and fifteen minutes from the last bank I'd be visiting on the outskirts of Melba.

Once I dropped the cash at Little Eddy, it would be another hour's drive back to the house to transfer the two million in Bitcoin. That part would actually be easy compared to the bank withdrawals. All I'd needed to do was set up a Coinbase account, and that had taken me fifteen minutes. However, it would raise the biggest red flags the second anyone from the city realized what I'd done. There was no doubt the kidnappers had anticipated this, saving it for my final step.

My mind spun, calculating and recalculating. There was just a little over an hour of play in the plan. Throw in a couple of quick bathroom breaks, a little traffic, a detour on the road, and even that buffer would dwindle to nothing.

Prickles of sweat turned my pajamas sticky against my underarms.

I knew they'd made the schedule tight on purpose. So I wouldn't be tempted to deviate—or bring in the authorities.

Eyes grainy and mouth dry, I opened yet another tab on my phone and typed in "Ransom kidnapping police involved."

Maybe I was hyper-focusing on the stories Dad had told me about his time as lieutenant. I needed to know what else was out there—and if I was making the biggest mistake of my life by going along with the ransom note.

The headlines were worse than I expected. I scrolled, unblinking, through the gauntlet of horrors.

Kidnapper Executes Hostage After Police Ignore 'No Cops' Demand.

Failed Rescue: Victim Found Dead After Police Intervene Against Ransom Note Instructions.

Police Raid Turns Fatal as Kidnapper Follows Through on Threats.

Family Devastated as Police Involvement Leads to Hostage's Gruesome Demise.

Kidnap Victims Slain After Police Misread Ransom Demands.

I couldn't bring myself to even open these articles. The headlines were already too much.

I glanced at the time on my phone once more—just past 1:30 a.m.—before forcing myself to turn the screen dark. This wasn't helping, even a little bit.

I closed my eyes and pictured Bonnie and Sage. Were they together right now? Were they still in Idaho? Were they sleeping?

I refused to imagine anything else. So I pictured them tucked together like ducklings, breathing soft and deep, their impossibly long eyelashes fluttering while they dreamed.

I told myself that the image was real, over and over again in the darkness until the words lost all meaning. Because my mind already felt like a horse about to bolt. And I wasn't sure I could hang on if it really took off headlong into all the dark possibilities.

27

SIX HOURS, THIRTY MINUTES BURIED

I jolted awake when I heard a car door slam.

"Shh," I hissed automatically, my eyes fluttering open before I realized what I was saying or why I was saying it.

At first I thought it was morning, even though the darkness made everything feel like night time down here. But after a second, I knew in my bones it was still the middle of the night. My body felt heavy and slow and sticky. My eyes wanted to close, but my heart was pounding harder than ever.

It took me only a second to remember why everything smelled bad, why the ground was wobbling around underneath me, why I couldn't see even a tiny bit of light in front of my eyes.

We were still down in the hole. And I was lying on the mattress stack. That's where I'd fallen asleep, my body finally relaxing on the dirty, stinky mattress at the very top of the pile even though I'd thought there was no way I would since the inside of my thighs, where I'd peed my pants earlier, still itched and burned. But one second I was awake and listening as hard as I could to the silence out-side the bunker, and the next I was drifting, listening to the other kids as their breathing turned deep again.

Another car door slammed, followed by slow footsteps. My heart beat faster. Something was happening.

I leaned up on my hands and knees, straining my ears.

At first, I couldn't hear much more than I had before we stacked the mattresses. Just shuffling and muffled words I could barely make out.

My stomach sank. At first I thought my plan of stacking the mattresses to hear the men better hadn't worked. But it turned out that was only because the men were quiet for a really long time. Maybe they'd been sleeping and were trying to wake themselves up, too.

I lifted myself up a little higher on the unsteady pile of mat-tresses, stretching up on my knees like I was doing a yoga move I'd seen Mom do on Saturday mornings.

I was still too afraid to try standing up on the springy, lumpy mattresses, so it was impossible to know how close I really was to the top of the bunker.

I was close enough, though.

"Don't speed," Jeepers was saying, his voice just loud enough that I could hear the words. "Not even a little."

Greasy Hair said something back that I couldn't make out.

"Should we check on them?" It was Jeepers again. His voice sounded thick, tired. The way Grandpa's voice sounded when he just woke up.

I froze and listened as hard as I could. *Them* meant us. They were talking about checking on us. My heart hammered harder. Did I want the men to check on us? Part of me was dying for fresh air, for that hole to open up, even if the night was dark outside, too. The air wasn't quite so thick and stuffy at the top of the mattress pile, but it was still stale and icky and smelled like dirt.

A bigger part of me wanted the men to stay away from us and the bunker. It had taken us a while to get the mattress pile just right so it wouldn't tip when I climbed on top of it. Ben and Ked had given me a leg up. Ms. Jessa hadn't helped at all. At one point I had my foot on Ben's head, and I could tell he was trying not to cry but he barely made a sound. I decided I'd love him forever for that.

Don't open the hole, I begged, deciding I'd rather take smelly, stale air than try to get back on top of this wobbly mattress pile again.

If the men opened the hole, we'd have to knock the whole stack down fast and start over.

I breathed harder when I thought about trying to get down the side of the tippy tower of mattresses by myself in a rush, maybe landing on top of Bonnie or the other kids. I probably wasn't up that high—the dark made everything feel more intense—but high enough to have to put my foot on top of Ben Whitlock's head was plenty high. What if I landed wrong and hurt myself or someone else?

"I'm not helping you move that heavy ass piece of metal again until we have to." Greasy Hair's higher, whinier voice rose just loud enough for me to hear every word. He laughed, like he'd just thought of something funny. "Or ... ever. We could just leave them down there, you know... Push some more dirt and junk over them ... It'd be a lot easier. Take the money and ..."

His voice drifted out of earshot and my tummy turned in circles. I closed my eyes and concentrated like my life depended on it.

Because maybe it did.

Jeepers made a funny noise. "Oh, for shit's sake. Just go do your pickup." He didn't disagree with Greasy Hair, though.

Footsteps crunched closer to the hole. There was a scraping sound right above my head.

I flattened my body against the mattress, ready to jump down if that sheet of metal began to scrape across the ground.

Instead, Greasy Hair spoke again, his voice closer but still quiet. "How long could they keep breathing down there if I covered up that hose?" he asked.

The hairs on the back of my neck stood on end. I could barely hear what he was saying, up on top of the mattress stack straining my ears. I hoped the other kids couldn't hear him at all.

Jeepers made a wordless noise again. He must have answered, because Greasy Hair's footsteps crunched away.

"We could just leave them down there, you know." That's what Greasy Hair had said.

My heart pounded so loud for a few seconds I couldn't hear anything except the blood whooshing around in my ears. My head spun, like I might topple over, so I lay down on my stomach.

Greasy Hair wanted to leave us down here. He wanted to know how long it would take us to suffocate if the air hose closed up.

Jeepers didn't tell him no, either.

A few seconds later, a car engine turned over.

"One of the vans is leaving," I stammered, finally finding my voice as the rumble of tires picked up then moved farther away.

At the bottom of the mattress stack, the other kids were shuffling again, waking up. "I heard, too. What did they say? Where are they going?" Mindy asked, as if I could know the answer.

"Shh," I whispered. There was the creak of another door opening, then a soft slam as it closed.

Then there was only silence again, except for the sound of kids moving around below me. Bonnie made a familiar little snuffle, and I knew it was taking everything in her not to call out my name.

I forced my mind to wake up, take notes on everything I'd learned after the last few minutes: *Greasy Hair just drove away to "do a pickup."* *He wants to leave us down here to die. Jeepers is inside the other van now. Maybe sleeping again.*

"What's happening?" Mindy asked again.

I told them about the first van leaving. I didn't know how to tell them the rest, though. I was the oldest kid here, and even I was so scared I was shaking.

I couldn't tell the little kids what Greasy Hair had said. I had to protect them.

I felt another rush of terror.

I wanted to tell Mom and Grandpa everything. And if I couldn't tell Mom and Grandpa, I wanted to tell Ms. Jessa.

None of those things were possible right now, though. So I needed to do what was best. And as far as I could tell, that meant finding a way out of here—or at least trying.

"They're really bad men," I finally said, choosing my words carefully. "They said … they said some scary things."

Bonnie's snuffles turned faster and sharper. "What did they say, Sage?" her little voice asked, and I could just imagine her holding her hands against her cheeks, eyes wide like a cat's in the dark.

"I'm going to see if I can stand up all the way," I said, ignoring the question and rising back onto all fours, getting my legs underneath me. So far, I'd only crouched, afraid I'd lose my balance. The mattress pile shuddered, and I bit down on my cheek to keep from yelping.

The mattresses shifted and made a quiet groaning sound as I managed to get on my feet.

My legs shook. I lifted my hands into the air, pawing and grasping for anything above me.

I found nothing but air.

I stood on my tiptoes and tried to reach again, higher. However, before I could fully extend my arm, I lost my balance and plunged forward.

It took everything I could not to scream as my body flew through space. *I'm going to die right now. I'm going to fall and break my neck.*

Instead, I landed hard with my back on the mattresses, one arm and one leg poking halfway over the far ledge. The pile tipped, and I grabbed hold of the saggy material. "Help, help, help," I whispered through my clenched teeth. The tower shuddered, and I could hear scared whispers at the base of the mattress stack.

Then Ms. Jessa's voice, a few feet from my ear. "Sage, breathe. It's okay. You're okay." The mattress pile stopped shaking, and I gulped in air.

"I'm not coming back down," I said, breathing hard and keeping hold of the mattress, even though getting down was exactly what I wanted to do.

To my surprise, Ms. Jessa didn't try to convince me, or pull me down. She just whispered, "Tell me what you heard the men say."

So I told her, reluctantly, because I hadn't expected her to ask. And because I didn't know what else to do.

When I was finished, Ms. Jessa was quiet for a few long seconds.

Then she said, "How tall are you, Sage?"

I frowned. "Five-foot nine."

She sighed like that wasn't what she wanted to hear. "Okay. You're five inches taller than I am. If I hold onto the sides of the mattresses with the other kids, can you try reaching for the ceiling again? Stand in the middle. That way if you fall, the stack won't tip."

I nodded, even though I knew she couldn't see the motion, and crawled back to the middle of the pile. Footsteps crunched overhead again, followed by the slam of a van door, then silence.

I was pretty sure Greasy Hair was gone. From the sound of those footsteps, Jeepers was a safe distance away too. But the desperate, flopping feeling in my stomach—like a goldfish out of water—was worse than ever.

All this time I'd wanted Ms. Jessa's help. Wanted her to stop telling all of us to be quiet and do what the men told us to do, so we'd stay safe.

Now here she was, wanting to help all of a sudden.

But all I could think about was how scary it was that Greasy Hair's words were bad enough to change her mind about trying to get out of here.

28

JESSA

SIX HOURS, FORTY-FIVE MINUTES BURIED

We could just leave them down there, you know.

Those terrifying words Sage had whispered into my ear as she leaned over the edge of the mattress stack thawed something in me.

And that thawing felt truly awful. Burning and prickling like I'd just plunged frostbitten feet into a tub full of warm water.

I wanted to slink away from the mattress stack and tuck my body back into a ball, like I'd been doing until Sage called down from the top of the mattresses. I'd somehow even managed to fall asleep for a little while. But now, the panicked voice in my mind was fully awake, screaming that there were no more good options, so I might as well try to disappear inside my head. That, at least, I could do.

You can't win. Just find a way to get through this.

There was another voice though, too. The same one I'd listened to three years ago. A dangerous, urgent voice that had come alive when Sage told me what she'd heard. It insisted, *You won't make it through the night. You have to try.*

I gritted my teeth. Sometimes, the consequences of trying—of fighting—were just as bad as the thing you were trying to escape.

I let the painfully hot fear wash over me until the frozen feeling unclenched a little more.

"Sage?" I stood on my tiptoes and ran my fingers along the edge of the top mattress until my hand found her arm.

"Yeah?" she asked in a tiny voice, but she didn't move.

The other kids were impossibly quiet, except for the sound of their breathing. I squeezed my eyes shut. The darkness made it impossible to see, anyway.

"Can you stand up again?" I asked. "Try to reach the ceiling?"

More silence. Her warm arm shuddered beneath my hand.

"What if I can't do it?" she asked, her voice so soft I had to strain to hear every word. "I'm scared."

This wasn't the defiant Sage I'd heard whispering to the other kids a few hours ago.

I swallowed. "I'm scared, too," I admitted, not remotely sure I was doing the right thing by saying it out loud.

She didn't reply for a long moment.

I squeezed her arm gently, not sure what else to say.

"Maybe you were right," Sage finally whispered into the silence between us, still not moving. "Maybe we should do what the men say, and we'll be safe. Like you told us before."

A tear leaked from my squeezed-shut eyes and rolled down my cheek. She sounded almost apologetic, like a contrite child.

Because she *was* a child.

I knew that if I wanted to right now, I could lean into the reprimands I'd given her earlier, coax her down from the stacked mattresses, hug her, let her cry, tell her and the rest of the kids to get some sleep and that the men would let us go soon.

I could almost feel the weight of her tired, sweaty frame lean against me in surrender. My arms ached to stroke her hair, tell her that yes, we'd be okay. We'd get through the endless hours like that.

I'd gotten through that way before. Tucked flat underneath Soph's bed with a blanket like a game of hide and seek, counting on Matt to stop pacing the hall outside her room and retreat for another finger of whiskey at some point.

The nights he reached under the cupboard for that amber-colored bottle were the nights I headed upstairs to Soph's room. I'd wait to hear his heavy footsteps on the stairs then down the hall to stand outside her door. He knew I was in there.

Every few minutes, he'd mutter threats just loud enough for me to hear through the door. Never loud enough to wake Soph.

He didn't want to hurt *her,* disturb *her* sleep.

Only *me.*

It'll be worse tomorrow ...

Coward ...

I knew you had something to hide ...

I'd never dared put my hands over my ears to block out the sound of his voice. Because every once in a while, he would put his hand on our daughter's bedroom doorknob to jiggle it a little, letting it catch against the flimsy privacy lock that we both knew he could open with a coin or a butter knife in a matter of seconds.

I'd always told myself that I wouldn't respond to him unless he actually opened the door. Then I'd have to go with him wherever he wanted, so Soph wouldn't wake up.

Sometimes, even now, I still wondered if things would've turned out differently if I'd stuck to my plan. Just stayed frozen underneath that bed with the sound of my daughter's soft breathing in one ear and the ominous sound of the doorknob clinking in the other.

However, each night it happened, Matt stayed outside her door a little longer, clinked the knob back and forth a few more times.

Sometimes he stayed perfectly still until I relaxed, thinking he'd finally gone to bed.

Sometimes, he had. Other times, right as I was about to close my eyes and give in to sleep, he'd stomp a few steps so I knew he was outside the bedroom.

Then one night, the pins inside the privacy lock clicked to release the bolt.

The doorknob turned freely.

I held my breath and tensed my muscles. *No, no, no.*

Soph shifted in bed above me like she was waking up. "Mommy," she murmured, and I prayed she was talking in her sleep.

Matt snorted softly but didn't push the door all the way open, like this was a game he was enjoying and wanted to last a little longer. Suddenly the thought of *Just get through the night* switched in my head to *What if tonight is all you get?*

That was when something in me snapped, and I scrambled out from underneath Soph's bed and across the floor toward the sliver of yellow light coming from beneath the door.

He still hadn't actually opened the door yet. Not fully. I just knew he would, though. And if he was willing to come for me in the one sanctuary I had left, that meant he was willing to show our daughter a glimpse of the face he'd only shown to me so far.

It was only a matter of time, and time was running out.

"I thought that might flush you out," he said in a soft, almost kind voice when I stood face to face with him in the hall. "Maybe after tonight, you'll behave."

My knees nearly buckled. Instead, I gently closed Soph's door and let him grab me by the arm.

That's when I saw the fireplace poker in his hand.

When Matt raged, called me a bitch, pushed me sideways as he rattled off the supposed evidence that revealed I'd been cheating on him, he was scary. But those outbursts were predictable, at least.

They flared and peaked, then slowly fizzled out like the threats and insults themselves had a half-life of destruction.

It was when he got quiet and measured that I knew something truly awful was coming.

It was always the veiled, unspoken threats that were the most dangerous ones, in my experience. So when Matt said, *"Maybe after tonight, you'll behave,"* in that ultra-calm voice, part of me lit up. A blinking *danger* button reserved for when things were about to go off the rails.

It was the same part that had lit up down here in the bunker, when Sage told me what the kidnappers said.

We could just leave them down there.

Those words repeated like a heartbeat, louder and harder in my mind.

I swallowed past the sticky grit in my throat. "No, Sage. You were right. I was wrong. I'm sorry. I'm here for you now."

She sniffed, like she was crying, too. Then the mattress pile shuddered as she shifted to her hands and knees. "Okay. I'll try to stand up again."

I spread my arms and braced my body against the folded mattresses. "Come on, kids," I whispered. "I know we're all tired, but let's make a circle around the stack to keep it steady, okay? Everybody lean in so Sage can stand up and reach for the ceiling."

"Oh my gosh. Ms. Jessa, I can touch it," Sage suddenly hissed from above my head, sounding triumphant.

For the tiniest fraction of a second, I let myself feel the excitement in her voice.

Then came a fresh breaking wave of terror.

Because even if we did manage to claw our way out of here, we weren't free. We'd just come face to face with the men who'd put us down here in the first place.

And when that happened, the quiet threat of, *We could just leave them down there,* would reveal its true colors.

29

SIX HOURS, FIFTY MINUTES BURIED

My heart pounded as my fingertips moved across the rough wood of the ceiling hole.

Plywood. The word popped into my mind, and I pictured the board I'd seen when Jeepers closed up the bunker and dragged something heavy across the hole that led up to the chimney.

I could barely press the tip of my finger flat against the ceiling, let alone push it with the palm of my hand, but I refused to let that fact get me down.

Harriet the Spy wouldn't let it get to her. She'd think—and keep trying.

And now that Ms. Jessa was on my side, too, I felt sure we could figure something out.

I brushed my fingers along the rough wood surface of the ceiling, back and forth. The wood felt splintery, like there were lots of little pieces of wood smashed together, and some of the splinters were sticking out enough for me to grab hold of them.

As an experiment, I stretched onto my tiptoes as much as I could and used my fingernail to dig into one big splinter and pull.

It came loose under my fingernail with a soft ripping sound.

It wasn't much more than a chip. About the size of a penny. There were hundreds, maybe thousands of those papery splinters holding the plywood together. I was suddenly sure that if I had some kind of knife or tool, I could chip more of them off, little by little. And if I could scrape more of them off, maybe I could make a hole in the plywood big enough for my body to fit through.

"Is there anything else I could stand on?" I asked, trying not to think about how scary it would be to add yet another object on top of this unsteady tower. The mattresses weren't wobbling nearly as much with Ms. Jessa and the other kids bracing against them, but it still felt like I might topple over any second.

"What about the bathroom bucket?" Evelyn Marks whispered.

Her suggestion was followed by a few excited murmurs and one "Ew."

I listened to hear what Ms. Jessa would say, still waiting for her to change her mind and insist I sit back down on the mattresses.

She stayed quiet, but I could feel her presence a few feet below where I stood, holding the mattresses steady along with the other kids. It made me feel braver, like instead of being Cook in *Harriet the Spy* she was willing to be Ole Golly, Harriet's nanny and mentor, for a while.

"There's two bathroom buckets," I said, thinking out loud. They were wide and big, like the buckets Mom kept in the garage for pulling weeds. If I tipped one of them upside down, I could set it on top of the mattresses and stand on top of it so I could reach the ceiling better.

"Evelyn, can you get one of the buckets?" Ms. Jessa asked in a shaky voice, and my heart soared. She meant what she'd told me earlier. She was going to help me and be Ole Golly. "If there's anything in it, pour it into the second bucket. Everybody else, keep holding the mattress stack steady with me, okay?"

"Okay," Evelyn said, sounding doubtful. A few seconds later I heard something slosh, then the sound of trickling and a soft "Gross."

"It's okay, Evelyn," Bonnie piped up, and I was proud of her for how brave she sounded. "Everybody poops and pees." I just knew she was quoting that dumb book Mom read us when we were babies. But then she added, "Sage will get us out. It won't be stinky for too much longer."

My throat tightened, and I made myself a promise that I'd do everything I could not to let her and the other kids down.

"Here, Ms. Jessa. Here's the bucket," Evelyn said a few seconds later. "I dunno if it's big enough to stand on, though. I don't want Sage to fall down."

My brain was moving faster and faster, even though my body felt so tired. "Bonnie, could you come up here and hold the bucket steady—like the yoga ball game?"

I knew she'd understand just what I meant. Mom kept a yoga ball in her office, and Bonnie and I liked to play with it when she wasn't working. Our favorite game was seeing who could balance on it the longest—no touching your feet to the ground. The other person's job, besides counting seconds to time you, was to wrap their arms around the base of the yoga ball until you said, "Go." That way you had a chance to get your balance before you tipped over.

If she could do that with the base of the bucket, I'd be brave enough to stand on top of it. One of the older kids might be stronger, but I'd seen Bonnie hold onto the wiggly yoga ball like a barnacle, and I trusted her more than I trusted the others.

"Oh, yes," Bonnie said, her little voice as cheerful as if I'd just asked her to play the yoga ball game. I felt a pinch of guilt. She'd stopped asking me to play that game with her a few months ago, because I'd said no so many times. *We already play together enough, because you follow me around the whole time at Bright Beginnings,* I'd said once when she begged.

I crouched and Ms. Jessa handed me the bucket. I felt it with my hands to memorize its shape even though it was dripping with pee. A few seconds later, the mattress pile jiggled a little as Bonnie crawled up beside me.

I tipped over the dripping bucket, shifted it into the middle of the mattress pile, and moved Bonnie's arms around the base. "Hold on right there, okay? Try not to let it wiggle."

Without complaining about the smell or asking for more directions, Bonnie sprawled out on her stomach and wrapped her arms all the way around the base.

For some reason, that made me want to start crying again.

"Thanks, Bonnie," I said, my voice hitching. Then, before I could get too scared, I put one foot on top of the flat bucket bottom and pushed my body up toward the ceiling where I'd felt the plywood.

Like I'd hoped, my palm hit the plywood flat. "I did it," I whispered excitedly. "I can reach the ceiling really good now." I pushed harder this time with my fingernails, scraping away more of the big plywood splinters.

I shifted my weight to my other foot on the bucket, and it tipped just a tiny bit. "You got it, Bonnie?" I whispered. "You're doing really good."

"Yeah, I got it," she whispered back, her voice full of pride.

A few more plywood splinters came off in my hand, and I dug for more even though my fingers were starting to hurt. I frowned and tried to think. If I was going to make any progress, what I really needed was a sharp edge.

"Does anybody have something sharp so I can scrape the ceiling better?" I felt stupid for even asking. We were elementary school kids. We didn't have tools with us.

Concerned murmurs drifted around the dark room. Then Ms. Jessa said, "I'm wearing a belt. The edge of the buckle is sort of sharp. Let's try that."

I shrugged. "Hand it up to Bonnie."

There were more shuffling sounds as Ms. Jessa undid her belt and handed it to Bonnie, moving slowly so the mattress pile didn't shake.

Balancing as carefully as I could, I bent down just far enough to meet Bonnie's outstretched hand.

The second the warm metal of the buckle grazed my fingers, I smiled for the first time.

The process of scraping the splintery wood off the plywood was going to be awful. Even with the belt buckle, my fingers were going to get scratched and raw and maybe even bleed.

Still, this was a tool a spy could use. The perfect size for me to hold in my hands, with squared-off corners I could really dig into the wood.

Harriet the Spy would have been giddy.

And so was I.

30

EIGHT HOURS BURIED

I scraped and dug and clawed at the plywood with all the energy I had left.

With every few strokes of the belt buckle, I felt the ceiling for a sign that I'd finally broken through the piece of wood. It felt like I was making progress, especially after I got used to the best way to hold the belt buckle. However, I had no idea how thick the plywood was. All I knew was that, little by little, the place I was digging was turning into a shallow crater in the ceiling.

I kept my eyes closed while I dug, to keep the tiny wood splinters that were falling onto my face from getting into my eyes. The bucket I was standing on stayed steady, but every few minutes I still called down to Bonnie, "You awake?"

"Yeah, I'm awake," she said, but as the minutes ticked by and my legs and arms got shaky, I worried that I was going to need a break before she did.

A song from *Sesame Street* kept trying to work its way into my brain, but I didn't quite know the words. Something about putting one foot in front of the other. I'd stopped watching *Sesame Street* years ago, but Bonnie had been obsessed with Snuffleupagus since she was a baby, and she turned the show on whenever she beat me to the TV.

My hands shook and my shoulders burned as I dug the belt buckle into the wood with one more satisfying scrape. My foot wobbled on the bucket, but I didn't fall.

"Are you okay?" Bonnie whispered.

"I can try doing it, if Sage is tired," Rose piped up, but her words were split in the middle with a big yawn.

I shook my head. "I'll be okay," I told Bonnie. Then, "Thanks, Rose. Everybody else is too short though—except maybe Ms. Jessa," I said, "but she's shorter than me, too." Saying it made me want to cry. I wasn't sure how much longer I could go without a rest.

"I could try," Ms. Jessa said slowly. "But I weigh at least three times what you do, Sage, and I'm shorter. I'll sink lower on the mattress pile."

I swallowed back a lump in my throat. The mattresses were limp and bendy—which made them easy to fold in half. However, that also meant they sank down when you put any weight on them. Ms. Jessa was "curvy," the word Mom told me and Bonnie we were supposed to use instead of "chubby." She wouldn't be able to reach the plywood, no way.

It was all up to me.

I shifted to the other foot, trying to keep my legs from shaking, then switched to my left hand.

As I made the next scrape into the plywood, pushing up as hard as I could to get the belt buckle in contact with as many splinters as possible, two things happened:

First, I heard the faint sound of tires moving along the dirt and gravel, getting louder by the second.

Then, I felt the belt buckle sort of pop upward while I pushed it into the ceiling. My knuckle scraped across sharp bits of wood, but I held on and pushed harder until I heard a cracking sound.

I gasped, which made a few of the kids—and Ms. Jessa— whisper, "What happened?" at the exact same time.

With the sound of the approaching tires in one ear and that beautiful cracking sound from the plywood in the other, I pushed with all my might, making sure to brace on the ceiling with my other hand so I didn't topple over onto Bonnie beneath me.

I gasped again as more splinters prickled against my skin, and something warm and wet trickled down my hand.

But then it happened.

My fingers pushed through the fist-sized hole I'd just made in the plywood ceiling.

I suddenly felt so dizzy with excitement I worried I was going to fall down on top of Bonnie.

The tires stopped and a door—this one creakier than the others I'd heard—opened, then shut a short distance away. Was this a different car than the gray van and the white van? Neither of their doors had creaked. What was going on? Should we scream for help?

I took a big, deep breath. "I made a hole," I hissed down to the others. "And there's a new car up there right now, but I don't know if we should—"

"Can you—" Ms. Jessa whispered, but all of a sudden I could hear voices coming from somewhere past the hole.

"Shh," I said, then listened as hard as I could.

"Don't freak out, okay? It is what it is," Greasy Hair said.

My blood chilled, even though I was as sweaty as I'd ever been in my life. Greasy Hair was back. What was he talking about? What would make Jeepers freak out?

Please don't look down here, I begged them in my mind, hoping that whatever Greasy Hair had to say would keep them away. If I just had a little more time, I was sure I could keep scraping until the hole in the ceiling of the bunker was big enough I could somehow wriggle my body up into the big wooden chimney we'd climbed through with the ladder earlier.

"Why would I freak out?" Jeepers asked, his voice harder to hear.

"Just don't freak out. It's too late for that."

"For shit's sake, just tell me what happened," Jeepers said, louder this time.

Then another door opened and slammed.

Greasy Hair said something else, but I barely registered it because my mind had suddenly put two puzzle pieces together.

I knew who Jeepers was.

Jeepers was Mr. Edward. The bus driver at Bright Beginnings, who swore at all of us when that apple went rolling down the aisle and got stuck up front.

"For shit's sake." That was what he'd said that day. I'd never heard anybody else use that swear, and the way he said it was strange … drawing the phrase out, making it a long sentence instead of just three words.

He'd only been driving the bus for a week when the apple disaster happened.

That was the last time he drove the bus. Rose said her mom called Bright Beginnings and complained, which meant Mr. Edward probably got fired.

Was that why he put us down here? Because he was mad about getting fired?

For shit's sake. The words and the way he said them rolled around in my head. He'd been saying that exact same thing, that exact same way, all night long.

31

I slept in the van for maybe an hour while Andy took the shuttle for his 1:00 a.m. pickup, but it felt like minutes. When I woke up to the sound of tires, I scrambled upright, disoriented and groggy.

I shoved my hands in my hoodie pockets, got out of the van, and blinked into the approaching headlights.

That was my first clue that something was wrong.

Those lights were way too low for the shuttle.

I tensed as the vehicle slowed then stopped—and Andy emerged.

Relief, then confusion, then anger, zipped through my system. "What the hell happened?" I asked. "Where's the shuttle?"

"Dude, calm down," Andy said, leaning against the two-door Honda Civic I recognized now that my eyes were recovering from being blinded by the headlights. He fished in his pocket for a cigarette and lighter. "Some lady freaked out. It was just some dirt … and trash."

If I was angry before, I was livid now.

"Tell me what happened," I said. "Don't leave anything out."

So he did. And when he was finished, I sat down on the hood of the Civic to calm myself down. *Fuck.*

Andy's 1:00 a.m. passengers had called the Speedy Shuttle desk to complain fifteen minutes after he'd dropped them off at the airport.

The floor of the shuttle had been filthy—dusty smears and footprints everywhere, from when I'd dragged the detour sign in and out of the back. Not only that, but Andy had wadded up the sweaty pantyhose and stuffed them under the driver's seat—where they'd rolled backward.

A woman had actually picked them up, before he snatched them from her hand.

"For shit's sake," I muttered for the fifth time. I kicked at a rock that went scuttling in the direction of the metal sheet covering the hole.

"Calm *down*," he repeated again, like I was overreacting.

I couldn't calm down, though. Not when he'd fucked up this bad.

Andy lit the cigarette and turned his head toward the buried bunker. "Any peep from the little assholes?"

"What do you think, dumbass?" I said, with more acid in my voice than I meant.

Andy's mouth twisted into a sneer around the lit butt of the cigarette. "I mean … your bedtime is usually like, nine o'clock, isn't it?"

I ignored the jab and swiped at a fat raindrop that splashed down on my head and rolled down my cheek.

I didn't want to fight with Andy—not when we were this close to the finish line. How could he have been so stupid, though? I couldn't help adding, "Seriously, how many times did we run through this? You were supposed to give the airport shuttle a once-over wipe down before you picked up any passengers."

I should have done it myself, I added silently, hating myself for leaving it to him. But this was supposed to be a team effort. If he was getting half of the money, he had to hold up his half of the plan.

"Well, if you hadn't taken so goddamn long babying those kids down into the bunker, I wouldn't have been in such a rush earlier," he snapped back, flicking the still-glowing cigarette onto the rutted dirt at his feet.

I forced a deep breath and told myself that all in all, things hadn't gone that far off the rails. They could have, though, and that was the real problem.

"Did she say anything about the pantyhose?" I asked. I wanted to hear him reassure me again. Wanted to believe he wasn't leaving anything out.

A gust of wind picked up some of the fine dirt near The Pit. More raindrops splatted against my cheeks, and I could hear the pings hitting the sheet metal and junk now.

Shit. It wasn't supposed to rain. My skin felt hot and my muscles kept twitching.

"Hell *no,* I already told you. She was dumb as a box of rocks. Didn't even realize it was pantyhose. Thought it was a fucking *scrunchie.* Asked me if it was *mine* then got mad at me when I grabbed it out of her hand. *Idiot.* Who sits in the front seat when there's room in the back, anyway? She was a dumb bitch, I'll tell you that for sure."

He hadn't mentioned the part about the "scrunchie" the first time he told the story. I forced my shoulders to relax. We were both back at the quarry. We were safe. I cut my eyes toward the sheet metal covering the hole, reminding myself of everything we'd gotten away with already.

I hadn't heard a peep from the kids. Maybe they were asleep.

I'd expected some bangs and yells in the silence while I waited for Andy to come back from his airport drop-off, but there was nothing.

I pictured the kids sleeping on the mattresses at the bottom of the hole, full of the peanut butter and jelly sandwiches I'd used part of my last paycheck to make, and that made me feel weirdly good. Like they were my pets just for the night, tucked safe and sound until I let them go.

"It was actually kind of dope when I got fired," Andy said, breaking into my thoughts.

My shoulders tensed up again and I forced them to unclench. Not only had he completely failed in making sure the van was clean —and free of fucking masks—before he picked up his passengers, but he made a scene and got fired, too.

Not waiting for me to respond, Andy kept going. "Any other day, I would've been shitting a brick and kissing Mr. Kessler's ass when he started tearing me a new one over that lady's complaint. Because the shuttle job's pretty good money, right? But since … you know, we're gonna be rich by tomorrow, I let him have it."

I rolled my eyes, but I wanted him to keep talking so I knew exactly what'd happened while he was out with the Speedy Shuttle. "What did you say to him?" I asked.

"When he told me that bitch complained about the dirty shuttle, I told him maybe she had something stuck up her ass."

I clenched my jaw to keep in a yawn.

Andy snickered. "So I said, 'Maybe you could help her out. One tightass to another.'"

I knew I was supposed to laugh, so I did, but I was still pissed.

We were supposed to be lying low. Not making a scene.

"It's fine, Teddy Bear," Andy sang as he opened the door to the tiny hatchback and got inside. The rain was falling harder now. Not a downpour, but enough that we'd get soaked standing around in the open.

"Don't call me that," I mumbled, but I was starting to calm down.

"Okay, Teddy Bear," Andy muttered, then yawned so wide his hair-rimmed mouth showed all his teeth. "Let's sleep for a few hours, yeah?" He gestured toward the sheet metal, prickling with raindrops. "Big day tomorrow."

I nodded and headed for the gray van without answering.

We needed to be sharp for the ransom pickup. And the kids weren't going anywhere.

None of them, not even the bus driver, could reach the top of the bunker without the ladder. Not even close. Even if they could somehow, there was no way they'd be able to move the plywood covering the first hole. I'd centered that hundred-pound battery on top of the plywood and nearly thrown out my back doing it.

There was no way, I reassured myself for the thousandth time. But if they did, we'd be right here waiting for them.

I opened the door to the gray van and rolled down the window a crack so I could hear any kind of commotion. A few raindrops rolled down the inside of the glass, but I just leaned against the console and rested my head on the passenger seat. A blanket would've been nice, but I had my sweatshirt at least.

Not the most comfortable night I'd ever spent—and that was saying a lot, because the cramped bedroom in Mom's trailer was about as comfortable as my jail cell. But in a few more hours, all of this would be over.

I'd be rich.

And then I'd be gone.

32

NINE HOURS BURIED

A muffled pinging sound came from above my head, and I held my breath. What was that?

There was another pinging sound, then another, until they combined into a dull roar.

Raindrops, I realized. It was starting to rain hard.

There was another slam of a door. Then another. Mr. Edward and Greasy Hair had probably just gotten into their cars, so they wouldn't get wet. I forced myself to take a deep breath. The loud rain was good. The sound of the water droplets falling on the metal would make it harder for them to hear the scraping sound of Ms. Jessa's belt buckle against the plywood.

I hadn't said anything yet about Jeepers being our old bus driver, Mr. Edward. It felt like something I should whisper in Ms. Jessa's ear instead of announcing it to the other kids, and I couldn't bring myself to climb down and stop scraping yet.

It already felt like we were out of time.

"Sage, I can't hold the bucket very good," Bonnie said, on the verge of a whine, her voice rising so I could hear her above the raindrops splashing down on the sheet metal above us. "You're moving too much and my arms are really getting tired."

"Let's rest for a few minutes," I said reluctantly, because my legs were shaking hard enough that I was worried I'd lose my balance and tip the bucket over any second. It felt like trying to balance on a skateboard.

"You doing okay, Sage?" Ms. Jessa asked.

I opened my mouth then closed it. "I'm just tired," I said quietly, struggling to keep my balance as I lowered my body into a crouch and got down off the bucket, careful not to step on Bonnie's arms.

As I did, an image of Mr. Edward's smashed-up face covered by pantyhose zoomed into my mind.

I remembered what Ms. Jessa had told us earlier, when I was trying to scratch the hole in the paint to see the men. That they wouldn't be wearing masks to hide their faces unless they really didn't want us to know who they were. Because then, if we ever got out of here, we could tell on them.

So I decided that maybe I shouldn't tell anyone, even Ms. Jessa, what I'd realized. She'd been helping us try to escape, but what if she stopped when she found out I knew who Mr. Edward was?

I frowned and tried to think it through.

Unlike Bonnie, I'd never thought Mr. Edward was all that mean. Just a little bit grumpy, like Grandpa could get when he hadn't gotten his nap or when he forgot something he knew he was supposed to remember.

That was before, though. Bonnie had been right all along. Mr. Edward was mean. He'd pointed a gun at all of us and made us come down into this hole.

I'd still take Mr. Edward over Greasy Hair, though.

He seemed like *"The lesser of two evils."* That was what Grandpa said one time when Mom burned the garlic bread and over-boiled the spaghetti. He was only joking, but sometimes those words still popped into my mind. I'd been wanting a chance to say them out loud, but I'd never really found the right situation.

Until now, anyway.

"Sage?" Ms. Jessa said again when me and Bonnie scooted toward the edge of the top mattresses.

"One sec," I said, staying low to the ground so I wouldn't lose my balance or tip over the edge like I nearly had earlier.

The mattress stack was tottering a lot more now than it had been. And from the sound of soft snores coming from the base, most of the other kids had fallen back asleep.

I didn't blame them. My head felt so fuzzy and dizzy I was starting to see dancing gray spots in front of my eyes when I blinked in the dark. It had to be really, really late by now.

My body told me it wasn't just dark because we were in a hole. It was dark because it was the middle of the night.

Bonnie grabbed for my hands as she lay on her stomach and let Ms. Jessa help her down off the mattresses. I squeezed her hands twice and held on a little longer than I needed to, because I was proud of her for holding that gross bathroom bucket so long when even some of the older kids had fallen asleep.

When it was my turn to come down off the mattress stack, I finally answered Ms. Jessa. Although I left out the part about Jeepers being Mr. Edward, at least for now. "I tried to listen to what the men were saying, but the rain made it hard. I can poke my fingers through the plywood though," I said. "Just a little bit. I can make it even bigger. I just need to rest a minute."

I knew I needed more than a minute, though. Now that I was standing on solid ground, I felt so tired I just let my legs give way and crumbled at Ms. Jessa's feet where Bonnie was already sitting.

My lungs hurt like I'd just run the mile at school without stopping. Maybe it was just my imagination, but the air felt the teeniest bit less thick now that I'd made that hole in the plywood. That made me less scared.

"You're a brave girl, Sage," Ms. Jessa said, her voice so sincere and proud that I blinked my eyes open in surprise. The way she said it made me wonder if she was a mom, because it sounded just like the way Mom talked to me and Bonnie when we'd done something that made her really happy.

"Thanks," I said, my eyes already closing. "Bonnie? Are you still awake?"

The bunker had gone quiet all around us in the dark, except for the sound of more snores and heavy breathing. "She's by my foot," Ms. Jessa whispered so quietly I could barely hear her over the drumming of the rain on the metal above us. "I think she's already asleep."

I nodded, wondering if I should scoot over next to her so she wouldn't have to sleep on the hard, bumpy metal floor of the bunker. "How long should we rest for?" I asked, suddenly afraid that if I let my eyes close for even a second, I'd open them to find out that days had passed and we'd lost our chance to escape.

"I'll stay awake and get you up in a few hours. You'll work faster when you're fresh, anyhow." She paused then added, "There's thirty sandwiches left. I think they're planning on keeping us down here for a couple of days," she said.

"You're a spy, too," I mumbled, impressed she'd thought to count the sandwiches.

There was a rustling sound, and then Ms. Jessa handed me a plastic cup of water and half a sandwich. "Here," she said quietly. "So you can get some of your strength back. You've been working really hard."

My stomach rumbled gratefully. "Thanks." I smiled and took the cup and sandwich from her, gulping both down so fast I hardly tasted the peanut butter. Then I wiped my mouth and tried to find a position to sleep in.

It was impossible to get comfortable on the hard ground, but I wasn't about to wake everybody up to pull a mattress down from the top of the stack. So I sat up and leaned my head against the lumpy mattress tower as Ms. Jessa sat down between me and Bonnie. That position wasn't very comfortable either, though.

Ms. Jessa was quiet for a few seconds. Then she said, "If you want, you can lay your head on my shoulder."

She said it almost like a question. Like I might say no. But I was so thankful for a comfortable place to sleep, I just shifted my body and lay my head down against her without even opening my mouth to say yes.

33

NINE HOURS BURIED

You're a brave girl.

Those words felt sticky and wrong the second they came out of my mouth.

They weren't untrue. Sage *was* brave. So what, then?

My heart lurched and I suddenly realized that it was the same thing I'd said to Soph that awful night.

For once, I let my memory go all the way back.

Matt pulled me halfway down the hall—headed for the stairs. I wanted to scream, wanted to pull away, but that would just make things worse. He only stopped digging his fingers into my arm when we heard Soph's tiny voice call out, "Mommy? Daddy?"

This time, I knew she wasn't talking in her sleep.

She was scared, wondering why her bedroom door was cracked open, wondering why there were scuffling noises and low voices coming from the hallway.

"Tell her to go back to bed," Matt hissed in my ear, his breath hot and sickly, whiskey-sweet and sour.

"Soph, it's okay, I was just checking on you and forgot to close the door. Go back to bed, baby," I said in a voice that didn't sound like it belonged to me at all.

"But I had a bad dream," she replied. *"I need a hug."*

I took a step away from Matt, toward her half-closed bedroom door, thinking that surely he'd back down now that Soph was awake and scared.

Instead, he tightened his fingers on my arm again and pressed the fireplace poker against my side as he whispered in my ear, *"You're using your own daughter like a human shield, Jess."* He nudged me with the poker and I swallowed my scream. *"Stop it. You're the one who fucked up, not her."*

If it weren't for the countless times he'd accused me of cheating on him, I would've had no idea what he was talking about. I hadn't done anything. Saying so wouldn't help me, though. I knew that by now, from long before I'd started hiding under Soph's bed.

"Soph, Mommy is tired," I said, doing everything I could to keep the tremble out of my words. *"Go back to sleep, baby. I'll see you in the morning."*

If I see you in the morning. *I couldn't stop the thought from blooming before I shoved it away.*

There was silence. Then that tiny voice again. "Okay, Mommy."

"That's a brave girl," I managed as Matt pushed me forward a few steps, pointing at Soph's door.

I reached out a hand and closed it slowly, so slowly, hoping maybe she'd call out again.

Instead, she sighed. A soft, little sigh that told me she really was going back to sleep.

Now, to my right, Bonnie sighed in her sleep, and the sound of it was enough to make the memory of Soph feel so real again that for the first time in ages, I didn't try to stop the tears that poured down my cheeks and into my mouth, wide open in a wordless wail.

For just a few seconds, I let myself pretend that Sage—and Bonnie, who had nestled herself halfway onto my lap—were my daughters.

I tried to brace against the shuddering that came with the silent sobs, not wanting to wake any of the kids, but they were all so exhausted I suspected I could cry all night like this without waking them.

What were we going to do? Was there any way out of here?

My tears flowed faster, harder, as the panic in my stomach turned heavy and electric the same way it had that night in the hallway when I turned around to face Matt. That feeling that screamed *run, get out, fight back, do something.*

Except that the odds were so stacked, what could I even do?

I lost everything the last time I felt that particular flavor of desperation, urging me to *do something.*

I had, and I'd lost my sweet Soph who had once loved horses and friendship bracelets and bubblegum ice cream. Did she still love those things at nine like she had back when she was six? I didn't know, and that thought made me cry even harder.

Getting custody again was technically possible. Only *technically*, though. As far as the courts were concerned, it involved saving up enough money to move out of the halfway house and into my own place. It also meant passing muster with the social worker who'd been assigned to supervise our visits for six months.

I'd quickly learned that those were the easy parts. For one thing, nobody wanted to hire a felon fresh out of jail. I'd started putting my maiden name and my sister Lisa's address down, praying they only ran in-state background checks.

When I actually got the job with Bright Beginnings, I'd whooped with joy.

When I told Soph—at one of our supervised visits—that I'd be able to apply for custody again in six months or so, she'd cried.

They weren't happy tears, though.

"She'll come around," Lisa had assured me. "She's just having a really hard time. The therapist says she's doing lots better. Soph just has to process all of this in her own way."

It was a pretty way of saying an ugly truth.

And the truth was so, so ugly.

Soph had been living with Lisa in Idaho the whole three years I was in prison in Utah. And as much as I adored Lisa for that—and for everything else she'd done for me—I secretly hated her for it, too. Because the only letters I ever got while I was in jail were written in her handwriting, not Soph's. I loved and hated the photos I saw of my little girl, getting older and more grown up and farther away with each passing month, smiling at my nieces and nephews and sister like the lifelines they were.

Soph had never wanted to talk to me over the phone. Not even once, the entire three years I'd spent locked up.

The rain pounded harder overhead on the metal sheet covering the bunker, drumming louder and more violently.

I cried more violently too, letting the sound cover my sobs.

I'd only ever told the story of what I'd done that night one time. On the third day of the pre-trial hearing, when I'd changed my plea to guilty.

Things weren't looking good for me. The jury was going to convict. There were no witnesses who could testify to seeing evidence of physical abuse. I'd covered my bruises far too well. And as for the emotional and sexual abuse? It was my word against a dead man's.

That morning, the prosecution offered me a plea deal with an expiration of four hours. Three years in prison, versus the possibility of life if the case went to trial.

My lawyers urged me to take it. They'd never seen a deal that good.

It would mean that my daughter—a witness for the prosecution—wouldn't be forced to testify against her own mother in a trial that might drag on for months. She was the only one who'd seen what had happened that night.

Accepting the plea would mean I'd get out of prison while she was still in elementary school. The other alternative—that I'd never see her again—was unthinkable.

So I'd accepted the deal. Then I stood in front of the judge at a plea hearing and told him everything that happened that night. Every awful thing, in exchange for a charge of voluntary manslaughter and three years in prison. I told him how I'd pulled away from Matt when we were halfway down the stairs, when he dug the fireplace poker into my side just hard enough that I whimpered. How then he'd done it again, harder, as if to prove a point. "Shut up," he'd said. "You've been putting this off long enough."

How I'd known then, deep in my bones, that I might have said goodnight to my daughter for the last time.

How that was enough to make the panic burn so hot, I'd snatched the poker before I fully realized what I was doing.

I grabbed the staircase banister with my free hand, leaning against the wall and kicking wildly at Matt, connecting hard with his groin.

I hadn't aimed there.

I'd just been trying to get him away from me, trying to create enough space so that I could run back upstairs and lock myself in the bedroom with my cell phone, call the police, anything but let myself be dragged down to the basement.

Matt made a strange, high-pitched oof sound, and I knew instantly that I'd hurt him and embarrassed him at the same time.

While he was drunk. While he was already on a mission to punish me.

The fireplace poker flew against the wall with a bang as he stumbled down a step. The handle landed at my feet.

As he reached for it, he sucked in a breath and said the words that turned my panic up all the way into the red. "I'll fucking kill you for that."

He let go of my arm as he groaned, bent in half on the stairs.

I ducked and grabbed the poker.

I swung as hard as I could, knowing I'd have one chance before he grabbed it back. I didn't want to hit him. I didn't want to hurt him. It was as if I were watching myself from somewhere outside my body, like in a TV show.

The sharp end struck his neck, ripping into the soft skin where his pulse was popping fast.

He made a gurgling noise. "Jessa, stop—" and reached for the poker. I pushed him away, watching little drops of red fly back at me from the sudden gush of blood that had opened up at his neck.

I stared in horror at what I'd done.

As he fell, before the crack that broke his neck, he screamed my name one more time.

It almost covered up the sound of the tiny voice at the top of the stairwell screaming, "Daddy!"

34

Closed.

I pulled into the front parking space of the credit union and stared at the sign on the door until the black letters blurred in front of my eyes. There were people moving around inside, employees wearing green-collared polos, getting ready for the day. It was only 8:45 a.m., and the bank didn't open until 9:00 a.m.

Just open a few minutes early today, I begged them mentally, each time one of the employees walked past the glass entry door.

My face felt puffy and drained at the same time. I was a soggy husk of the person I'd been two days earlier.

I hadn't slept last night. Not even for a few minutes. Because when I closed my eyes, all I could see were Sage and Bonnie's faces. All I could see was Dad's look of defeat and betrayal when I'd left him at Cherished Hearts, promising I'd call in the morning. All I could imagine were the headlines I'd read about botched ransom kidnappings and the stories Dad told me where he wished he'd gone with his gut over protocol.

Listen to your gut, Sheen. Screw the rest. That's what I kept imagining Dad's voice telling me, words he'd said a hundred times. I just wanted my children home safe and sound.

I blinked hard, trying to focus, trying to pretend I wasn't about to embezzle bond money from the city while my two daughters were being held for ransom God knew where.

I let myself look at the dash clock for the hundredth time that morning. Eight forty-seven. Everything was moving too slow and too fast at the same time, like that heady feeling right as the roller coaster car started to zoom down the first hill.

To my right, another car pulled into a spot in the parking lot directly beside me. An elderly woman with a little black dog on her lap. She turned off the ignition and rummaged in her purse, squinting at the closed sign. I averted my eyes and unbuckled my seatbelt, getting ready to move, unwilling to take any chances that I wouldn't be the first customer in the bank.

Keeping one eye on the old lady, I unlocked my car doors and reached for the folder I'd prepared this morning with all the evidence I'd need to withdraw $9,758 dollars from the first bank—the exact amount of the bid I'd confirmed for new play equipment at Longfellow Elementary.

It wasn't *quite* ten thousand dollars. The other five banks would be the same. In the end, I'd have a shortfall of $8,752. But there was no other way to make the math, the budget, *and* the vendor bids line up.

I had three thousand dollars of my own money in an emergency savings fund. I'd pull that out at my last stop for the day. However, even that would leave me a shortfall of more than five thousand dollars.

Just get it done, I told myself, unwilling to think about the fact that I was brushing up against failure already. *It'll be enough. You'll figure something out.*

A flurry of movement to my right caught my eye, and I jerked up my head in time to see the elderly woman opening her car door. Without hesitating, I grabbed my folder and purse, flung open my own car door, and ran the short distance to the front door of the credit union.

Behind me, the dog barked and the woman snapped at it to shut up. Then, more quietly—but not so quietly I couldn't hear her—she muttered to herself, "Raised wrong. Nobody respects their elders anymore, do they?"

I clenched my jaw and ignored her, refusing to turn around and make eye contact with her. Instead, I mentally rehearsed what I was going to say when that closed sign finally swung to open.

Walk inside. Show them your ID.

Smile and fill out the withdrawal form.

Tell them you're doing just fine when they ask.

Give them the folder with the Longfellow playground expenses if they hesitate at all.

Get the hell out and get to the next bank.

There was no reason to think this would be anything but easy. I'd withdrawn sums larger than this before, plenty of times. I'd even forged my boss's signature before—with his permission—to satisfy the "dual signature" requirement that usually felt like cutting a corner on red tape. As city treasurer, I was in charge of a revolving door of payments, vendors, and projects that sent me to the bank at least twice a week to deposit or withdraw different sums. Usually in the form of a cashier's check, but cash wasn't unheard of.

The woman behind me edged a few inches closer to my back, still tutting to herself. I moved forward too, so close to the doors that I was basically pressing up against the glass. A teller who looked to be maybe twenty-five years old looked up from his place behind the desk and made eye contact with me. I smiled as big as I could, hoping it would draw him out to open the door.

He just smiled back, then resumed whatever he was doing behind the desk, taking his time moving papers around and turning to chat with a coworker.

I let out a measured breath but didn't let my smile fall. I turned my body so the woman behind me wouldn't see my phone, so I could check the time again.

Eight fifty-one.

There was no way I was going to make it through the day. This was torture.

Desperate for a way to make the time move faster, I opened my phone and scanned the missed calls and text messages I'd ignored from this morning. There was a short one from Bright Beginnings, promising more updates and pleading with parents to refrain from coming into the rec center trying to get information. A missed call from the police officer I'd spoken to in the parking lot yesterday, then a text asking me to come back into the station at my earliest convenience for a more thorough interview.

That one made my blood run cold.

If only that officer knew what I was doing right now.

A familiar shiver of doubt prickled down my back. Was I doing the right thing? The question thundered through my brain again, finding the same panicked desperation in response.

The last text was a long one from Chez from next door, about how sorry he was about the girls, and to let him know if I needed any help with Dad.

Guilt grabbed me hard by the throat, and I took another deep breath and closed my phone. Two minutes until opening.

I'd call Cherished Hearts on the way to the next bank.

The teller behind the desk looked up again, accidentally catching my eye through the glass once more. His mouth quirked down ever so slightly. Without thinking, I lifted my free hand in the air and waved frantically. "You're open?" I called, even though it was still two minutes until nine—and he probably couldn't hear me through the door.

He glanced at the clock on the far wall, then laughed and said something to his coworker in a way that made me realize this probably happened all the time.

Then he set down the paper he'd been holding in one hand, strode out from behind the desk, and waved at me to come in. He must have remotely unlocked the door, because the latch clicked.

"Thank you, Jesus," I said out loud, forgetting that the old woman was still just a few inches behind me.

She snorted. "Raised *wrong,*" she muttered again, but I was already reaching for the door handle to go inside.

"Thank you, seriously, I'm in such a crazy rush this morning," I blurted out, smiling as big as I could.

"No problem," he said, waving me over to the desk he'd been standing behind moments earlier. "How can I help you?"

I told him what I'd rehearsed, proud and horrified by how easily the lies rolled off my tongue.

All that mattered was that this worked.

It only took him about five minutes to tuck the wad of cash into an envelope and hand it to me, still smiling, over the desk. "Is there anything else I can help you with, Ms. Halverson?"

"That's all," I chirped, tucking the folder back underneath my arm. "And really, thanks again. You're a lifesaver."

My throat nearly caught on the last part.

I'd never meant those words so literally in my life.

35

TED

When I woke up to the sound of tires rolling down the quarry road, my first thought was, *It's over.*

Sheena Halverson had gone to the cops. Or maybe I'd fucked up and left a fingerprint on the ransom note somehow, even though I'd worn gloves whenever I touched it. Could the cops run prints that fast? How would they know to find us here, though?

Fucking hell. I sat up and looked in the rearview mirror—nothing yet—then over at Andy in his Honda Civic—still asleep. "Dude, wake the hell up," I hissed through the cracked window of the van. "Someone's coming."

For a second, I thought about cranking the key in the van's ignition and leaving Andy to fend for himself. However, there were two problems with that plan. One was the stick shift. Two was the van was facing the wrong way to make a run for it. In half a mile, this section of the quarry dead-ended at the old dump pit—which had been closed a couple of years ago when it got full.

I shook my head. "No, think," I muttered to myself.

I hit the power button on my phone and scanned through the dozen or so notifications I'd set to come through from KTRB's crime beat.

The last one still read "UPDATE: Northridge Elementary Bus Found, Abducted Students Still Missing." There was no mention about me or Andy. But would they really announce it on the shitty local news if they knew it was us? Especially when they hadn't found us?

The tires were getting louder. Andy was awake now, looking over at me with that dumb deer-in-the-headlights look he got on his face when he didn't know what to do.

I gripped the steering wheel and stared, waiting to get a glimpse of the vehicle on the straightaway before I did anything stupid.

My fingers relaxed as old Paul Scaug's truck came into view, splashing through the puddles that had formed in the ruts overnight with all the rain. Paul was annoying as hell, but he minded his own business.

"For shit's sake," I muttered and glanced back at Andy, who was already opening the door to the Civic and waving.

I hurried out of the van to join him. We'd planned for this possibility—somebody stopping by the quarry over the weekend for some reason—but I didn't feel like leaving the ad-lib to Andy. Not after what he'd done last night.

Paul's eyes, two raisins underneath skinny gray eyebrows in his wrinkly face, flicked from me to Andy. He didn't seem suspicious though. He looked thrilled to see us, which was almost as bad.

"Don't say anything stupid," I muttered to Andy out of the corner of my mouth and lifted a hand up to wave at Paul.

Andy grunted. "Screw you."

I forced myself not to look at the piece of sheet metal lying on the ground twenty feet away as Paul stopped the shiny blue Tacoma—his pride and joy—a few feet away from us and cranked down the window, squinting into the sun. "Didn't expect to see you two idiots out here this morning," he grunted.

I rolled my eyes and forced a laugh that sounded real enough to my ears. I lifted up my shirt to show him my gun then pointed to the van and the beer cans on the ground I hadn't bothered to clean up from last night. "Redneck Friday night. Came out here to hunt wood-chucks and got wasted." I raised my arms as if to say, haven't we all been there before? Since it was Idaho, Paul probably had. He'd worked at the quarry since Andy's dad had opened it twenty years ago.

I ribbed Andy in the side and gave him a look. He grinned and said, "Don't say anything to my dad, okay? He has a soft spot for whistle pigs."

It was true. It was a running joke among the guys who worked at the quarry. Andy's dad braked whenever he saw the cat-sized ro-dents. Everybody else sped up. Last year, Paul had gotten one taxi-dermied and stuck it in his office.

Paul laughed like this was the funniest thing he'd ever heard. "You get any?" he asked, and my heart nearly pounded out of my chest when he glanced toward the sheet metal. Sweat started to bead down the back of my hoodie.

"Nah," I said, forcing another laugh. "We bagged more beer than woodchucks last night. Might hang out a while and try again though."

Paul nodded and craned his head out the window a little longer. For a second, I was afraid he might ask if he could join us. Or that Andy might offer. But then he said, "Well, good luck. I won't say nothin'. Bag one for me, all right? I told my son I'd bring him some scrap rock for his yard. Don't you be telling your dad about that, nei-ther," he said to Andy with a wink. He tilted his chin at the camper shell of his truck.

Andy grinned like an idiot, and so did I. "You got it."

Then Paul waved and drove past us, and I finally let myself look over at the sheet of metal.

I let out a big whoosh of air. "You think we should check on the kids?"

Andy snorted. "Yeah, let's open it up right in time for Paul to drive back through and see us doing it. You're such a pussy about those little shits."

I rolled my eyes, but he was right. If they'd gotten a little wet down there, they'd dry out. And if everything went like it was supposed to with the ransom later tonight, they'd be back home by tomorrow morning.

"Guess we gotta shoot some whistle pigs now," Andy said, scratching the back of his head and looking in the direction Paul's truck had bumped down the road.

"Nah, too much noise," I said. "Let's have a couple of beers. There's sandwiches on top of the cooler, too. We've got all day before we gotta leave for Little Eddy anyway." The truth was, I had a soft spot for the rodents, too. Not that I'd say so to Andy because he'd only call me a pussy again.

"Breakfast of champions for a couple of goddamn kings," Andy crowed as he walked away without telling me that I should be the one to get the beers from the cooler in the lean-to. We were both in a better mood this morning, thanks to a few hours of sleep.

I pulled out my phone and checked the time—and my news notifications.

"Abducted Students Still Missing" hung on the screen in its little alert bubble.

As if to drive home the point, there came a muffled thud from the direction of the bunker.

It wasn't the first bump or thump I'd heard. There were eleven people down there after all, and it was faint enough that even if Paul had heard it, it wouldn't have drawn his attention unless he was listening for it. The sound made my tense shoulders inch higher toward my ears anyway, though.

Paul would get his scraps and leave soon, I told myself, shoving down a growing sense of unease. The sun had come back out, the rain had stopped, and we just had to hang tight for a few more hours.

Then we could get the ransom—and finish what we started.

36

NINETEEN HOURS BURIED

After the rain, the smell in the underground prison was way worse than before.

The one remaining bathroom bucket on the ground was full, and some of it had spilled over. The air was hot and damp, and it smelled like one of the camp toilets we had to use when we went to Grayback Gulch with Mom, and Bonnie was so scared she'd fall in.

None of us knew how long we'd slept, not even Ms. Jessa. Was it morning or night now? Nobody had a watch or a phone. When I woke up with my head on her lap and Bonnie's hand curled into mine, I didn't move right away. My whole body hurt from digging into the plywood, and I was still so tired. But hearing the crunch, crunch, crunch of the men's shoes walking around up on top of the ground woke me right up.

"Boost me back up on top of the mattresses," I'd whispered frantically, and everyone helped.

NOELLE W. IHLI

A car came by pretty soon after that. From the top of the mattress stack, I could hear Mr. Edward and Greasy Hair talking to somebody named Paul about shooting "whistle pigs."

At first, I wanted to holler and scream, because what if Paul was a good guy?

Then I started thinking about how maybe "whistle pigs" meant *us* down here in the hole.

If we all started screaming, they'd open up the hole and maybe even see what we'd been doing with the belt buckle.

Just thinking about that made me get my tired, aching body back on top of the bathroom bucket and start digging at the wood even harder.

This time, the other kids took turns holding onto the bucket while I scraped away.

After Paul's car drove off, I couldn't hear much of what Mr. Edward and Greasy Hair were saying to each other. Mostly, it sounded like they were smashing up pop cans—or maybe beer cans—and belching and laughing.

Go away, I kept telling them with my mind. *Leave.* But they never did.

So I just kept scraping, splinter by splinter, quiet as I could for what felt like forever.

After a while, I started counting time by the number of scrapes I made in the plywood, because anything else was pretty much impossible.

When I got to three hundred, Rose, who was taking a turn holding the bucket, started to cry. "I can't breathe very good. We're gonna die, aren't we?" she said in a whisper, then a louder voice. "This isn't working, we're gonna die."

The bucket teetered, and my stomach flipped as I tried to get my balance again.

228

Ms. Jessa's voice cut through the dark. "Rose, it's okay, honey. You're doing a really good job, but I think you need a break. Let's share some more of the sandwiches, okay? Remember how good they are. Sage, do you need a break?"

All I could think was that Ms. Jessa sounded just like Mom, so I wanted to cry again, too. I kept thinking I was close to making a hole in the wood big enough to push my hand through, but it was harder than I thought it would be. And I'd thought it would be pretty hard.

My head felt fuzzy, and there were a few times I'd been sure I was going to fall over and land right on top of Rose or whoever was taking a turn holding the bucket. So I didn't argue with Ms. Jessa when she asked if I needed a break. *Just for a few minutes,* I told myself firmly. Harriet wouldn't take a longer break than that, and neither would I.

"Can we play the vacation game again?" Bonnie asked while we ate the pieces of sandwich Ms. Jessa handed out.

"Yeah," Charlotte said eagerly. Her nose sounded stuffed up and her voice was hoarse like she'd been crying again. "I don't remember how, though."

"Well, you just say a thing you wanna bring on vacation, and then …" Bonnie trailed off. "I don't know how to explain it. Sage, will you play with us?"

I frowned and shook my head, even though nobody could see me in the dark. It felt like my brain was turning to mush. It was like the stinky hot air was sucking the life right out of all of us. How long had we been down here? A day? More than that?

"I don't want to play anymore games," I mumbled, sitting against the mattress stack and popping a crumb of the sandwich in my mouth. Scraping at that plywood for so long was taking every little bit of energy I had. My hands felt like one giant blister.

"Okay," Bonnie said without a fight, and that made me feel bad, but I just couldn't muster up the words.

Then Ms. Jessa spoke up. "I have a game," she said. "For whoever wants to play while we rest. Can you all make a circle around the mattresses and hold hands?"

As I scooted away from the mattresses, Ms. Jessa added, "Sage, my sweater is next to the sandwiches if you want to lay your head on it for a bit."

"Thanks," I said, hoping she'd understand that I meant it for more than just the sweater. Ms. Jessa felt like a real grownup now. Which meant that I could be a kid again, even if I was still the one who had to scrape at the plywood because I was the only one who could reach it.

I kept my eyes closed and listened to the sound of bodies shuffling around the mattress stack. Ms. Jessa was lining the kids up— everyone but me, as far as I could tell.

I breathed in and out as slow as I could and tried to pretend I was somewhere else, even while I listened with one ear.

"Okay, this is a game I used to play with my daughter when she wasn't feeling well," Ms. Jessa said, and the way she said it made me wonder whether she still had a daughter.

"We're going to tell a story, one word at a time. You can say any word you want—"

"*Any* word?" Ava asked.

"Any word," Ms. Jessa insisted.

"What about bad words," Ked asked solemnly, drawing a few giggles.

"Yeah, there's no swearing on the bus," Ben said like the know-it-all he was.

Ms. Jessa laughed. "Well ... we're not on the bus anymore, so say whatever word you want, okay? Just don't tell your parents."

That made everyone laugh again.

"I'll start. As soon as you say your word, squeeze the hand of the person next to you so they know it's their turn." She paused, then started the game. "We."

I kept my eyes shut and listened as everyone added their words with pauses and a few giggles in between them.

"We. Are. Here. It. Is. Stinky. But. I. Like. Dogs. I. Want. Some. Good. Food. Farts. Suck. Mermaids. Sing. Like ..."

"Chickens," Ms. Jessa finished, and this time everyone laughed, including me.

I rubbed my hands and sat up. "I can dig again," I said. "Can somebody hold the bucket for me?"

"I'll do it," said Bonnie real quick, before anybody else could answer, and I promised myself that I'd never call her a baby again if we ever got out of here.

* * *

Twenty-five, I counted in my head, pushing the belt buckle up into the wood as hard as I could.

I'd stopped paying too much attention to what the men were saying, mostly because they were talking about such dumb stuff when I paused to listen. Like the best tires for a dirt bike, and how many beers they could drink without getting drunk, and whose mom was the worst. Stuff like that. Nothing to do with us kids, which felt sort of strange since they were keeping us down here.

Crack.

I held in a gasp as the plywood gave way beneath the buckle and my hand suddenly pushed right through the wood.

It hurt, scratching my blistered, bloody fingers even more than they already were, but I didn't care one bit.

Because now I could fit my entire hand through the hole I'd just made.

"Did you get all the way through?" the other kids were asking, along with Ms. Jessa, but I was trying to listen for footsteps. Had the men heard that crackling sound? It was loud next to my ears, but how loud was it outside the hole?

I held my breath, but it only took a second to realize that the men's voices hadn't changed at all. They were still talking to each other about beer.

They had no idea what I'd just done.

"Yeah, I got through," I whispered down, steadying my other hand against the ceiling. "I think I can rip through it faster now," I added, realizing that if I made the hole a little bigger, I could peel off bits of wood with my fingers while using the buckle at the same time.

Before long, I'd be able to get my whole arm past my elbow through the hole. Then my body, if somebody gave me a boost.

"Good job, Sage!" Bonnie squealed in a quiet, excited voice.

"Amazing," Ms. Jessa added, even though I could tell from the way her voice shook that she was starting to get scared again. Because if we could make a big enough hole in the plywood, we might actually be able to get out of this stinky bunker. But then we'd have to face the men. "Do you need another break?" she asked.

I shook my head. "No, I can keep going. Bonnie, you wanna let Rose take a turn?"

"No way," Bonnie said, and I loved her for it.

My fingers burned, and my legs were shaking hard like they had before, but I wasn't going to rest again.

There was no telling how much time we had left.

37

I called Cherished Hearts while I sat in gridlock traffic, on my way to the last bank in Kuna. Technically, I was still doing okay on time. If anything, I was ahead of schedule.

I suspected that the kidnappers had sent me out of town into the thick of commuter traffic intentionally, to keep me busy. But as the cars slowed to a crawl and then a dead halt, that knowledge didn't stop the panic from making me breathe like I'd been running for my life. In a way, I was. If I lost my girls to this slowdown, I didn't know how I'd go on.

I'd been inching along at five miles per hour for the last twenty minutes. I wouldn't be exiting the freeway for at least another twenty.

The receptionist at Cherished Hearts picked up after the first ring. She must have had caller ID because she said, "Mrs. Halverson, oh I'm so glad you called. Ron has been asking about you all day."

Guilt—and the long stretch of red on my Maps app—made my stomach tighten painfully. "I'm really sorry. It's been … it's been a hard day. I'm so sorry it took this long to check in."

Do not cry, I instructed myself. *Do not show up at this bank looking like a mess.*

"No, no, honey. That's not what I meant," she said, and the kindness in her voice nearly sent the tears over the edge. "He's in good hands. It's good you called, that's all. He's feeling a little lost and lonely. That's totally normal for his first day. Hold on a minute, okay?"

I tried to respond before she put me on hold to get Dad, but the lump in my throat wouldn't let me.

"Hi." When Dad came on the line a few minutes later, he didn't sound lost and lonely. His voice had a hard, clipped edge to it, like I'd interrupted him in the middle of something.

"It's so good to hear your voice," I floundered, no longer sure what I should say. What did he remember from last night? Should I apologize again? Explain my decision to take him to Cherished Hearts? I couldn't say anything about the girls. That would make everything worse. But it was the whole reason I'd done this so suddenly.

A fresh wave of guilt—this one a tsunami—rolled over me so hard I had to swallow the bile rising up.

The semi-truck behind me laid on its horn and I jumped, realizing that traffic was moving again. "Dad, do you remember when I was a little girl and you told me to trust you—and stay very, very still on that camping trip?"

It was a longshot question. However, I'd learned that sometimes those old memories were etched deep, in a way nothing else seemed to be.

I could still picture the orange-blue flicker of the coals in the fire ring, the way Dad's eyes had gone wide as he glanced in my direction then barked at me not to move an inch. I wanted to whirl around and jump up from the rock I'd been sitting on. But his voice —and the way I trusted my father—rooted me right where I was.

"Yes," he muttered gruffly, and I smiled despite myself.

"There was—" I began, but he cut me off and started telling the story himself.

"There was a spider on your neck," Dad said, his voice losing some of its edge. "Knew it was a widow, because of those legs with that big old body. Must've been on the rock when you sat down. And you must've felt it crawling, because you had your hand up and moving toward it. If you started poking at it, it would've bit you."

"Yeah, I remember how it felt," I said. "I was so scared. But I trusted you. So I didn't move, even though I wanted to panic."

There was silence on the other end of the line. "Yeah," he finally said.

"Before I knew it, you'd flicked it away with a branch. You didn't even tell me what it was until we got home from the trip."

"Yeah," he repeated again, his voice softer.

"I need you to trust me, okay? Even though it feels bad and doesn't make sense. I just need you to trust me. Because I love you and I'm coming back for you, okay? I—I'm trusting my gut, like you always told me to do. I'll explain later, okay?"

He was quiet for so long I thought maybe he'd hung up. Then he said, "Well, why didn't you say that last night? I'll stay put, Sheen. You know I love you, too. And the girls. Tell them hi from their papa."

"Thanks, Dad," I choked out. "I need to go, okay? I'll see you really soon."

* * *

As I drove away from the final bank fifteen minutes later, I glanced at my reflection in the rearview mirror.

I'd been expecting to see a haggard shell of a woman—like how I felt inside. To my surprise, the Sheena who looked back at me was pretty put-together. My eyeliner still tipped-out in subtle wings that I'd applied at 4:00 that morning, not wanting to give the bank any excuse to raise a red flag about my withdrawals. Foundation and powder hid the blotches I knew were lurking underneath on my dehydrated skin. Even my lipliner hadn't smudged.

I cut my eyes back to the road and nudged the car five miles over the speed limit. Headed this direction, back toward Boise, the traffic was sparse, but I wasn't willing to risk going any faster. Not when someone might be watching me. Not when I had barely over an hour to get home, organize the money in a backpack like I'd been instructed, and write a note pleading with the kidnappers to accept the shortfall.

I had, in the footwell of the passenger side of the car, a total of $44,243. It was $5,757 less than the kidnappers had requested, but even that sum felt like I was just asking for the police—and the feds —to perk up and start looking in my direction at any moment. The thought barely raised my heart rate, though. Nothing mattered anymore except saving my girls.

I glanced in the rearview mirror again as I finally exited the main freeway and pulled into traffic along State Street and pointed the car toward home, this time scanning for police.

I was so close.

I'd successfully made withdrawals at all five banks. As soon as I got through Boise and passed out of city limits, I would be headed straight for Little Eddy Campground. After that, the only thing left on the kidnappers' list of demands would be the two-million-dollar Bitcoin transfer—which would definitely alert the authorities.

What if they don't give the kids back? the voice in the back of my head piped up as I imagined dropping the money and walking away.

That voice had been getting louder with each successful bank withdrawal, each minute that ticked closer and closer toward the ransom drop.

I gripped the steering wheel harder, heart beating so fast I was afraid I might have to pull over.

What if they're already dead? asked the voice that I knew was my own but felt like a stranger's. *These are bad people. They don't keep their promises.*

"But there's still a chance," I cried out loud, blinking away the tears that finally spilled down my cheeks and finally smudged the carefully applied eyeliner.

I had no idea where my girls were, or even if they were still alive. All I knew was that as long as there was a sliver of hope I could get them back, a chance they were still okay, I'd move heaven and earth to make it happen.

Ping.

I glanced at my phone long enough to clock that the text update included the words *kidnapping* and *person of interest* were part of the headline.

I pulled the car over to the shoulder of the road so fast without signaling that a truck to my right laid on the horn as I put on my hazards and grabbed my phone.

The headline read, "Police Name Person of Interest in Daycare Kidnapping."

My mouth went dry as I scrambled to click on the article. Did this mean the police were closing in on a suspect? Was there a chance I might not have to pull off this insane ransom on my own?

When the article opened, I shook my head in confusion. The photo beneath the headline showed the mug shot of a skinny woman with dark circles beneath her brown eyes. She couldn't be much older than me, and it looked like she'd been crying in the photo.

I scrolled down, desperate to read as fast as possible, but unwilling to skip a single word.

In a shocking development, authorities have named 38-year-old Jessa Landon as a person of interest in the case involving ten children kidnapped while enroute to Bright Beginnings Rec center for after-school care. The children, aged between 7 and 11, were last seen boarding the bus at their elementary school on Thursday afternoon but never arrived at the daycare center.

Jessa Landon, who had been working under her maiden name, Jessa Palmer, is now at the center of an intense investigation. Gregg Landon of Herriman, Utah, her ex-brother-in-law, has come forward with alarming information about her past, revealing that Jessa recently served three years in jail for voluntary manslaughter after killing her husband. Following her conviction, Ms. Landon lost custody of her daughter.

"When I saw the articles about the kidnapping and read her name, I got this huge pit in my stomach," Gregg said in a statement recorded this afternoon. "I thought, 'My God, what has Jessa done now?' I've seen firsthand what that woman is capable of. She's a master manipulator. Not someone who should be anywhere near children."

Bright Beginnings released a statement expressing their concern and disbelief. "We are horrified to learn that Jessa Landon intentionally misled us by using her maiden name and used her sister's address on her application. This deception allowed her to bypass our background check process. Our primary concern continues to be the safe return of the children."

As the search for the missing children continues, authorities are urging anyone with information to come forward. Law enforcement officials have stated that this news article will be updated as new information becomes available. "We are doing everything in our power to locate these children and ensure their safe return," said a police spokesperson. "Our thoughts are with the families during this incredibly difficult time."

When I finished the last sentence, I forced myself to put the phone back onto the dash mount and pull back into traffic.

I couldn't stop shaking, though.

That woman's face stared back at me from my mind's eye while bits and pieces of the article swirled through my head.

Voluntary manslaughter.

Master manipulator.

Lost custody.

For the first time, an undercurrent of anger rippled through my fear. Was *this* the person who had written the ransom note that had showed up on my doorstep with that pizza? She was apparently capable of heinous things. She'd killed her own husband—and lost custody of her daughter.

I didn't want to admit it, even to myself, but there was also the strangest bit of relief that my children might be with a mother. Even horrible people still loved their children sometimes, right? Surely, someone who had gone through the blood, sweat, and pain that even the most cursory kind of motherhood involved couldn't be completely devoid of empathy, could they?

I refused to remember the stories Dad had told me about exactly that kind of mother. Women who locked their children in the closet for days, fed their babies dog food, drowned their toddlers in the bathtub.

Surely there weren't many of these women, but I knew for a fact they existed.

I blinked away the horrifying thought and stared into the tear-filled eyes in the pixelated photo on my screen.

Were those tears of hate, selfishness, deceit?

Or was that a little bit of her soul bubbling to the surface? If so, maybe, just maybe, this woman would be willing to keep her word and return my children to me if I followed her instructions to the letter.

My phone screen lit up with an incoming call—saved to my phone earlier as simply POLICE.

I shoved the phone away unanswered, then pulled back onto the road and nudged the gas pedal to bring the car up to seven miles over the speed limit, my blood boiling hot and heart pounding hard against my ribcage.

"Fuck you, Jessa Landon," I choked out, even while I silently begged her not to hurt my girls.

38

"Holy *shit,*" I muttered for the third time as I scrolled up on my phone.

"Oh my god, *what is it?*" Andy asked, finally irritated enough to get his drunk ass up off the cooler and march over to where I sat on a rock beneath the lean-to shelter.

I shook my head, half-regretting saying anything. But the news story had caught me completely off-guard. This was unbelievable.

"The bus driver," I said, setting down the warm beer I'd been nursing for the last hour, checking myself over mentally to make sure I wasn't drunk anymore. The cooler was almost empty, but that was mostly Andy's doing. Despite my warnings, he'd slogged down nearly the entire stash. I was pretty pissed about it, actually. I was doing the ransom pickup, but he couldn't be so shit-faced he lost his cool if somebody came around the quarry while I was away.

"What *about* the bus driver?" Andy slurred and took another step toward me, belching and patting his thick middle, then tossing his empty can in front of him and smashing it with a *crack.*

I stared at the mug shot in front of me. "She's a felon, dude. Look at this." I held the phone out so he could see the news headline.

"The police just named her a person of interest. They think *she* did this." I pointed in the direction of the buried bunker.

Andy let out a wet belch of sound that was half-burp, half-laugh. "No way. *No way.*" He kicked his latest smashed beer can and ran his fingers through his long, dirty hair. "We have to use this, dude. This is too perfect. Like, God giving us a sign or something, right?" He belched again, long and loud, then guffawed. "She could take the blame for the whole thing," he said, talking faster and faster like the one time we'd done a bump together. "They'd never come for us if they thought she did it."

I shook my head. "Shh, okay?" He was practically yelling now. And he wasn't thinking straight. "Nah. Even if she takes the blame, the kids are gonna remember the two dudes with pantyhose on their heads who marched them off their bus ..."

"But only if we let them out ..." Andy trailed off in a singsong, stopping in front of me and looking me dead in the eyes. With his hands still tugging his hair upward into a crazy-looking ponytail, his belly spilling over the top of his jeans, and his eyes popping wide in his scruffy face, I had to stop myself from cringing away from him. He looked—and sounded—like a nutcase.

"No," I said firmly. "We already decided. Nobody gets hurt."

Andy snorted and kicked another empty beer can my way, like we were playing a game together.

For a second, I was afraid to meet his eyes. I knew now deep in my gut that I shouldn't have told him about the news article. *Or tried to pull this plan off with him,* my brain hissed.

"Just hear me out," Andy said, still hell-bent on this new plan. His eyes gleamed, alcohol-shiny. "We could convince them that the lady bus driver was the mastermind behind the whole thing. She doesn't look like a mastermind, not with that face, but if the cops already think it ..." He lowered his voice and followed my gaze to the sheet metal lying in the dirt at the edge of The Pit. "We could take her out of the hole and talk to her like she's in on the whole thing, so the kids hear, then put a gun to her head and ..."

My mouth went dry. Impossibly, Andy's eyes went even wider and shinier. "This is such a good idea," he hissed. "Do you have some paper? We could make her read something to the kids. Like ... like about how we'd fucked everything up and she wasn't gonna share any of the ransom money with us anymore because we're incompetent dipshits. Fire two gunshots, like she killed us both, only we'd fire them right into her head. The kids would tell the cops the lady bus driver killed us and then got away."

"And then what?" I mumbled, even though the knot in my stomach told me exactly where this conversation was headed: Right off the rails.

"And then we could, you know, disappear her body into The Pit and get away with the money," Andy screeched softly, swaying in front of me and all but clapping his hands with glee.

He looked at me expectantly, like surely I couldn't object to this brilliant plan.

I stood up from the rock and backed away a few steps, glancing in the direction of the buried bunker yet again. It was time for a subject change. I didn't want to kill anybody. "Come on. We need to leave for Little Eddy. We're going to be late." I took a step toward his Honda Civic. "We can talk in the car."

"*We?*" Andy narrowed his eyes and laughed. "Hold on, I thought *you* were going to pick up the money." He belched as if to prove it.

I thought fast, trying to come up with a reason. He was right. The plan—before he got fired and lost the airport shuttle—was for *me* to pick up the money while he stayed behind at the quarry. When we plotted all the final details of that plan weeks ago, I'd couched it like I was doing him a favor. He could stay put and drink beer. I'd be putting myself at risk by going out into the open a second time.

But the truth was, I'd never trusted him to pull off the money pickup by himself. Andy was impulsive, especially when he was drunk. If something went sideways, I wanted it to happen on my watch—not his.

Which was the same reason I didn't trust him to stay here alone with the kids by himself anymore, either. Not after what he'd just said, not with that plan baking in his stewed mind.

There was a red, flashing warning in my head that if I left him to his own devices with his current thoughts worming through his drunk brain, I'd come back to a scene that all the money in the world couldn't cover.

I couldn't leave him here. I couldn't let him drive, though—he was way too drunk for that.

Think. Apply yourself, Ted.

"Dude, your Honda is a wreck," I said, latching onto a semi-solid reason he needed to come with me. "I was supposed to drive the *airport shuttle,* remember?" I ad-libbed, gaining momentum with the train of thought. Unlike the van, the Civic was an automatic, so I could technically drive it, but the ignition *was* messed up, and I'd seen Andy spend ten minutes swearing at it, trying to bully it into starting, after he picked me up for work from the trailer park.

Andy considered this thought and took another swig of beer. I wanted to rip it out of his hand and slap him.

"Oh for shit's sake." I barked. "Just get in the car."

"That sounds like it'd suck ..." he drawled, and my stomach dropped even further. "I'm gonna stay here and relax." He turned away from me and kept staring at that covered hole near The Pit.

I gritted my teeth and tried not to panic. *Shit, shit, shit.* We were so close to finishing this. I was so close to getting out of here with the money—and a halfway clean conscience. Clean enough for me, anyway.

As if reading my mind, Andy darted his eyes toward me and lifted an eyebrow, reaching for the handle of the gun shoved sideways into his belt. "You're such a bleeding heart, Teddy Bear. It'd be *so* easy to do it my way…" he trailed off, slurring.

"It's a bad time to improvise," I insisted.

He laughed softly then stood, cocking his head like he'd just had a new, brilliant thought. "Maybe you're riiiiight." He finally lowered his voice and dropped his shoulders. "We're not done talking about this, though. Think about it. She's just a dumb bitch. She killed her husband, for Christ's sake," he said, grabbing me by the arm. "It's just too perfect. God is practically dropping this in our laps."

I kept my face neutral. It wasn't perfect. Not by a longshot, and I doubted God was pleased with anything we were doing. Besides, even if I *were* on board, this wasn't the kind of plan we could throw together on a whim. "Let's just get the ransom," I insisted again. "Come on. We can talk in the car—"

"Fine," Andy said, and to my relief he stretched and turned to follow me.

I moved toward the Civic, eager to get in and drive. I was sure I could talk him down if I just had a little time. We didn't have to hurt anybody. This could still work.

After a couple of steps though, I heard Andy mutter something under his breath.

My stomach tightened and I spun around to see what the holdup was.

But instead of looking back at me, Andy was lifting up a finger and pointing at the other side of the dirt road, in the opposite direction of the Civic.

"What?" I asked in confusion, craning my neck thinking that maybe Paul or somebody else was back again, trying to access the slag rock or something.

Andy ignored me and took an unsteady step in the opposite direction, angling toward the van. "Those little *shits*."

"Andy, come *on*, we're seriously going to miss the actual money drop," I burst out, starting to get mad now. We didn't have time for this bullshit.

I stepped forward and grabbed his arm, but he shrugged it off and kept moving toward the gray van, walking fast, pointing at something. "Those little shits," he said again, louder. "Look what they did."

I jogged to catch up with his stumbling walk, trying to figure out what the hell he was looking at.

Then I saw it.

My insides turned to rubber cement.

There was a quarter-sized hole scratched into the black paint we'd used to coat the inside of the van. The setting sun was coming through the back windows at a slant, which meant that the angle was just right to make a faint little white halo in the shadows gathering behind the bumper.

"Fucking hell," I breathed, feeling like the ground was shifting under my feet and my mind was trying to swim faster and faster to keep from being dragged under some invisible current.

Andy opened the van door and hoisted himself inside.

Half a second later, the hole in the paint disappeared, replaced by the pupil of his wide brown eye staring back at me.

My stomach seized. How much had those stupid kids seen? I scrambled to think through every second that Andy and I had taken off our pantyhose before we marched the kids into the hole. I'd kept mine on, but he'd been barefaced when I got back to the quarry.

And if Andy's cover was blown, so was mine.

Fucking hell. Shit, shit, shit.

"You still think we can just let them all *go*?" Andy muttered, the sound muffled from within the van. "They saw our faces. Shit, we should cover up the air hose right now, go get the money and just drive away. Nobody will ever find them—or us."

Acid burned its way up my windpipe and the undertow in my gut pulled harder.

This was bad.

This was really, really, *really* bad.

"We still need to talk this over," I stammered and tilted my chin toward The Pit. As much as I hated to admit it, I was feeling pretty damn rattled now, too.

Andy reopened the back door of the van and fixed me with an unreadable expression that made me take a step back.

For the first time, I seriously considered whether he'd do something to *me*, if he didn't get his way. If his back went against the wrong wall.

"They're not going anywhere until we get back here," I managed, forcing my voice to stay as steady and steely as his. "Let's just get the money and then do what we have to do, okay?" Sheena Halverson wasn't expecting us to actually have the kids with us at the cash drop. She knew she had to make the Bitcoin transfer first, and then wait for instructions regarding their release. We still had a little time to figure this out.

He stared at me from the back of the van with a cocked eyebrow. "Okay, Teddy Bear. If you say so. Let's go."

39

TWENTY-THREE HOURS, THIRTY MINUTES BURIED

They saw our faces. We should cover up the air hose right now ...
Nobody will ever find them ...

They'd seen the scratched-out peephole I'd made in the paint.

There was no question anymore of whether they were going to do something horrible to us. Mr. Edward and Greasy Hair were going to leave us down here—or kill us.

And soon.

Even worse, it was at least partly my fault.

I'd made that hole in the paint, even though Ms. Jessa had told me not to. And for all my Harriet-the-Spying and scraping away at the plywood with sweat pouring down my skin and feet aching from standing so long, the hole still wasn't big enough for my body to squeeze through. I could fit my arms, but I'd wasted precious time digging at the place beneath whatever big, heavy thing they'd shoved on top of the plywood to hold it in place.

Car doors slammed, the two men's voices disappeared, and the sound of tires hummed into silence away from us.

I listened hard, barely breathing. They'd said they were both going to get the money. After that, there were no more sounds from above. They were both gone, for now.

"What did they say?" Bonnie asked, where she lay on the mattress with her arms wrapped around the bucket.

I didn't answer. Just swallowed, frozen where I stood on top of the bucket with my legs shaking. I was glad Bonnie didn't hear what I'd heard. But not hearing wouldn't save her—or any of us—from what was going to happen when the men got back from picking up the ransom money.

The fear that we might die wasn't just a horrible idea anymore.

It was real. Roaring toward us. A matter of *when,* not *if.*

"Sage?" Ms. Jessa called out when I didn't say anything.

"I have to talk to you," I choked past the strangling feeling in my throat.

Then I climbed down from the mattress stack, leaned close to Ms. Jessa's ear, and repeated everything I'd just heard and everything I'd figured out—including the thing about Mr. Edward being the old bus driver. Including what they said about her. How she'd been arrested. Which I knew meant she'd been to jail.

That last part didn't even scare me anymore, because I was too busy being terrified about the first part.

Ms. Jessa stayed quiet and let me lean against her and choke the words out so the other kids wouldn't hear. I didn't want anyone else, especially not Bonnie, to be as scared as I was right now.

She didn't pull away even when I knew that my snot and tears were dripping like a gross faucet while I pressed my mouth against her ear.

The horrible thought came again: We were all going to die, and it was my fault.

"I couldn't hear most of what Mr. Edward said, and only some of what Greasy Hair said," I hissed into her ear, realizing I was probably repeating myself but needing to make sure Ms. Jessa knew how bad things were. "But he definitely saw the hole I scratched in the paint on the van window. I'm sorry, I'm *so* sorry I didn't sit down when you told me to. They're going to kill us when they come back, and it's all my fault."

I was close to having what Grandpa called a "conniption." I couldn't stop it, though. I was too panicked and too scared.

I tried to keep talking, but all of a sudden Ms. Jessa was pulling me to her chest and into a tight hug. Then she leaned her head down and whispered in my ear, "It's *not* your fault. It's *their* fault, Sage. Only theirs. You understand?"

The way she said it reminded me of Mom all over again. The way she'd gotten mean and fierce on the phone the time Bonnie got pushed off the monkey bars and the recess monitor tried to tell Mom that Bonnie should have been more careful.

It wasn't Bonnie being careless. It was the fifth-grader who pushed her, that was the problem. That's what Mom said in the exact same voice Ms. Jessa was using now.

My tears came even faster.

No matter whose fault it was, and I was still pretty sure it was mine, we were still going to die.

"What's wrong?" tiny voices kept asking all around us.

"Sage? Sage?" Bonnie was repeating, over and over, as a small hand that felt like hers stroked the back of my sweaty T-shirt.

I only cried harder.

"Sage is feeling really tired," Ms. Jessa said, sounding like she was sucking in air through a straw. It was so stuffy and hot by this point, all of us were breathing that way. Heavy in, heavy out. Ms. Jessa kept her arms tight around me though, and I was glad she did even though it was a lot sweatier and it hurt the blisters and skin on my raw hands. "That makes sense, because this is a hard time." She drew in another painful-sounding breath. "I think we're all having a pretty hard time, huh?"

There were a few murmurs of "Yes," and "I am," and "Me too, Sage," and "It's okay to cry."

"Even though we're all having a hard time, I need everyone to do something for me now, okay? We all need to help Sage," Ms. Jessa said.

Murmurs of agreement rippled through the blackness in the hole. "How can we, though?" Rose asked. "We can't reach the ceiling like she can."

I forced myself to stop sniffling so I could hear better.

I hadn't been expecting Ms. Jessa to say what she had, and I had the same question Rose did. How could anyone help me?

I swallowed the sob-scream trying to squeeze through my throat. Part of me was sure I was going to suffocate right here, right now. It felt impossible to make air go into my lungs. Ms. Jessa and Bonnie and the other kids were all counting on me, but I was so tired and so scared. How far away was the ransom money the men were talking about? How quick would they return? The questions spun sticky like sugar in a cotton candy machine at the fair.

Even if I *could* get out of the hole, how long would it take me to find help? I had no idea where we were.

Maybe I could pull some of the taller kids up with me if I could get on top of the plywood?

I shook my head in despair. That narrow chimney we'd first climbed through wasn't very wide. It was just big enough for the sheet of plywood I was digging away at and whatever heavy thing was plunked on top of it that I kept running into.

"Sage, how big is the hole you've made in the plywood now?" Ms. Jessa asked, interrupting the terrible thoughts.

"I can fit both arms all the way through it," I said, clearing my throat so the other kids could understand me.

"That's really, really good," Ms. Jessa said. Then, louder, "We're going to help Sage by doing something I learned how to do once when I was having a really hard time. When I had to be apart from my daughter for three whole years." Her voice broke. "And I missed her the same way you miss your mommies and daddies."

There were a few quiet "Oh" sounds from around the mattress pile.

I wiped my eyes, thinking she must be talking about the time she was in jail.

"The thing I learned," she said, talking faster, "that a really smart counselor told me to do, was to imagine what I *wanted*. Instead of thinking about what I *didn't want*. Like, I was always thinking about how long it would be until I saw my daughter Sophie again. Or how much I missed her. But that just made me feel stuck and scared. So instead, the counselor told me to think about the two of us eating cereal together for breakfast, or running through the sprinklers on a hot summer day, or just saying goodnight at bedtime." Her voice caught. "So can you all help me do that for Sage while she tries really, really hard to get us out of here?"

I noticed that Ms. Jessa said the counselor *told* her to do it. Not that she actually did it.

This didn't sound like it would work.

"Yes," Bonnie said, without even missing a beat, and her *yes* was followed by a chorus of voices repeating the same thing.

For a second I wanted to tell them not to bother. It wouldn't make me dig any faster. That we didn't have enough time before Greasy Hair and Mr. Edward came back.

The other kids didn't know that part, though. That worst, most awful part.

Somehow, that made me want to try again, though. I wanted so badly not to let them down, and I'd protect them from this bad thing as best I could because they believed in me so hard. I'd never had that feeling about anything before, and it made more tears drip down my cheeks.

"I'll start," Ms. Jessa said. "When we get out, I'm going to eat an ice cream sundae with all the toppings. Whipped cream and cherries and so much hot caramel."

Ked jumped in, his voice quiet and firm. "When we get out, I'm going to give my mom and dad a big hug. So tight they'll laugh and say, 'Whoa there, tiger!'"

Then Bonnie. "I'm going to watch TV with my sister, Sage, and she gets to pick the show. I won't say I don't like it. It can even be *Family Guy*, and I won't tell Mom on her."

I smiled even though it hurt. To my surprise, Ms. Jessa was actually right. It felt good to think about what was waiting for us outside this hole in the ground, even if it was maybe far-fetched.

We just had to get there.

"Help me back up," I croaked, getting to my feet.

40

TWENTY-FIVE HOURS, THIRTY MINUTES BURIED

The kids and I kept talking while Sage scraped away at the plywood like a machine.

I thought of the slick blood I'd felt coating her hands, the way she'd winced when I touched her torn-up fingers.

Over and over, we told her about all the good things waiting for us when we escaped.

When we escaped.

Never *if* we escaped.

Lies, my mind kept snarling. *False hope.* However, to my surprise, what we were doing actually seemed to be working. Above the sound of our affirmations, Sage scraped and clawed at the wood, faster and faster.

Distantly, I realized that all ten of these children, especially Sage, knew my secret. I was a convicted felon. If we got out of here, my tentative attempts at starting a new life would shatter. I'd lose my new job. I might even go back to jail, since I'd broken my parole by lying on the job application.

I'd still *have* a life, though. If we escaped this hellhole, we all would. And that was what mattered.

I was so dizzy and tired I could barely stand. I refused to sit down, though. If Sage was the one up there on top of that mattress stack hour after hour, digging harder than ever, I could at least stay within arm's reach in case she needed me.

Despite the prison counselor's advice—which I'd so confidently given to the kids—I'd never actually applied it to my own life. But the sound of those little voices calling out with so much courage and optimism in this hot, airless hellhole made me think that it had been a mistake.

Maybe there was something to hope for—all kinds of hope— after all.

41

TWENTY-SIX HOURS BURIED

I couldn't tell how much time was passing while I made the hole bigger. I just knew I had to hurry as fast as I could.

I didn't let myself think about how much my body hurt. Or what Mr. Edward and Greasy Hair had said. Just what the voices underneath me were saying. Until finally, to my surprise, the hole in the plywood got so big I stretched both my arms and shoulders through and pressed them against the jagged edges of the ripped-up wood. The fingertips on my right hand brushed against another plank of wood—that chimney chute we'd crawled down earlier. The fingertips on my left hand brushed against the warm, grimy metal of the big thing on top of the plywood.

"I—I think I might be able to pull myself up through the hole now, if someone can give me a boost," I stammered, hoping so hard that I was right.

It would be a tight squeeze, but I was pretty sure I could get up into the chute if I wriggled through. When Grandpa still lived at his old house, Bonnie and I found a hole in the cupboard of his downstairs bathroom, leading up to a hole in the cupboard of the upstairs bathroom. Mom said it was a "laundry chute," and told us not to play in it.

We did anyway, the first chance we got, giggling while we shimmied up and down through the narrow square tunnel.

I was pretty sure that the hole I'd made in the plywood was about that big, but just barely, and the edges weren't smooth like the laundry chute.

"Yes, Sage. That's amazing. Can everyone hold onto the sides of the mattress stack?" Ms. Jessa asked. "Evelyn, do you think you can keep the bucket steady for Sage if I climb up onto the mattresses and lay beside you so I can give Sage a boost up?"

"I can do it," Evelyn said, like she was born for this moment.

"Okay, Ben and Rose, come give me a leg up. The rest of you, push against the mattress stack so it doesn't wobble too much. I'll go slow."

I braced my hand against the edge of the jagged hole as Ms. Jessa climbed up to me. It was easier now that I had an edge to grip, even when the mattresses and the bucket shook a little under my feet.

In no time, I felt Ms. Jessa's hands feeling around for my shoes on top of the bucket. "You ready, Sage?"

My stomach tightened up, and a fizzy hot feeling zipped around through my veins, like I'd just downed a bunch of Pixy Stix. "Ready."

The mattresses rippled again as Ms. Jessa got to a crouch and moved her laced fingers underneath the foot I was holding up for her to take hold of.

I gripped the splintery sides of the plywood hard. "Okay, go," I said.

My arms and my head went up through the hole.

When my armpits hit the jagged edges, I started to panic.

I wasn't going to fit. Bits of sharp wood dug into my under-arms in two places, feeling like they wanted to break through the skin. I was going to have to start scraping all over again.

"Sage, when you get up to the top you're gonna be so proud," Bonnie called from below me, and I wriggled harder, even though the rough edges hurt.

"Keep pushing me up," I told Ms. Jessa, because she'd stopped for a second.

I twisted my chest, feeling the splinters dig in as Ms. Jessa pushed my feet up.

I bit back the *ouch* I wanted to scream, and managed to get my hands planted on the topside of the plywood.

Yes, yes, yes.

With my palms splayed on top of the dirty, splintered wood, I pushed as hard as I could and leaned on Ms. Jessa's hands. The skin on my tummy hurt so bad that for half a second, I imagined the splin-tery edges punching through my ribcage and into my lungs.

That wasn't what happened, though.

Little by little, the pressure from the sharp edges went away, and I was moving all the way into the chimney.

"I'm up, I'm up," I hissed, barely able to believe it.

Soft cheers rose up to greet me.

"Sage, you did it!"

"We're going to get out!"

42

SAGE

TWENTY-SIX HOURS BURIED

"Ms. Jessa, can you boost me up now, too?" Ben asked. He was the next tallest.

"Yes, as soon as Sage finds a way up the shaft."

I gulped in a ragged breath. It was already easier to breathe up here, closer to the surface. The tiniest breeze tickled the hair on my arms.

My shaky arms dripped with a fresh layer of hot, wet blood as I scooted my feet around the narrow ledge of the plywood. Then I tentatively climbed up on top of the big, heavy square-shaped thing in the center of the wood, bracing my hands against the sheets of warped plywood that formed the walls of the narrow chute.

There was a little light coming into the chute from above me. Little slivers around one edge of that big piece of metal that covered up the entrance to the hole.

I stood slowly, barely daring to hope that I'd be able to reach the sheet of metal. It wasn't that far away.

I held out my hands, fingertips stretching skyward.

My heart sank.

It was still a good two feet above my fingertips, even standing on top of the heavy object. "I still can't reach the top," I called down.

"Can you pull Rose or Ben up there with you?" Ms. Jessa asked hopefully. "I think I can boost them through the hole if there's room to stand."

I shook my head and squinted at the plywood walls bowing in toward me. It was narrower in here than I remembered from when we'd climbed through earlier. It had been a struggle just to get my arms and legs in position to stand. I wasn't sure how the ladder had ever fit down here. I remembered the chute being bigger, the plywood walls straighter. I definitely wouldn't be able to lift someone else up here with me.

I ran one hand along the plywood and frowned. It was wet.

I suddenly remembered the sound of the rain from last night, pinging fast and hard on the metal sheet above us before we went to sleep. "I don't think there's room for more than one person. The rain … it soaked the wood walls, they're bending in a lot. Could you hand me the bucket? I think I could put it on top of this …" I kicked at the big black thing I was standing on, testing how solid it was. It didn't move. "There's a big square thing I can put the bucket on top of."

There was a soft rattle beneath me as Ms. Jessa tried to push the bucket up through the hole, then a hard *thunk* as she tried to force it through.

"The shape is wrong," Ms. Jessa said. "We'd have to make the hole bigger. Can you break off more pieces of the plywood?"

I ignored her for just a second, because I was too focused on an idea that had jumped to the front of my mind.

It was a Harriet-the-Spy kind of idea, and it sent a little fizz of hope through me.

"I don't think I need the bucket. I know how to get out now," I called back.

43

I pulled into the Little Eddy campground turnoff, so sweaty and winded you'd think I'd been running instead of driving up the mountain road.

I was exactly seven minutes early.

I swiped at the back of my damp neck and flicked my eyes toward the fast-disappearing wink of daylight sinking behind the mountain peak's furthest tree line. It wouldn't be true sunset for another half an hour, but with the sun down past the mountains it felt like dusk had already settled in earnest. The thick stands of lodgepole pines scattered throughout the dispersed campsites of Little Eddy made it hard for me to see whether anybody was coming down the narrow dirt road into the campground, but I kept flitting my eyes back and forth anyway every few seconds, thinking that the dark after-image was a person.

I took a breath and tried to calm myself down. As I released the whoosh of air, a sudden flash of movement through the trees made me curl my fingers tighter around the steering wheel and sit up straight again.

It was just a little girl—maybe eleven, close to Sage's age—riding her bike down the bumpy dirt trails.

I wanted to roll down my window and scream that something bad was happening in this peaceful little spot in the forest, to get back to her campsite and ride away on her two-wheeler as fast as she could.

Instead, I kept my teeth clenched and watched her coast down a slope, long pale hair streaming wild in the gray light, chin tilted upward and a smile on her face as she passed the sign for Bull Creek Trailhead and disappeared among the trees.

I opened the car window a crack, and the smoky, savory smell of campfire dinners wafted through the air, making my stomach growl despite the ever-present sick dread churning. I'd drunk a half-cup of day-old coffee that morning, but that was all I'd had today. My stomach felt tight and sour, full of acid.

Four minutes. I had to stay put until then.

My eyes moved to the backpack of cash on the passenger-side floor, then back to the clock on the dash. In exactly four minutes, I was supposed to get out of my vehicle and leave all of it for the kidnappers.

I knew what I was supposed to do. The instructions couldn't have been more clear. And I'd memorized them since the first time I saw them last night.

You will bring the cash, in a backpack, to the Bull Creek trailhead at Little Eddy campground at exactly 7:00 p.m.

Then drive away. We will not retrieve the money until you leave.

However, with each second that ticked by, unease gripped my insides like a vise hitched tighter. How could I actually bring myself to drive away, trusting that the person who'd taken my children would hold up their end of the bargain and contact me to return the children as soon as I made the Bitcoin transfer when I got home?

Because it's all you have, my weary gut replied.

The bus driver's dead-eyed mugshot from the article flashed into my mind.

My stomach coiled tighter and I flicked my eyes back to the clock on the dash.

Three minutes left.

"Shit," I whispered, half-word, half-whine. I'd actually thought that getting the money would be the hardest part.

It wasn't, though. Being here in this moment alone, not knowing if I was doing the right thing or completely fucking up, with my daughters' lives on the line, was the hardest part.

Whatever happened next was entirely my responsibility. I'd done exactly what the ransom note had asked, to the letter. I hadn't called the police. Hadn't told a soul. I had the money—most of it, anyway. And I was about to drive home like a bat out of hell to transfer that Bitcoin.

I desperately wanted someone to tell me I was doing the right thing. That by tomorrow morning, Sage and Bonnie would be wrapping their arms around my neck so tight I could barely breathe.

Then I finally let myself picture the alternative. The police and FBI showing up on my doorstep tonight, surrounding the house, when that Bitcoin transfer emptying the bond money out of the city's accounts triggered a digital tripwire.

They'd realize pretty quickly what was happening when I completed that final step of the ransom. They'd find out who I was and that my children were on that bus.

I imagined a red-faced FBI officer in a suit asking me to tell him again why I'd been so stupid as to stay quiet, think that I could do this on my own. Surely I knew better. I imagined him telling me that the backpack of cash was the last tangible link to the kidnapper.

And now my children—and the other parents' children—were simply gone.

Listen to your gut, Sheen. Think of Mindy Falcrest. The 'right' thing isn't always the right thing.

I was biting down so hard on the inside of my cheek I could taste blood. Was that really what Dad would tell me if he was in his right mind? Or was that just a story I was telling myself because I was too terrified to think straight?

What had I done?

Two minutes.

Hands shaking, I unlocked the car doors and reached for the backpack handle.

As I moved, a flicker of gold caught my eye from the car cup holder.

Dad's broken Rolex knockoff.

I reached for it, overwhelmed by emotion and panic. "What the hell should I do, Dad?" I whispered.

I wasn't expecting an answer.

But then an idea flickered faintly in the corners of my mind.

The second hand of the watch ticked toward seven o'clock as I let the length of the links unfold, a cold sweat breaking in rivulets down my back.

"Shit," I whispered again, my voice cracking. Was this a good idea or a bad idea? My tired brain floundered. There wasn't nearly enough time for me to think this through.

One minute.

Do it, my gut urged, louder and firmer than anything I'd felt all day.

I threw the watch back down on the seat and grabbed a pen and a bank receipt, lying beneath a pair of sunglasses on the dash, praying the device still worked.

Then I scribbled out a note, wrapped it around the broken watch, and placed both items at the top of the backpack.

I couldn't get all the cash. $5,700 short. This is my dad's Rolex. It'll be really easy to fix the clasp, and it's worth $12,000, easy.

I looked at the clock. *Zero minutes.*

Before I let myself fall apart, I grabbed the backpack, swung open the car door and walked the few steps to Bull Creek Trailhead.

From somewhere farther down the dirt road in the campsite, the sound of an RV generator droned quietly. Someone called to a barking dog. The faint smell of meat and potatoes cooking on somebody's campfire got stronger.

But all I could see, tucked into the woods by the trailhead, were dark trees and a darkening gray sky.

My legs shook, but I pushed them forward until I stood beside a cluster of huckleberry bushes, their leaves already tinged with red from the cool nights at higher elevation. I set the backpack down among them, then stepped back to see if it was visible from the edge of the dirt road.

Just barely. Only if you knew what you were looking for, though.

Then I forced myself to walk back to my car with measured steps, nothing that might make a hiker out for a walk through the woods look twice.

I didn't glance back over my shoulder.

I didn't hesitate as I pulled out of the campground and onto the rural highway in the direction of Sunset Springs.

I didn't drive back home, though.

44

Andy leaned his head out the open passenger-side window of the Civic like a dog, practically salivating. Then he lowered his binoculars—same ones we'd used earlier in the day—and pointed at the dark, narrow deer trail that intersected with Bull Creek. "Dude she's gone, let's go," he hissed impatiently for the third time.

His hair, which hadn't been combed in the last twenty-four hours—maybe longer—looked wilder than I'd ever seen it, framing his jowls. He was definitely still beer-drunk.

"She really drove away already? You're sure?" I asked, reaching for the key to cut the idling engine.

He pulled his head in the window and shoved the binoculars onto my lap. "I'm buzzed, not a fuckup. Yeah, bro, she's *gone.*"

"And she didn't seem like she saw us?" I demanded.

"It's getting dark. She didn't see shit," he insisted flatly, holding up his hand Scout's honor.

My heart thumped as I pulled the keys out of the ignition, got out of the car, and followed him down the scrubby trail that led to the far end of the campground, where the real trailheads and campsites were located. This side of Little Eddy was all vault toilets and over-grown campsites, with a CLOSED sign and a chain across the path.

"The backpack looked sort of small," Andy grumbled. "Bitch better have brought all the cash."

"Shh," I hissed. There wasn't anybody nearby. All the updated campsites were a quarter of a mile away, near the main dirt road. Anybody out for an evening hike would probably be headed for one of the marked trails—like Bull Creek. But sound carried in the quiet, and there was no sense being stupid.

"I'm sure it's all there," I whispered, not wanting to sour Andy's mood again. "She wants her kids back."

Saying it felt like a brick dropped into the pit of my stomach.

We still hadn't settled on what to do with the kids and the bus driver—even though we'd argued about it the whole drive.

Andy still wanted to "Take care of them," as he put it in his slurred voice.

I didn't know what to think anymore. Not since I'd learned those kids might've seen Andy's face. And the quarry.

Sure, there was no way any of them could know who Andy was. However, if the bus driver or any of the kids could point the cops to the quarry—and Andy—*I* was screwed. Everybody knew that me and Andy were thick as thieves. If they caught him, they caught me.

For shit's sake.

I pushed the thoughts away and told myself we'd pick up the money, then figure things out, somehow. At that point, our plan—except for the trick of disappearing with the ransom—would be complete.

There weren't any cars around as we approached the Bull Creek trailhead on foot. No people, either. Just the dark, settling deep into the tall pine trees.

"Look," Andy hissed, crashing through the brush. A startled bird made a *chee* sound and flew in the opposite direction of our feet.

I stood and stared as Andy bent down, muttering something I couldn't hear.

A dog barked somewhere from the direction of the campsites, and I cringed but forced myself not to look around like I was doing something sketchy.

Even though you fucking are, said a voice in my head that sounded like Mom.

I pushed it away. Like she had any room to give me advice on morals.

Andy had the black backpack in his hands. To my relief, he didn't open it. Just slung it over his shoulders like we'd talked about and made a beeline back to the spot where we'd left the Civic. He wasn't exactly walking in a straight line, but he wasn't falling over either, and that was good enough for now.

"It's heavy," he huffed, shuffling so fast I almost had to jog to keep up. "That's good, right?"

I didn't reply. Not until we got back into the car and locked the doors.

The second we were inside the vehicle, Andy had the zipper down and was staring into the backpack with an expression on his face I'd never seen.

Adoration, maybe. And a little confusion.

He reached into the bag and picked up something gold-colored. There was a piece of paper folded around it, and it made a soft, metallic clinking sound.

I wrinkled my nose. It was a wristwatch—with a broken clasp.

Andy opened the paper, read it, then shoved it toward me with a laugh.

"Dumb bitch. How are we supposed to split a watch, even if it's worth twelve thousand? And cash won't be even now," Andy complained, but he was laughing. "You think it's real?" he asked, bringing the watch close to his face. "It feels heavy. It's probably real, right? She wouldn't fuck with us like that, would she—"

I forced out a real-sounding laugh. "You take it."

Andy wrapped his fingers tighter around the watch and studied me. "Why would you do that?"

"Just let me finish," I said, thinking faster. "We split the cash even, and you get to take the Rolex." Then I added, "I get to decide what happens to the kids."

He frowned, and the wrinkles between his eyebrows deepened into dark elevens. "I'm not getting caught just because you don't have the balls to do what we gotta do. A fuckin' *Rolex* isn't gonna do me any good in prison."

I shook my head firmly. "No shit. You think I want to get caught? I'm not saying I *won't* do it if we have to … I just want a chance to think. We've got time. Tomorrow is Sunday. A whole day, while the quarry's still closed for the weekend."

Andy sat back in the passenger seat and shook his head but didn't respond.

I started up the car. "Do we have a deal? You keep the Rolex—and stop talking about killing kids until I think this through?" I hesitated then said, "I'll come up with an even better plan."

This made him smile—a big, crooked, toothy thing that made my skin crawl. He slipped the Rolex into the front pocket of his jeans. "Well, when you put it like that …"

45

SHEENA

I flew down the mountain road switchbacks in the gathering dark, praying that the dusk-colored shapes lurking on the shoulder would stay there.

The last thing I needed was to hit a deer and go off the road.

It already felt like things were spinning out of control, with that stunt I'd just pulled putting Dad's watch in the bag of cash. Did they suspect anything?

No. They wouldn't. Why would they? It looked just like a real Rolex.

Even so, I couldn't shake the dread that built with every passing mile. Every direction I looked, failure lurked in the brush.

There were no headlights behind me yet. In the past ten minutes, I'd only passed two other vehicles headed the opposite direction, toward Little Eddy. But there was only one highway that bisected these mountains. And unless the kidnappers planned on driving the opposite direction down I-55—deeper into the national forest for a hundred miles—they would be right behind me as soon as they got the money.

That's what I was counting on, anyway. Because if they were planning on using their cell phones to check whether I'd complete the Bitcoin transfer—the real ransom compared to fifty-thousand dollars they asked for in cash—they couldn't stay in the forest.

Please, God, they couldn't stay in the forest.

If they did that, that watch wouldn't help anyone.

Every few seconds, I glanced at the SOS-ONLY message on the screen of my phone, begging it to give me a single bar.

"Come *on*," I finally screamed in frustration.

And, as if it had just been waiting for me to ask, the bar appeared.

"Fuck yes," I hissed.

I could track them now.

I slammed the brakes and started scanning for a forest-service road, anywhere I could pull off and tuck my car out of sight for a few minutes to look at my phone.

I didn't know what the kidnapper's vehicle looked like. However, I was sure they knew mine. If they saw me stopped along the side of the road instead of hurrying home to transfer the Bitcoin—everything would go fully off the rails.

The pale dirt of a narrow gravel road appeared in my headlights a moment later, and I hit the brakes so hard the tires squealed.

I managed to make the turn, then pulled around a bend flanked by pines and undergrowth until I was certain my car would be out of sight from the main road. Then I killed the headlights, cracked the driver's side window an inch, grabbed my phone, and turned the brightness down low.

I still had that one bar of service.

"Please work," I muttered in a shrill whisper, fumbling through the apps on the screen until I found the familiar icon of a gold watch face.

276

I held my breath while it loaded, hoping for the best but bracing myself.

I hadn't bothered to charge Dad's watch at night since the clasp had broken yesterday and he'd gone to stay at Cherished Hearts.

Surely it still held at least a little juice, though.

The faint sound of tires on the road—followed by a flash of headlights—brought my eyes up. Was that the kidnapper? My heart banged in my chest as the sound and lights disappeared without any sort of wobble that might indicate they'd seen my car.

I darted my eyes back to the loading app. "Come on, hurry up," I begged.

After a few long, agonizing seconds, the login screen appeared. I scrambled to type in my password, mercifully getting it right on the first try—and stared as the splash page loaded.

My eyes moved to the notification in the top corner that read LOW WATCH BATTERY—8%.

I let out a soft gasp. There was still some juice left in the watch.

This was going to work. But I didn't have long.

I stared at the dot on the main screen that showed the word DAD, above a rapidly-moving dot on ID-55.

1.4 miles away.

My breath caught in my throat. The car that just blazed past me *had* been the kidnapper. And there was zero indication they knew I'd pulled off here. I'd been wondering all day whether I was being followed. Now I knew it was an empty threat.

Fresh tears welled up in my eyes and I wiped them away furiously, reaching for the ignition.

My car hummed back to life, and I pressed my foot to the gas pedal, keeping one eye on the road and one on that tiny moving dot as I brought my car up to speed and closed the gap to one mile.

No matter how much I wanted to floor the gas pedal and drive like a maniac to overtake it, I didn't dare get any closer.

For one thing, there were hardly any other cars on this lonely highway right now, and the second the kidnappers turned off somewhere—and I followed—it was only a matter of time until they started paying attention to the car behind them. And then they sure as hell weren't going to lead me to the kids.

For another, I couldn't count on the watch battery.

I looked at the moving dot on the app screen again. Seven-percent battery. The longer the watch's connection with the app was active, pinging between my device and GPS to give me its position, the faster the battery would drain.

Swallowing hard, I forced myself to shut down the app and drew in a shaky breath, flicking my eyes to the speedometer.

This would work. If I didn't give into panic with my need to constantly check, and run down the watch's battery, it would work.

Dad's tracker ran on GPS, which meant that the range was excellent—but the battery drained pretty quickly when it was actively being used by the app. The website where I'd ordered it a couple of months earlier had explained all the advantages and disadvantages of different tracking devices. GPS meant that I could track the watch almost anywhere it went—as long as the charge held. With a full battery, that meant hours. With a tapped battery, that meant minutes.

I decided to open the app for a few seconds at a time only, taking screenshots of each location. As long as the kidnappers kept that watch with them, they were creating a literal map for me—and police—to follow.

I just couldn't let that battery run down.

I gripped the steering wheel and held the car steady, resolving not to reopen the app again for at least five minutes.

Each time I felt the panic rise up in me, the urge to stomp my foot down on the accelerator, I thought about that beautiful blue dot waiting to guide me to my daughters.

If I lost that connection, I was back to square one—relying on a psychopath's word that she would return the children safely.

I shook my head and focused on the road. For right now, the only thing I needed to think about was doing what the ransom note had asked. Complete the instructions. So I would rush back home and make the Bitcoin transfer.

And then I would—what? Call the police, even though the note had explicitly warned me not to?

After the Bitcoin transfer, I wasn't sure what my next move would be. That terrified me. I didn't know what the hell I was going to do, but I was going to have to figure it out soon.

Just before the mountains opened up into foothills and the pin-prick of lights from the first houses on the outskirts of the Treasure Valley, my headlights bounced off a deer moving into the road.

"*Shit.*"

I slammed on the brakes. The animal lifted its head and stared into the headlights, eyes wide and nostrils flaring. A doe.

"Move, please move," I begged her, hitting the gas again to inch the car forward, in hopes I could startle her into running away. With the mountain road behind us, it was anyone's guess where the kidnappers would go next, and I was desperate to check their location again. What if they were planning to drive all the way to Kuna or Caldwell, twenty miles beyond Sunset Springs?

The deer shuddered but planted her feet and stayed where she was, swinging her head back toward the shoulder of the road.

"Move, goddammit!" I screamed and hit the horn. I'd come this far complying with their every demand. Before I could go off-script, I needed to drive straight home and make that transfer.

Because there was still a chance they'd let the children go when I did.

And, if they didn't, I had their location—but only as long as the watch kept pinging.

Movement from the weeds of the steep embankment drew me back from my desperate, frazzled thoughts.

Two gangly fawns—maybe a few months old—trotted to follow their mother into the middle of the road in front of my high beams. As soon as her babies were by her side, she picked up her feet and disappeared into the brush on the other side of the highway.

The horror of the near-miss sent a sharp prickle down my neck. I blew out a shuddering breath, wiped the fresh tears running down my cheeks, then pushed the car back up to speed in the direction of the first city lights.

46

TWENTY-SIX HOURS, THIRTY MINUTES BURIED

It was working. It was really, *really* working.

The bowed walls of the plywood in the chimney were completely soaked through—with thick mud behind them. Which meant that I could dig into the wet wood way more easier than I'd been able to do with the dry plywood covering up the ceiling of the bunker.

When I'd realized how crumbly and flaky the wet wood was, an image had flashed into my brain of the playground in Sunset Springs. The one that had little footholds and handholds carved into a wall you could climb up.

Still using Ms. Jessa's belt buckle, I dug into the soggy wood and mud faster and faster, ignoring how much blood I could feel oozing between my fingers and down my arms.

I made two footholds, then three, then four, up higher and higher. Then I dug my feet into the soggy wood and mud footholds I'd made and pushed myself up to dig more.

In what felt like no time, I was nearly to the top.

We were *so* close.

We were almost out.

The light coming from beneath the big sheet of metal above me was fading by the second. It was getting dark outside. That meant a whole twenty-four hours had nearly gone by since the men had stuck us down in this horrible bunker.

And they were going to be back any second, I just knew it.

But soon, I could run for help. The men might not even know I was gone if they didn't check.

"I'm at the top," I rasped after another few minutes, barely able to believe it.

My fingers brushed the top of the metal sheet while I clung to the last soggy foothold I'd made, praying the sides wouldn't give way.

Excited voices whispered beneath me as I clawed at the dirt under the sheet metal, digging for the last time.

The sliver of dim gray light widened.

I kept digging like an animal, gasping and crying, pushing myself up bit by bit. It was getting hard to angle my body to keep digging beneath the sheet of metal from this angle. I had the thought I should make one more foothold, but if I just leaned a little more, I was sure I'd be able to make a final hole big enough I could scramble out from under the metal.

My eyes were so bleary from dust and sweat I could hardly see what I was doing anymore. The air hose looked like a little black snake in the corner of my eye, dangling down into the chimney beside me. The opening was small enough I could have covered it with the palm of my hand. It didn't look nearly big enough to bring enough air into the hole for eleven people. No wonder we'd all been struggling to breathe.

But all I cared about anymore was that I could finally see a big slice of the steely gray sky, right in front of me. The hole I'd created between the mud at my fingertips and the big piece of metal above my head was nearly wide enough that I was sure I could fit through it if I was just able to wriggle my body upward and through it.

I heard a faint groaning sound but ignored it. My hands scooped, clawed, dug, like I'd seen the neighbor's dog do when it was after a gopher in the hills by our house, panting and yelping out loud because my fingers and hands hurt so much.

I pushed hard on the last foothold with my sneaker, fighting for the last inch I needed for leverage.

"I did it," I cried, grabbing hold of the metal's jagged edge with one hand. Ignoring the muscles screaming in my legs, I propelled myself upward one last time.

Squirming hard, I twisted onto my back, using my shoulders to help me squeeze myself inch by inch out from underneath the sheet of metal.

Another strange groaning sound that didn't make sense came from beneath me.

I wriggled my shoulders and ignored the metal cutting into my hands as I braced against it and pulled myself all the way out of the hole.

I was free. I was finally, one-hundred percent free. I gasped in the fresh, clean air and rolled onto my belly. Then I hurried to my feet, turning around to call down to the others—at the exact second the groaning sound was replaced by a cracking noise and a low rumble.

I watched in horror as the bowed plywood walls that had been holding the chimney together crumpled in on themselves.

My mouth dropped open in confusion, then horror.

I saw just enough to make sense of what had happened.

There was no chute anymore because the mud behind the soggy plywood sheets had broken through where I'd just climbed up, filling the space completely with wet, packed dirt.

"Ms. Jessa? Bonnie?" I called, then clamped my mouth shut so I could hear a response.

Any response.

There was only silence.

"Bonnie," I cried again and again. "Bonnie!"

Had the bunker filled up with mud, too? Had everyone just been crushed? Were they alive? My heart beat so loud in my ears and my legs started shaking so bad I could barely stand.

I couldn't hear anything from down in the hole. Nothing.

But I *could* hear the sound of tires coming back down the dirt road, headed right for me.

"No," I cried, grabbing the stubby end of the black air hose that was still sticking out beneath one side of the sheet metal.

I put my ear to it, then my mouth, seeing if I could draw in a breath.

My lungs filled with a little bubble of air.

My heart lifted the tiniest bit.

I sucked harder on the hose—and then my lungs hit a wall, like when you suck the air out of a plastic water bottle and it starts crinkling up because there's no oxygen left.

Even if the mud hadn't completely collapsed the bunker like it had the chimney, the air hose wasn't bringing any air down to the bunker anymore.

And the sound of those tires was getting closer with each passing second.

47

Andy was happy as a clam the whole way back to the quarry. Kept reaching his hand inside the backpack and touching the bills. "I'll wait until we're back to count it, bro. So you can watch. Make sure it's all there. We can split it together, so you know everything's even," he cooed.

"Sounds good," I said, making sure the tone of my voice matched his. However, the closer we got to the quarry, the tighter the knots in my stomach twisted.

Think, for shit's sake, I begged my own brain. But the only ideas it spit back landed me in prison for the rest of my life—or put so much blood on my hands, I might as well lock myself up and throw away the key.

They were kids, for fuck's sake. *Kids.*

For the first time, I didn't try to push away the prickly feeling of regret trying to elbow its way into my fantasy about disappearing with my cash, starting a whole new life, and getting out of shithole Idaho. And once I gave that regret an inch, it slammed me in the chest so hard I could barely breathe.

Fucking apply yourself, Ted.

What if my mom was right, though? That I was just a stupid, reckless kid. That's what the owner of the motorcycle I'd wrecked said when he testified at my hearing. As if he pitied me, even though he hated me, too.

I had no future, in any direction. I was trapped, just like those kids I'd put underground.

My mouth started to taste sickly sweet, the same way it did when I had too many beers and was gonna throw up. So I rolled down the window even though Andy started giving me shit because he had to close the backpack. "I don't wanna puke in your car," was all I could think to say, and that shut him up for a few minutes at least.

All said and done, the quarry was a little more than an hour's drive from Little Eddy campground, but it had felt like minutes while my mind spun.

What the hell was I going to do? My palms felt slick and clammy on the steering wheel, and the smell of Andy's body odor— steeped into the Civic—was making my stomach churn even more.

Before I knew it, our headlights were reflecting off the rusted-out aluminum sign marking the back entrance to the quarry.

And I still didn't have a plan.

Could I really kill somebody—or let them die, which was basically the same thing?

Not just somebody. There's eleven somebodies down there, my mind insisted.

If you don't do it, you'll spend your entire life in prison, a deeper, darker part snarled.

I couldn't go back to jail. I *couldn't*. Even a few months felt like hell. Like forever. Like I was one of those dogs on an ASPCA commercial that somebody locked up in a tiny crate so long the animal turned all shaky and terrified and didn't even know how to be a dog anymore. I could practically hear Sarah McLachlan singing in the background.

Those memories of jail brought me right back to square one.

It felt like there was a bomb strapped to my chest. I could either blow myself up, or I could unstrap it and throw it away from me —knowing exactly who it would hit: Those kids.

"Should we count the money right here in the car, or should we like, spread it out on the van floor—?" Andy started to say the second I yanked the key out of the ignition.

He was still slurring a little bit. And I had no doubt he was going straight for the cooler to slug the last of the warm beers now that we'd returned with the ransom money, triumphant.

I felt so disgusted by him, by myself, that the bile in my throat actually spilled onto my tongue. Without a word, I unbuckled my seatbelt and lurched away from the car before the burning, sick mess in my stomach came up.

I thought I heard Andy snicker, but he stayed where he was in the passenger seat while I half-stumbled, half-ran in the direction of the buried bunker.

Then I doubled over and spewed my guts—a disgusting soup of peanut butter and jam sandwiches and beer.

I heaved again and again, blinking back hot tears I couldn't stop from pouring down my face like when I got a really bad stomach bug. It was the only time I cried.

Then I sat on the dirt, wiped my mouth, and stared at the sheet metal.

Another wave of sick hit me, but not the kind that would make bile rise up in my throat again. The prickly, sweaty kind that won't go away even if you vomit.

Because I'd just realized that something—something new— was very, very wrong.

The big piece of metal didn't seem to be sitting quite the way it had the last time I'd seen it.

I rose from a crouch, trying to convince myself that my eyes were playing tricks on me in the dark. The sun had just barely set, so it wasn't fully dark yet. There were still faint shadows around the edges of the sheet metal. One of those shadows was bigger than the rest, though.

Big enough that, as I got closer, it looked less like a shadow and more like a hole.

It couldn't be a hole. There was no way. The buzzing, electric feeling in my chest got stronger, sharper, like there were invisible nails pushing down all over my skin.

I took a step closer and leaned down, so my face was just a couple of feet away from that suspicious shadow. "Fucking hell."

It *was* a hole.

The car door slammed behind me. Andy's footsteps were heading toward the lean-to and the cooler of beer. He was saying something, but I couldn't focus on the words.

I couldn't focus on anything but that hole. It was just big enough for a small person—a kid—to squeeze through.

Then my gaze wandered to the right and I saw the faint, muddy footprints in the damp, hard-packed dirt, leading toward the edge of the trash pile—and the road.

The sight of those imprints, barely visible in the darkness, snapped me out of that frozen, prickly feeling, and I whipped my head left and right.

Andy's footsteps were crunching toward me now. I heard the pop of a beer's tab and loud slurping. He was saying something, but I didn't listen. Instead, I followed the path of the footprints toward the edge of the junk pile, searching the shadows, scanning past the angular shapes of random rubble and broken equipment.

I walked for maybe fifty yards, until I got to the far edge of The Pit, where the hulking frame of a half-broken excavator leaned at an angle, its tires hanging onto the edge of the dirt road that led out of the quarry. It was the same excavator we'd used to dig out the hole for the bunker. Same one we'd scavenged for its door.

And then, so quiet I would have missed it if my senses weren't suddenly sharp as knives, came a quiet shuffling sound from behind it. Like somebody was shifting their weight.

I darted toward the sound.

"Dude, where are you? Your puke stinks—" Andy was saying from the darkness behind me.

I ignored him. Because my eyes had just locked onto a shadow that moved—while the rest of the shapes in the junk pile stayed put.

I took four quick steps forward, around the excavator's frame.

Then I saw her.

A tall, skinny girl covered from head to toe in dirt—and something dark that must have been blood on her hands, arms, and even smeared across her face. I didn't know her name, but I knew who she was immediately: one of the kids I'd recognized from when I drove the bus. And there was absolutely no doubt now, as we locked eyes, that she recognized me, too.

Her knees were bent in a slight crouch, and I could tell I'd caught her right as she was about to launch into a run. But now, she stared at me frozen, like a gangly baby deer in the headlights.

"Dude, where *are* you?" Andy's voice came from behind me again, loud and annoyed and headed toward mean-drunk. He clearly hadn't seen the new hole or the faint muddy footprints leading away from the buried bunker.

The girl's eyes, already huge like a doll's, widened so you could see the whites all the way around her pupils. There were pale lines streaking down the dark gunk on her cheeks from crying.

She leaned away from me, coiling like a spring.

"Mr. Edward," she said, her voice all shaky and whispery. That was all she said, but it was enough to make my guts seize up so violently that I nearly doubled over again.

"*Please,*" she begged, putting her hands in front of her body. Her eyes flitted toward the dirt road.

If I jumped forward, I was pretty sure I could grab her. Honestly, I didn't know why she hadn't already bolted.

I took a small step forward, and she darted her eyes to her foot.

I followed her gaze and suddenly realized that her foot was caught in some tangle of dirty Styrofoam and broken cement behind her at the edge of The Pit. "Please," she said again, slowly reaching her bloody hands to her ankle to pull it free.

As she did that, her eyes moved away from the road, looking past me. At first, I thought she was afraid of Andy—who was making a racket in the direction of the bunker. He must have seen the dugout spot by now, because from the grunting and clanging, he was trying to move the sheet metal by himself to get inside the hole.

Then the girl, her voice small and trembling, said, "The walls caved in from mud. My sister and the kids and Ms. Jessa ... they don't have any more air. Help them. Please."

I blinked at her as she pulled her foot free.

No, that was impossible. She was just trying to distract me and get away.

But then Andy crowed, "Holy shit, the hole's filled up with dirt."

He didn't sound upset, necessarily. Just astonished.

The girl mouthed "Please" one more time.

I parted my lips to scream for Andy to help me grab her, then figure out what the hell had happened.

But the part of me that had just spewed my guts all over the dirt, the part of me that heard her say my name with that pleading look, kept me rooted where I stood, even as the little girl took two steps away from me. She finally managed to kick her foot free of the debris, backing onto the road now. If it hadn't been for the excavator's frame, and the settling darkness, Andy would have seen her by now, too.

"What the hell are you doing over there, you dumbass?" Andy's voice, and the crunch of his footsteps, were getting closer now. The little girl's eyes turned to saucers.

And then she ran.

Fucking *booked it.*

Chase her, my brain screamed. *Do something.*

I just stood there, though.

"Hello? Asshole?" Andy called as he came around the dump truck. He was wearing the ransom backpack, and he was talking fast and excited as the fresh beer buzzed him up. "Bro, the whole thing *collapsed.* At first I thought one of the little shits got out, because the dirt is all caved-in on one side. I guess not, though. God stepped in and decided for us. They're probably dead down there."

I blinked at him, feeling my mouth twitch but unable to make words. Then I turned my head to stare back down the dark, dirt road, and along the deep shadows of the steep quarry walls. I couldn't see the little girl anymore. Had she already gotten that far?

Apparently, Andy hadn't noticed the faint, muddy footprints. He didn't know that, right this second, there was a blood-and-dust-covered skinny little girl running as fast as she could down the dirt road away from us.

"Come on. I counted out all the cash. Your half's in the cooler. We gotta get out of here, see if that bitch made the Bitcoin transfer," Andy was saying, adjusting the pack on his back and moving away from me again.

Tell him.

No, keep your mouth shut.

But the other kids might still be alive down there. Not for long, though.

No! Get the hell out of here and don't look back.

On the outside, I was numb and frozen, but the inside of my head was a whirlwind of contradicting demands coming hard and fast.

Earlier, when I saw that little hole scratched into the paint on the van's back windows, I thought the plan was spiraling out of control.

But things were much, much worse now.

Andy's footsteps stopped when I didn't follow him. "Did you have a stroke or something? Stay here all night if you want I guess, but I'm getting out of—" Then he sucked in his breath. "What the hell is that?"

I didn't have to ask what he meant. When I followed his gaze, I could see it too.

The silhouette of a skinny person—tall enough to be an adult, but so painfully childlike in the way she pumped her arms and legs like a gangly baby horse, that there was no mistaking what she was even in the near-dark.

"One of them got out? One of them GOT OUT, and you let her go?" he roared. Andy ripped the gun from his waistband, sprinting past me in a stumbling mad-dash. "Help me, you fuckup," he screamed over his shoulder when I didn't follow, nearly tripping on a piece of plywood.

"Fuck you," I seethed, loud enough for him to hear.

Because I knew it would make him turn around.

And because I meant it. *"Fuck you."*

He slammed to a stop, pointed the gun at my head, and held it there.

I didn't move a muscle, though. His eyes widened in shock, like he'd expected me to cower—and then help him. When I did neither, he cocked the gun, hesitated in confusion, then whipped his head around and ran. Because she was getting away.

Run, my brain screamed. *Run as fast as you can.*

Once for myself, and once for that terrified little girl.

48

TWENTY-SIX HOURS, FORTY MINUTES BURIED

The ringing in my ears receded just enough that I tried to sit up.

It was a mistake.

I couldn't move at all.

Five minutes earlier, I'd been balancing at the top of the mattress stack, heart in my throat, waiting for Sage to call down that she'd gotten herself all the way up and out of the chute.

I couldn't believe she'd done it. I was so proud of her. I was so proud of all of us. We'd fought, and we were going to win. We weren't going to die down here after all.

Then the roar, the crack of plywood, and the rush of dirt and mud that came pouring into the chute—and down on top of me—happened so fast I didn't even have time to brace.

The force of it had knocked me flat on my back, sending the mattresses we'd stacked up toppling to the sound of shrieks and screams all around.

"My arm is hurt," someone hiccup-cried.

"There's a big splinter in my tummy!" a high-pitched voice repeated again and again. "A big splinter!"

"Ms. Jessa? Ms. Jessa?" some of the kids kept asking, crowding around to push away the heavy, wet clods of mud that half-covered my body.

I blinked and tried to move again, terrified when my body still didn't respond. I didn't feel pain. I didn't feel anything at all, except for that ringing in my ears and thumping in my head.

Now you've reached hell, my mind whispered.

"Sage! What happened to Sage?" Bonnie's voice, shrill and terrified, kept asking above the other voices crying and yelling.

"She's going to get us help," I croaked, hoping Bonnie couldn't tell that I was crying every bit as hard as she was.

I didn't believe what I'd just told her. For all I knew, the force of those plywood walls caving in had pulled her back down into the shaft and buried her alive.

Like us.

If the bunker had felt like a tomb before, there was no question it absolutely was now.

"I feel dizzy," someone said softly as the screams and cries died to whimpers.

"Me too."

I closed my eyes, focusing on the feeling of the tears sliding down my cheeks. "Everybody lie down and breathe really slowly and calmly, okay?" I managed to choke out. "One at a time, everyone tell me who's hurt and who's okay?"

One at a time, they did, murmuring and snuffling as they felt around for each other in the dark and obediently lay down beside me.

I counted the voices until I got to nine. Everyone except Sage.

We were all still alive down here—but it wouldn't be for long now.

My tears fell faster. Even before the cave-in, I could tell that the carbon dioxide from our own breath was starting to compete with the small amount of fresh air coming into the bunker. How soon would we get so dizzy and lightheaded we'd pass out? How soon after that would we stop breathing altogether?

I'm so sorry, Soph. I'm so sorry.

It had all been for nothing. I'd lost Sophie three years ago, and I would never, ever get her back now.

And knowing that was unbearable.

I floated with that despair for a few breaths.

I was going to die down here. We were all going to die down here, and soon.

Then my mind drifted back to the advice that the prison counselor had given me.

Imagine what you want most.

I accept my past, understand my present, and look forward to my future.

The words turned over dull in my mind. I'd heard them—and even repeated them—so many times. They'd only ever been words, though. Something to play along with to please my counselor. And recently, something to comfort the kids.

But not this time. This time they hit hard. Because they were all I had left to cling to.

During all that time I'd spent in prison—and even when I got out—I couldn't stop rewinding. Obsessing over and mourning the moments I'd missed with Sophie.

I couldn't accept what had happened. What I'd *done*. Where it had landed me. I couldn't bring myself to look forward to a future that was tied to that horrifying past. Because what if my daughter never forgave me? What if she couldn't bring herself to love me anymore or call me "Mom" again? What if there was no way to repair the damage?

But all of a sudden, a switch seemed to flip. My mind zipped into fast-forward, to the moments I'd been afraid to visualize or even admit to myself. The moments I wanted so badly—and was about to lose forever.

All of those second chances, all of those hopes, all of those possibilities for the future, gone. Before I'd even let myself hope they could ever be real.

I'd kept myself so busy mourning the time and memories and trust I'd lost with Soph, so busy feeling discouraged over how much she'd resisted my first attempts at returning to her life, I'd barely let myself think about how many good things could still be ahead. A whole unlived lifetime that was now slipping through my fingers with every breath I took.

I gritted my teeth to keep the sob back, but I couldn't hold in the whimper.

"Ms. Jessa, you got hurt bad?" Rose asked.

"I'm sorry," I choked, not wanting to scare the kids any more than they were already. That was the least I could do in whatever time we had left. "No," I lied. "I just need a second."

"When I get out, I'm going to take a really good bath," Bonnie whispered next to my ear, her voice as shaky as mine.

I squeezed my eyes shut on the river of tears, not stopping any of them from cascading down my face. "Thank you, Bonnie." The despair that had become my constant companion over the past three and a half years swirled faster, harder, until it felt like an undertow. Inevitable, impossible to resist.

But to my surprise, something inside me still wanted to resist, kicking out against the current, even as my head started to feel dizzy and faraway.

I decided then and there that if I was going to die down here, I was going to die with hope. With my heart open, just like I'd asked these kids to do but had never actually done myself.

When I get out, I'm going to write Soph a letter, telling her how much I love her and how sorry I am, even if she never reads it.

When I get out, I'm going to decorate the spare bedroom in my apartment for her, even if she's not ready to stay in it yet.

I'm going to slip a dollar under her pillow every time she loses a tooth—even if she's still at Lisa's house.

I'm going to get her the best back-to-school shoes and a new dress, even if she won't come shopping with me.

I'm going to offer to hug her until the day she finally lets me. And when she finally lets me, it will be the best day of my life.

I'm going to show up for her every single day, every single moment, until she's ready to let me back in.

The tears slid down my cheeks hot and fast. One of the kids—I couldn't tell who—nuzzled closer to my shoulder. "We're going to be all right," I whispered, reaching for the last flicker of hope I could find.

49

SHEENA

The Bitcoin transfer wasn't nearly as straightforward as the ransom note made it sound like it would be.

By the third attempt, my hands were trembling so badly that I could hardly keep hold of the computer mouse on my office desk, let alone navigate through the endless menus and verifications. My heart pounded in my chest, each beat echoing in my ears like a warning. Handling funds for the city was one thing, but this ... this was truly something else.

It had only been eight short minutes since I'd arrived home. I'd promised myself I wouldn't check the watch tracker's location until I finished the Bitcoin transfer—but I was starting to lose my mind.

Every step of the process seemed designed to trip me up. I'd opened the bank's online portal plenty of times before, but the options—beyond those of standard transfers—were buried under layers of security, each one more frustrating than the last. Each one likely tripping warning alarms that would alert higher-ups. I was ready, though. I had my boss's credentials and codes for the two-factor requirements. I'd used them plenty of times to avoid red-tape. I'd never encountered anything like this before, though.

I kept telling myself I had to stay calm, that I had to focus, but every mistake felt like a countdown to disaster.

"Come on," I choked, desperately clicking another verification.

Every time I tried to link the city account to the Bitcoin wallet, another obstacle popped up—a security question, a two-step verification process, a delay in processing. The clock on the wall seemed to tick louder with each failed attempt, each setback pushing me closer to the edge of full-on panic.

I had to keep wiping my hands on my jeans, the sweat making my fingers slippery on the keys. I couldn't afford to make any mistakes. One wrong digit, one miss-click, and the money could vanish into the void.

But no. Here was the final confirmation code. *Are you sure you want to transfer?* read the message on the screen.

I clicked before I read any of the other details in the long warning text that appeared below it.

Transfer confirmed. Then a confirmation message.

I stared at it, overwhelmed with relief for a split second. But the feeling shriveled almost immediately, replaced by that building wave of dread and spiraling panic.

It had been nine minutes since I'd arrived home.

The money was gone, out of my control now. Which meant that the time to figure out what the hell I was supposed to do next had arrived. I still didn't know. Every single move I could make felt like pulling the pin to a grenade.

I stared at the phone as I unlocked the home screen with shaky hands, to reopen the watch-tracking app.

While I waited for it to load, I willed an unknown phone number to appear on my screen, someone confirming they'd received the Bitcoin transfer—and that my children would be released, safe and sound.

The phone stayed silent.

When the watch-tracking app opened, I was greeted by a notification warning me that the watch battery was down to four percent.

"No," I choked out in horror. The last time I'd checked the dot's location ten minutes earlier, the watch was twenty miles away —back near the place where I-55 started to wind into the mountains. They'd turned off a rural side road, one that wove parallel to city limits through the foothills.

I stared at the map, switching between topography and street view.

The blue dot was on the move again, but still in the vicinity of that rural foothills road—and creeping west.

I took a screenshot and was about to close the app when a named road—Sugarloaf Lane—flashed into the periphery of the map.

I felt my forehead furrow in confusion. Fear prickled at the back of my mind.

I was pretty sure I knew that street name, that general location.

Why were the kidnappers headed that way?

Words from the ransom note swam through my mind.

Do NOT contact authorities.

Follow these instructions TO THE LETTER.

Go home and wait for instructions. We will be watching. Once we have confirmed the cash delivery and Bitcoin transfer, we will release the children to you.

Adrenaline and fear started to make my legs shake. My gut was tied in knots, but I begged it to speak to me anyway. Do I call the police now? Wait a few more minutes? What if they were about to let the kids go, and I sent police sirens headed their way?

I typed 9-1-1 into my keypad, trembling so violently I kept my thumb a few inches away from the call button. Was I really going to do this, after everything? Did that mean I'd fucked up and should have notified the police from the start? Should I wait just a little longer to hear from the kidnappers?

"Contact me like you said you would, dammit," I cried.

Dad's cases, and the headlines I'd googled while I lay awake the night before were still burned into my brain, throbbing like a brand.

Police Raid Turns Fatal as Kidnapper Follows Through on Threats.

Families Devastated as Police Involvement Leads to Hostage's Gruesome Demise.

Kidnap Victims Slain After Police Misread Ransom Demands.

And then the worst thing happened.

That little blue dot disappeared, the "4% battery" message suddenly replaced by a notification in the corner of the app that read GPS DISCONNECTED. CANNOT LINK TO DEVICE.

"No, no, no," I cried out in stunned disbelief. I'd been so careful, checked so few times. The tracker couldn't just die like that. Not now. Not after everything.

But it had.

The watch was dead, the blue dot frozen in place at the intersection of an unnamed dirt road and Sugarloaf Lane.

Dead, dead, dead, dead, dead, my mind echoed louder and louder, even while my body stayed frozen in place.

I'd just lost my Ace.

A long-buried memory burst to the front of my swimming brain, like an after-image from staring directly into the sun. From the summer Bonnie was a toddler and Sage was six, and I took the girls to the Oregon Coast by myself. We were walking up the bluffs toward the rental condo after exploring tide pools—Sage soaking wet from jumping in, Bonnie wailing because she was ready for a nap—when I heard shouting from the beach behind us.

I turned in time to see the sneaker-wave roll back toward the ocean, retreating fast over the craggy tide pools.

There was a woman dashing barefoot across the lava rocks in hot pursuit of the retreating foam.

I wasn't sure what was happening until I saw a little red jacket tumbling in the churning white surf.

Horrified onlookers, including a man who appeared to be the woman's husband, screamed for his wife to stop, to come back. The sneaker-wave had rushed in—and out—so fast, it had already pulled that little red hoodie toward the sea cliffs and the wave break far beyond the innocent tide pools clumped along the sandbar. The waves beat against the rocky ledges of the cliffs. Anyone who tried entering the ocean there would be smashed against them.

My breath caught in my throat as I realized that if she entered the water, there was every chance I was about to watch two people die.

The man screamed again for the woman to stop, to come back, that someone had called the Coast Guard, that there was nothing she could do.

The mother didn't stop, though.

She swam hard toward that hoodie, impossibly fast in the churning surf, until she reached her child. Then she held on tight, pulling a mop of brown hair and grasping hands to her neck even when the next swell sent them both dashing against the cliff face.

Sirens wailed in the distance. Bonnie nuzzled against my neck. Sage whimpered, shivering, as she tugged on my hand.

And then, against all odds, that woman somehow swam her baby safely back to shore.

She'd been rash to attempt it. I could tell from the stunned faces and head shakes from the onlookers that they thought she'd nearly just signed her own death certificate. But sometimes, there was no other way.

Sometimes, the only choices are awful, with little hope that anything will ever be okay again. And you pick one anyway.

Like that desperate mother swimming toward her child being swept away, I was already in over my head. I had been from the moment I decided to continue following that ransom note's instructions to the letter.

It was dangerous and stupid.

I had no doubt that anyone who read the news report later would say I should have called the police and the FBI from the second I saw that letter attached to the pizza box.

But that mother on the Oregon Coast? Not her. She'd know that the only thing I could do at this moment was make a mad dash directly to the place where there was the smallest sliver of a chance I'd find a way to save my children.

So, with that bobbing red hoodie in my mind, I finally punched 9-1-1 into my phone.

Then, as I hit dial, I raced back to the garage, ready to drive like hell toward the last place I'd seen that frozen blue dot.

50

I ran faster than I'd ever run in my life.

I'd always been good at running. I was the quickest in my class, every fall when we had to run the mile. Everybody always complained, but not me. It was the one time Mia and the cool girls looked at me with something like jealousy.

Mr. Tamura, the PE teacher, told me I should join the track team in middle school. Grandpa said the same. *"Make the most of those gangly legs,"* he told me. *"You're like a little deer."*

I kept thinking that while I ran down the dirt road, away from mean Jesus. *Like a little deer.*

Crack.

A loud noise from behind me startled me so bad, I nearly lost my balance and went down hard on the broken rocks and dirt.

It took a second for me to realize it must have been a gun.

Greasy Hair was shooting a gun at me.

I leaped to the right, then the left, moving even faster. Anything but a straight line that would give him something easy to hit.

Like a little deer.

I had to be a deer. Because there was a hunter right behind me, his heavy footsteps thudding hard no matter how fast I ran.

"Stop, you little bitch," he kept gasping, breathing hard, but that only made me run faster. I could tell from his thumping footsteps that he wasn't running as quick as me.

Maybe he didn't have to, though. Because he had the gun.

Crack.

I waited to feel the bullet hit the back of my head, knock me down. Instead, I felt a rush of energy that was stronger than any Pixy Stix high.

Faster, faster, faster like a deer, I told my legs, and they listened.

I couldn't see very far ahead down the dark, narrow road. That was terrifying, but it was good, too. Because as long as I stayed ahead of Greasy Hair, he couldn't see me very well, either.

I didn't dare look back over my shoulder.

When I'd very first crawled out of the place where they'd buried us—before the dirt and mud collapsed into it—I thought I was so tired I could barely walk. But now, it felt like my legs were unstoppable. Like I could run all night if I had to without ever slowing down.

I didn't know where I was running *to*. At first, the towering cliff-like walls—the ones I'd glimpsed through the hole I'd scratched in the van's painted window—followed the dirt road closely on both sides. As I kept running, those cliff walls got lower and lower, and the dirt road started to branch off into other, smaller roads. They led to what looked like giant pits. And there were huge excavators and other machines in different places, like it was a construction site. I couldn't figure out what this place was—just that it was big and empty and full of dirt and rocks and junk, like some forgotten part of the world where no one was supposed to go.

All I really knew was that it felt like a nightmare, and if I ever wanted to wake up I had to keep running, had to stay ahead of Greasy Hair. Had to find help for Bonnie and Ms. Jessa and the others.

"Goddammit, stop!" Greasy Hair gasped again, but his voice was getting farther and farther away and only made me move even quicker.

I was faster than him.

There was a sliding sound behind me, then a thud, then the sound of his sneakers scrambling over gravel and a sharp *thwack* sound.

Maybe he dropped the gun, my mind told me. *Keep going, you'll lose him now.*

"Shit," he spat again, and there were more of those scrambling noises on the gravel.

I still didn't stop to look behind me, just kept pumping my arms and legs, praying I wouldn't slip like he just had.

Because if I did, he was going to catch me.

I whipped my head side to side as I ran. But there was nowhere to hide that I could see. Just rock and empty space and the dark. Mostly, everything around me looked the same—gray and dark.

After a few seconds, I couldn't hear him behind me anymore.

Just the sound of my own feet running, running, running.

I gasped for air. My chest hurt really bad all of a sudden—and so did my legs. I sucked in a big breath and tried to keep going, but that Pixy Stix energy was running out fast. And to make things worse, the road was going steep uphill now, making it even harder to keep up my pace.

However, as I staggered closer to the top of the hill, I saw something beautiful.

Flickers of light, small and distant. Like stars, but on the ground.

That's what Bonnie always said when we drove home from a camping trip at night and saw the first city lights twinkling in the distance. *Ground stars.*

There were houses and people that way.

I just had to get there.

My heart leaped, and I forced my legs to keep moving, even though they felt like they might give out any second. The ground started to change beneath me, still rough but less gravelly and more like a real road. My feet could move quieter here, as long as I didn't slap the ground with my sneakers.

In a few more feet, there was a gate—and a big, rusty white sign staked into the side of the road I'd just run up. It was tall, but it wouldn't be too hard to climb the fat, spaced-out rungs.

I swung myself up and over the rungs of the gate easy enough, except it made a loud clanking noise the second I started to climb, like that gate was yelling, "Here she is, come this way!"

My legs nearly gave out when I hit the ground on the other side of the gate, but I kept going. Bonnie and the other kids—and Ms. Jessa—didn't have much time. I had to help them, had to find someone who could dig out all that mud in the hole.

What if they were hurt down there? What if there was so much mud that they didn't have any air left at all …

I shut those thoughts out of my mind.

Thoughts like that were going to make my legs dissolve into jelly.

I turned my head to see the words on the rusty white sign as I passed it.

WEST ENTRANCE: NORTHSIDE QUARRY

I memorized those words and made myself keep running.

51

The last thing Andy had screamed over his shoulder at me before he disappeared after the little girl was, "Get the goddamn car. Move your ass!"

I could picture the keys dangling from the Civic's ignition.

I knew he meant that I was supposed to get the car and follow him. Help him catch the little girl who'd escaped.

But that's not where my mind went first.

It went to the idea of turning that ignition key and then driving away from the quarry *and* Andy as fast as I could, heading for Florida.

Because a notification on my phone had just informed me that there was the equivalent of nearly two million dollars in my Bitcoin wallet.

I stared in disbelief. I figured the Bitcoin transfer had fallen apart the way every other part of the plan seemed to be doing right now.

That part of the plan hadn't failed, though. The money was right there. More than I'd ever seen—or would see—in my entire life.

For a minute, while I stood there with my feet rooted to the ground, those dollar signs felt as tempting as they had the day me and Andy first came up with this plan to Robin-Hood that money away from the helicopter parents and bitch-ass management at Bright Beginnings.

All that money, ours for the taking, if we could pull off the perfect heist.

I pictured myself taking my share of the physical cash—probably soggy from Andy stuffing it into the cooler—then driving as far and as fast as I could, across state lines, until I could breathe again. Lying low for a while. Then slipping away into a new life with a clean slate.

Maybe I'd send Andy his share of the Bitcoin money eventually, but maybe not. Maybe, if I was really, really lucky, he'd take the fall for this whole mess. Or find a way to blame it on the bus driver.

I took a step away from the junk pile. Then another, and another as I pushed away the thoughts of what Andy was going to do when he caught that little girl.

My eyes moved to the sheet of metal I'd glanced at so many times over the past twenty-four hours, but I kept walking.

No matter what I did next, there was no getting away from the fact that I could feel my future about to cave in on top of my head, the way the bunker shaft had caved in on top of all those kids we'd buried twenty feet underground.

They were probably dead.

They had to be dead, with all that dirt, didn't they?

I thought about the way Mom's face would scrunch up when she saw me and Andy's names in the news. Those deep furrows in her forehead and cheeks that would nearly make her eyes disappear. Same face she made when she'd come to visit me after I got out of the hospital from the dirt-bike accident—and straight into jail.

Not surprised. Not even disappointed, really. Just fully disgusted. Like she had any moral high ground to judge me.

"What a waste," she'd say, as if she wasn't rotting from the inside out in her filthy trailer, high as a kite. *"Never knew how to apply himself."*

I clenched my jaw tight and walked faster, steeling myself for what I was about to do. What I had to do.

Because fuck it.

Everything had already gone to shit. That gangly little girl was a goner, and that was on her. Nothing I did would help those kids on Bus 315. Probably.

Probably. That word repeated at the end of every thought like a corrupted audio track in my mind. I slapped the side of my head to make it stop, but I wasn't walking anymore. I was just staring into space.

Apply yourself.

To my surprise, those words sounded like my own voice for once, not Mom's.

"For shit's sake," I whispered, feeling the adrenaline hit strong, like a bump.

Everything had gone to hell.

I glanced at Andy's Civic, parked on the side of the dirt road. Then I looked back at the spot where the bunker was buried, in front of the hulking shapes rising behind it in The Pit.

Apply yourself.

Something snapped inside me, and for the first time since everything went to shit, I knew for certain what I was going to do.

Right now, the only thing that mattered anymore was the feel of keys in my hand.

52

TWENTY-SIX HOURS, FIFTY-EIGHT MINUTES BURIED

"What's that?" Bonnie asked in a small voice, breaking into my thoughts.

My heavy eyelids tried to open, but it was too difficult a task. There was nothing to see anyway. So instead I just listened, trying to focus, even as my blurry mind kept drifting back to Sophie. There was a faint rumbling, the earth vibrating ever so slightly beneath our heads, and a dull growling sound getting louder overhead.

"No, no," the kids shrieked as more dirt began raining down onto us.

That made my eyes pop open. Whatever was up there was putting more pressure on the cave-in. A car, driving on top of the mud-filled shaft?

Something scraped across the top of the sheet metal in an eerie squealing sound, followed by the thump of something heavy.

More clods of dirt showered down through the hole in the plywood above us.

They're burying the entrance the rest of the way, my mind whispered. *So that nobody will ever find you.*

"Rose, Ben, Ked, hurry. Prop the mattresses up and make a shelter for us to hide underneath!" I shouted, doing everything I could to make my voice louder than the rumbling noise and the dirt clods pelting us.

That shelter would only buy us a few precious minutes until the thick plywood board Sage had dug her way through at the top of the bunker fully collapsed with the weight of the mud avalanche and the weight of whatever was making that rumbling noise above us.

A few minutes was a few minutes, though.

I closed my eyes and imagined taking pictures of Sophie and her date by the porch on prom night. Hugging her tight at graduation. Dipping our toes in the sand at Bear Lake, Soph's favorite vacation spot. The last place I remembered hearing her squeal with delight.

Just a few more hopes that were about to be crushed.

But that didn't mean I'd let them slip between my fingers.

53

I didn't know how far I'd run after I got out of the quarry. Probably only a few minutes, but the way my lungs were burning made it feel like forever.

The road had widened a little and turned from dirt to pavement, and the cluster of lights that had been pinpricks before were finally getting bigger now, brighter. The nearest ones, outshining everything else in the distance, were attached to a group of buildings up ahead, through the trees. They were tucked into the dark night, surrounded by a white fence.

Something about the place was familiar, but not enough that I could say where I was yet.

Almost there.

With all those lights and all those buildings, somebody had to be home. Somebody had to let me in, help me, take me back to Bonnie and that hole, where I'd dig and dig and dig even though I could barely feel my fingers and arms anymore.

I tried to think of what I would say, the quickest way to get someone to listen and come with me. "Help me! Call the police! There's kids buried over at Northside Quarry. There's men with guns. That way." Yes. Those were the words. They had to be the words.

I held them in my mouth, ready to let them out the second some-one answered one of those doors.

I staggered forward.

Then I heard a sound I recognized. Only this time, it was whisper-ing instead of screaming.

It was that metal gate I'd climbed over just a few minutes ago. It was making the same high-pitched, creaky sound it made when I hoisted myself over it. My bladder nearly let go as my mind shrieked, *He's right behind you. He's headed this way.*

I pumped my legs as fast as I could, which wasn't very fast any-more, for the white fence. As it got closer and closer, my breathing came faster and faster. Greasy Hair was going to catch me.

Any second, he'd be able to see me as the road dipped down to-ward these lights.

He'd know I would be heading straight for them.

I ran my hands over the white fence, looking for a latch, wanting to scream but afraid it would only lead him to me faster.

I was sure now that I'd seen this gate before, the same way I'd been sure I'd heard Mr. Edwards's voice before, but there was no time to sort through how.

I found the latch. There was a lock on the other side. A big, thick lock.

"No! No, help," I cried in a soft whisper as I jangled it. Climbing the fence would make a lot of noise, but I was pretty sure I could grab the top and pull myself over if I put my foot on the rail running along the bottom. It was nothing compared to climbing out of the bunker.

I was almost there, just had to get to the other side, then one more sprint and I'd be banging on that first door with the porch light blazing down.

I hesitated for just a second with my foot on the rail. Just long enough to hear a voice behind me say, "If you stay right there, I won't shoot you."

54

I sped through the dark streets with 9-1-1 dispatch on speakerphone, desperate to reach the last place I'd seen that frozen blue dot on the app.

I was still a good fifteen minutes from the top of Sugarloaf Lane, even if I kept up this pace.

"My name is Sheena Halverson," I said in a rush, knowing there was no point pretending otherwise. They'd likely already have my name and phone number on their screen. "My—my daughters were on the bus that went missing yesterday afternoon. And I have credible information about the location of the kidnapper—or kidnappers. Off I-55 and Sugarloaf Lane."

"Ms. Halverson, I'm having a hard time understanding you. I need you to slow down. Is that Sugarloaf Lane in Ada County?"

"Yes," I gasped. "I don't know where to start explaining. But I'm positive the kidnappers are in this area. I wasn't supposed to call the police. They said … they said they'd hurt the kids."

The tears were coming again, but I didn't take my hands off the wheel to swipe them away.

"I understand, and I'm sending help," the dispatcher reassured me. "You did the right thing by calling."

I swallowed hard. If only either of us knew that was true.

"Can you tell me—"

"How many officers are you going to send?" I asked, cutting the patient woman off. "They won't use sirens, right? Please, they can't use sirens. They could be anywhere near that location I gave you."

"Ma'am, I am dispatching multiple units now to the location you provided. I need you to stay on the line with me. What is *your* location?"

I hesitated just long enough, because her voice was stern when she said, "I need you to stay where you are and talk to me, Ma'am. You need to stay clear of the location you provided and talk to me."

I tried to speak, to respond, but the only sound that came out was a strangled cry.

"I'll be relaying everything you say to the officers headed to the scene," the dispatcher reassured me, her voice so calm I couldn't help but cling to it like a life preserver. "So I need any information you can provide that might help the police navigate the situation. Ma'am?"

I slowed down and pulled the car to the side of the road, feeling like I was sinking. Drowning, maybe, pulled under by the weight of the truth.

The police were enroute. Which meant that all I could do now was stay out of their way and hope like hell they could succeed where I'd failed.

I'd jumped into the surf, but I knew in my bones I wasn't going to reach that bobbing red hoodie on my own after all, no matter how hard I swam.

In my mind's eye, it was already disappearing beneath the waves.

Soon, it would be gone.

55

I froze with my hands on the white fence, not daring to look behind me into the dark.

The words replayed in my head on a loop. *"If you stay right there, I won't shoot you."*

How close behind me was Greasy Hair? His voice sounded as raggedy and tired as I felt, and his words sort of ran together.

My spy-mind whirled, telling me everything I needed to know in that split-second I hung there, frozen on the rail of the fence.

He missed you when he shot the gun before.

He's farther away now than he was then.

If you can get over the fence, it'll block him.

They just have to open the door fast enough before he reaches the fence and can shoot again.

I launched my body up like there were springs on my feet, scrambling and clawing as I somehow managed to throw my body over the white fence.

There was a sign near the walkway partially hidden by the bushes and flowers I ran past, but I didn't stop to read it. It didn't matter what this place was. It was all I had.

I heard Greasy Hair growl, then his heavy footsteps thudding on the ground, getting louder.

I ran for the porch as fast as I could, grabbing the handle—locked—with one hand, and pounding with the other. "Help, help, help, please help me!"

Between my shrieks, I could hear faint noises from inside the building.

Like someone was watching too-loud TV inside.

I drew in a breath and heard the faint pop of gunshots, then the sound of a horse neighing. Could they hear me in there?

Out of the corner of my eye, I saw a sign on the door: WEL-COME, FRIENDS. And that was what finally made me realize where I was. Mom had brought us here with her on a tour a few weeks ago. It was like a retirement home, but for people who had dementia and Alzheimer's. Like Grandpa.

Greasy Hair's body hit the fence, shaking it like he was going to plow it over instead of climbing over it like I had. Maybe he couldn't pull himself up the way I did. He was bigger than me, and he was so out of breath—

A light flashed on overhead—brighter than the porch light, so bright it made me squint.

"Help!" I screamed, no longer caring at all that Greasy Hair heard, waiting for him to shoot the gun again the second he saw me under the spotlight.

I cowered against the door, like if I just got close enough it would swallow me whole into the building.

The door creaked. Before I could blink, it opened all the way, sending me tumbling onto a pink tile floor.

My head spun, taking in the sound of the TV on blast and a man's deep voice yelling something about a "Wild frontier," the smell of cookies, and a woman crouching in front of me, her hair spilling over her cheeks, her clothing smelling sort of like a hospital.

"Oh my Lord," she was saying. "Child, what on earth ..."

I scrambled to my feet and looked around the long, dark hallway, focusing on the flickering lights coming from the room where the TV was playing. A half-door separated it from the hallway, so you could just see over the top. There was a small group of old people wearing pajamas and robes, gathering by that half-door.

I gasped and tried to stand up, slipping on the tile. All the words I'd tucked away in my head that I wanted to tell the lady, were suddenly so hard to grab hold of. Like each one was attached to a helium balloon drifting out of my grasp.

I opened my mouth to tell her about Greasy Hair, about Bonnie, about Ms. Jessa and the kidnapped kids in the buried bunker and the ransom, but all that came out at first were sobs and snot and tears.

"Hush, hush, hush," the woman was cooing. She had a radio in one hand, and she turned to it, "I need security here *now*." Then to me, "You're safe now, honey. It's gonna be all right."

That only made me cry harder. It felt impossible to get my words out.

"No!" I screamed, louder than I thought I was going to. "They took us. They took Bonnie! The dirt, the mud, it all caved in. The— the quarry! You have to go there now, you have to come back with me, you have to help them, they don't have air!"

The words were coming out now, but not like I wanted them to. I could see in her dark brown eyes and puckered lips that I sounded every bit as mixed-up as I thought I did.

"Just calm down for a minute, and we'll get this sorted—"

There was a commotion from down the hallway, louder than the TV. And then someone's voice interrupted the woman kneeling over me, bellowing, "Dammit, listen to the kid!"

The woman jerked her head up, shocked.

Everything in my mind went still.

I knew that voice.

I loved that voice.

Grandpa. He was here.

"And somebody open this thing." He rattled the half-door in front of him. "That's my granddaughter."

It was impossible, it made no sense. He wasn't supposed to be here yet. But there he was, with his wrinkly, freckled face and blue eyes staring at me from down the hall. There was a little white sign just beneath him on the door that read CHERISHED HEARTS STAFF AND RESIDENTS ONLY BEYOND THIS POINT.

"What's going on, Mindy," Grandpa said as a man wearing scrubs let him out into the hallway and he rushed toward me.

I didn't even care that I had no idea who Mindy was.

Grandpa was wearing his green flannel pajamas. The ones with the worn, soft fabric that smelled like licorice and toothpaste when he hugged me and Bonnie goodnight.

He knelt beside me and squeezed my hand, even though it was dirty and bloody and shaking. And then his head jerked upright as the front door made a soft creaking sound behind us.

The door was starting to open again.

Grandpa jumped to his feet, quick as I'd ever seen him move. Nothing like the shuffling, soft-spoken grandpa I remembered from before he got sick.

My body froze, and I realized that I'd never heard the door lock after the woman pulled me inside.

Nobody knew about Greasy Hair and the gun yet. Because I hadn't told them.

The world swam in slow motion as the nurse screamed something at Grandpa and he pushed past both of us to yank the door open so fast and hard it was like he wanted to pull it off its hinges.

Somebody made an "*oof*" sound from outside the door, followed by scuffling sounds and something rattling.

Boom. The gun went off, and some of the old people wearing robes screamed. I realized that I was screaming right along with them.

"Grandpa, no!" I imagined him crumpling to the ground—and Greasy Hair forcing his way inside the building and shooting me dead.

That's not what happened, though.

Instead, Grandpa pushed his way back inside, holding the gun and breathing hard. His lip was bleeding. "He got away," he muttered as he slammed the door shut, flipped the lock, and stood in front of it. And for the first time I could imagine him as the police detective he talked about in the stories he told.

Then, just as fast, his shoulders slumped and his brow creased as he stared at the gun in his hand, then he put it carefully down on a table near the door. "Nobody touch that. And … I think somebody should call the police," he added hesitantly.

Grandpa stepped closer and opened his arms wide to me. And that was just the thing I needed to make the chaos swirling in my scared mind settle.

I tumbled into his arms and he held me tight. I looked between him and the scared-looking woman holding the radio and said, "I'm Sage Halverson. Two men took me and my sister. And more kids on my bus. They're keeping them in the quarry."

Grandpa squeezed me again then turned to the woman with the radio. It kept beeping in her hand. "You heard the girl. Hurry and call the police!"

Somebody finally turned the TV off in the other room, just as two men wearing tan shirts burst through the door next to the reception desk, where another woman was scrambling for the desk phone.

She dialed then held it to her ear, beckoning to me and Grandpa. My heart beat fast, the same way it had while I'd been running, as she told the police what I'd just told her.

Then she got a funny look on her face, like she couldn't believe what she was hearing.

"I don't know how, but the police are already almost here," she stuttered, holding the phone out to me. "Here, quick, tell them everything you know."

56

I told the dispatcher everything I knew, rambling for ten minutes straight, with every single detail burned into the back of my mind from the past twenty-four hours.

I didn't know if I'd done the right thing anymore. Maybe there was no way to know until this nightmare ended, one way or another.

At that moment, my phone beeped in my ear, letting me know I had an incoming call. A quick glance showed an unknown number.

"I need to take this call," I gasped, sitting upright. "I think—I think the kidnappers are trying to call me."

I didn't wait to hear what the dispatcher said next.

What if it was the kidnappers calling me to say that they were releasing the children right now? Or, alternately, calling to tell me they knew I'd brought in the police?

Dread sent droplets of sweat trickling among the tears.

I clenched my jaw and accepted the call.

A female voice came on the line right away. "Ms. Halverson?"

At first, I imagined that stringy-haired, teary-eyed woman in the mug shot. Jessa Landon.

But no, the voice coming through the phone wasn't Jessa.

"Sheena, this is Rashida from Security at Cherished Hearts. I … I'm here with your daughter and—"

If I hadn't already pulled the car to a stop, I might have crashed right then and there. The words swam in circles in my mind, refusing to make sense. Those words couldn't be right. Dad was at Cherished Hearts. Not my children.

"My daughter? What?" I choked out, my body flooding with a dizzying cocktail of disbelief, relief, confusion, and horror.

"She says she was on that bus of missing kids. We just called the police—"

"Put her on the phone."

"We're trying to figure out what's going on—"

"Put her on the phone now!" I demanded in a voice that barely sounded like my own.

There was a brief silence. And then, impossibly, miraculously, a voice came on the line. *Sage.*

"Mom," she cried, her voice wobbly and thick with tears.

"Oh my god, Sage. Are you okay? Where's Bonnie?" I couldn't make sense of anything that was happening, but as long as the answer to those questions was yes, it was enough for this moment.

"I'm okay. I got away, Mom," she whimpered. "I'm with Grandpa."

For just a second all the horror and fear I'd been carrying lifted.

My hands automatically shifted the car into DRIVE, my foot hit the gas, and once again I was speeding in the direction of the blue dot I'd seen on the app: Sugarloaf Lane, which dead-ended on the outskirts of town. Barely a mile from Cherished Hearts, which was intentionally isolated from the hubbub of the city in case residents managed to slip past security and unwittingly wander off in a daze of confusion.

I still didn't understand why my children were there. All that mattered was that they were alive.

Then it hit me: Sage hadn't answered my question. And the security guard hadn't said anything about Bonnie, either.

My stomach churned and I fought to keep my eyes focused on the road in front of me.

"Sage, where's Bonnie?" I demanded as the world swam by in shadows punctuated by the glow of orange streetlights beyond the windshield.

"Mom, I tried to take care of her. I tried *so* hard—" Then she was crying so violently she couldn't even speak.

I floored the accelerator, listening to the sound of her sobs until I skidded into a parking lot lit up by blue-and-red lights from police vehicles for the second time in two days.

"I'm here, Sage, I'm here!" I called out through my own choked sobs, lifting my hands in the air as I got out of the Subaru and saw the police rushing toward me through the facility's open gate. I ignored them and looked around wildly, desperate for any sign of Sage or Bonnie, still clinging to hope that maybe I'd gotten it wrong, that Bonnie and the other children were nearby.

"I'm their mother," I screamed at the officer who held me back, as the tears and snot poured into my mouth, stumbling toward them down the walkway doorway where I'd said goodbye to Dad, just twenty-four hours earlier.

The nearest officer said something into his radio and softened his grip on my arm. Neither tried to stop me as I broke away.

The main door flung open, and there was a nurse—and Dad. And Sage, covered in dirt and blood from head to toe.

A rush of love and disbelief slammed against my heart so hard, I couldn't breathe.

All I could do was fall to my knees and pull her against my chest.

57

I didn't even hear the cop cars behind me over the rattle of the backhoe's engine.

That was how hard I was applying myself.

Foot on the gas, foot on the brake, left, right, left, right.

Dig, dig, dig. Get the kids out. Save them. Help them. Oh God, they couldn't be dead.

I'd told myself a long time ago that I wouldn't kill any more squirrels—or anything else—ever again. That hollow, sick feeling in my stomach was too much to bear. And these weren't fucking squirrels. They were kids.

If I left them down there when there was a chance they were alive, I knew that nothing would ever be okay again.

I was a bad person. I knew that. But I wasn't a killer. I *wasn't*. So I was going to get them out, even if I had to rot in jail for it.

All I had left was that. And all those kids had left was me.

Everything happened fast and slow as the police screamed into the quarry.

Fast, as they shined a spotlight in my face and told me to put my hands in the air and step down from the excavator. Slow, as they swarmed the hole in the earth and drew their guns when I refused to stop digging. Fast again, as one of them yanked me out of the seat and took over, desperately trying to reach the top of the bunker.

They slammed me to the ground and put me in handcuffs but didn't lead me away. Instead, a stout, bearded officer shouted questions at me rapid-fire over the noise of the big machine. "How far down are they? How long have they been down there? Describe the bunker."

And I did. Right down to the thick plywood roof on top of the bunker and the size of the battery holding it down.

I'd dug down far enough that it was barely a minute until they scraped the top of that bunker.

"There's a ladder over there," I called, pointing into the darkness of the junk pile as more cops swarmed the hole, pulling loose dirt with anything they could find to open up the space. I thought of where that heavy battery might have landed and felt sick to my stomach.

The exhaust from the excavator and the dread soaking through every cell in my body made me feel like I was suffocating, waiting for them to get the last of that mud out.

I wasn't suffocating though, and I was about to come face to face with the kids who had gone without air for real.

Because if they hadn't been crushed to death by all that mud, they'd been breathing in their own carbon dioxide for the past—how long had it been since Andy ran off after that little girl? Where was he now? I didn't know, but the flashlights combing higher through the foothills made me think the police were searching for him.

The excavator shuddered to a stop and went silent.

And then I heard it. The sound I knew would live in my bones until the day I died.

A weak little chorus of voices, begging for help.

58

The soft green shimmer of monitor screens in the dark hospital room made just enough of a night light that Bonnie and Sage finally fell asleep.

"Promise those glowy lights won't go off?" was the last thing Bonnie murmured, her voice raspy and quiet, before her eyes closed.

"I promise. I love you, Bonnie Bear," I told her, squeezing the one finger I could find that didn't have cuts on it, careful not to jostle her IV.

Her other hand was locked firmly on Sage's arm. The nurses had allowed us to push the two beds next to each other so the girls could still touch.

Sage hadn't tried to pull her arm away once.

I blinked back fresh tears as I stared at the shapes of my beautiful girls.

They were safe.

They were alive.

So were all nine other children on Bus 315.

"If you'd called the police even a minute later, some of those kids would almost certainly be dead."

Those words—from the chief of police—would haunt me for the rest of my life. The subtext, of course, was that I was a fool for waiting as long as I had. That I'd been lucky. So damn lucky.

The CO_2 levels in that bunker were close to fifteen percent, based on the severity of the kids' symptoms. Imminently lethal. They'd gotten them out of that hole just in time.

But then again, the luck of those few minutes weren't mine alone to claim.

If Sage hadn't made it to Cherished Hearts to point the police down that quarry road, it still might have been too late.

And if that nineteen-year-old kid—"Mr. Edward," one of the kidnappers, who'd been fired from Bright Beginnings—hadn't started digging with the excavator when he had, the officers, who only had one shovel among them, would have been forced to waste time scrambling to find the excavator keys. Or wouldn't have been able to find them at all.

I didn't know how to feel about that part.

I wanted to hate the punk. I was glad he was spending the night in county jail, awaiting a bail hearing. But all I knew was that when I thought about the number of dominos lined out in each direction from the choices I'd made, the choices the kidnappers had made, the choices my daughters had made, it was hard to find my own breath.

If I'd called the police the second I got that ransom note, would Sage's hands be bandaged up to her elbows? They were so completely covered in exposed muscle, scrapes, and blood, it looked like the skin had been pulled off like a glove.

Or would she and the other kids have met a different fate?

And if Sage hadn't clawed her way out of that hole over the course of a day, would it have stayed intact instead of caving in?

Or would the kids have been fish in a barrel when the kidnappers realized that their identities might have been exposed through that hole in the painted-over window in the van Sage had told me she'd scraped away before they put them in their tomb? I'd pieced the events together over the last few hours as Sage eked out the story to the police and FBI from behind her oxygen mask, lying in her hospital bed.

I closed my eyes and let the tears drip down my chapped cheeks.

"Mom," Bonnie whimpered in her sleep, and my eyes flew open.

I rubbed her arm, careful not to dislodge the IVs in her hand. "I'm here, baby. You're safe," I told her, and her eyelids stopped fluttering.

She sighed, and I scooted the hospital chair closer so I could lay my head beside her on the clean white sheets.

The sliver of light beneath the door, coming from the hallway, shifted, and I forced myself not to look at it. There was a guard stationed outside our door at all times.

At first, I thought he was there because the police still hadn't captured the second kidnapper—Andy McQuain—who had been named in the press as soon as the news of the rescue and arrest had broken. But when I left the room briefly to get a cup of coffee another officer escorted me there and back.

I still had answers—and maybe more—to give for my choices. Police had discovered exactly half the cash from my bank runs in a cooler near a lean-to near the bunker. And thankfully, Ted Barrett's lawyer had finagled the return of the Bitcoin funds back to the city treasury. The other half of the cash was still in the wind with Andy McQuain. I didn't know if that would be my responsibility to repay. I also didn't know if I would be facing my own lawsuit from the school district or maybe even the city in the coming months. But I didn't let myself go down that rabbit hole of worry quite yet.

Only time would tell.

Still, like a moth to a flame, I'd read the comments section in the breaking news articles. I hadn't been named as an involved party yet. It was too early for that. The press didn't know most of the details about what had happened tonight, but they would. I knew that some people would call me brave, a hero. Others would say I was the stupidest person alive. Reckless and foolish.

All I knew tonight was that I could hear the soft sound of my daughters breathing beside me.

At one point a detective working on the investigation had told me the driver, Jessa Landon, was under police custody here at the hospital, until they could clear her of any involvement in the kidnapping. But I knew in my heart she had nothing to do with endangering my children.

Sage and Bonnie had both sworn over and over that Ms. Jessa had treated all the kids like her own while they were in that dark, awful bunker. She had been a good mom to all of them.

Even though I hadn't slept for more than twenty-four hours, I knew that sleep was still a long way off for me. Between the coffee and the fear that if I closed my eyes the girls would disappear again, I could barely let myself blink for very long.

So, careful not to make too much noise, I pulled a pen and notepad from my purse on the floor and started a note to the only other person I thought might understand how I felt at that moment.

The white lines swam blurry in front of my tired eyes, but I put the pen to paper and started writing.

Dear Jessa ....

59

TWO DAYS LATER

Mom let me and Bonnie watch as much TV as we wanted while we were in the hospital.

Bonnie told me I could pick the shows. I chose the ones I knew she liked—*My Little Pony* and *Puffin Rock*—but neither of us were really paying attention to the screen above our beds.

Mom was with us most of the time, but when she stepped out of the room, Bonnie kept finding my arm across the gap in our beds. I could tell that she was still scared. And from the way I was glad she kept doing it, I could tell that I was still scared, too.

I'd thought that once we were safe, once we got out of that hole, everything would be okay.

And I was really, really glad we were out of that hole. But today was the second morning in a row that I'd woken up sweaty and panicked, twitching my bandaged hands up and down like I was still digging into the plywood.

For a few seconds when I woke up this morning, I wasn't sure whether the clean hospital room—or the bunker—was real.

Hot tears slid down my cheeks. *This is real*, I told myself again and again while I tried to get my breathing back to normal so I wouldn't wake Mom or Bonnie. It was still early—barely light outside the sheer curtains covering the windows in our hospital room.

But no matter how many times I repeated those words to myself, no matter how many times I looked around at the quietly whooshing machines and breathed in the smell of some kind of cleaner, it sort of felt like part of me was still stuck down in the hole.

So I did the only thing that helped when I actually was stuck down in that bunker. The thing Ms. Jessa told us all to do. I thought about the good things. And unlike two days ago, there were so many good things all around me now. I thought about what I was going to choose for breakfast from the hospital menu—waffles with whipped cream and Nutella. How good it would feel to jump on the trampoline when I got home, pumping my legs and swinging my arms until my fingers brushed the tips of the maple leaves above me. How I could feel Bonnie's hand in mine, clean and warm and no bandages when we both were better.

I could hear Mom sighing in her sleep on the other side of me, her dark hair spilling across the white sheets covering my legs. I was safe. Bonnie was safe. *This is real.*

I had barely closed my eyes again when a knock on the door sent them flying back open.

Bonnie startled and gripped my arm. Mom made an "oh" sound and sat bolt upright, her eyes blinking fast like she was waking up from something she'd rather not be dreaming about, too.

When the door opened, I saw the police officer from the hall, a nurse—and Grandpa.

Both me and Bonnie must've been making silly faces, because Grandpa tilted his head and boomed out a laugh in the quiet room. "Don't look so damn happy to see me," he said, shuffling toward us.

Then, "There's my girls," as he pulled Mom into a hug while keeping his eyes on me and Bonnie.

"Papa, you're here!" Bonnie squealed in surprise.

I was surprised, too. Although not as surprised as the last time I'd seen him—in the hallway at Cherished Hearts, with the gun in his hand that he'd taken from Greasy Hair. Mom had explained to me and Bonnie why he was there—and why she was driving toward Cherished Hearts already when I talked to her on the phone. That Grandpa's Alzheimer's had gotten worse, and then she'd gotten that ransom note from the kidnappers, and then something about a Rolex watch. I'd sort of stopped listening to all the details. Because seeing him—and then Mom—there that night felt like me and Bonnie were the runaway bunny from the children's book they read to us at bedtime sometimes. It didn't matter where the baby bunny went—his mom would find him, no matter what. And that's how I wanted to remember that night.

The nurse smiled and carefully closed the door while Mom guided Grandpa to a chair. His eyes crinkled at the corners, sending deep wrinkles fanning out above his cheeks the way they did when his mind was clear, and he was happy.

"We're still sorting everything out," Mom said to me and Bonnie, leaning in to make sure we were listening, "but one of the doctors at Cherished Hearts was reviewing Grandpa's medications and saw that two of them might have been making his sundowning a lot worse." She looked at me and Bonnie, like she wanted to know if we remembered what that word meant.

We nodded to show her that we did, so she kept talking, glancing between us and Grandpa. "Grandpa still has Alzheimer's," she said, and her voice broke. "And we're going to have to keep taking things a day at a time. But … the doctor is optimistic. So for right now, he's only going to visit Cherished Hearts during the daytime.

He'll come home every night when you two get home from school and sleep at home with us."

"When we get home from Bright Beginnings, you mean?" I asked, feeling a lump in my own throat when I said those words.

Mom shook her head and looked between me and Bonnie. "You two seem pretty grown up to me these days. Sage, I was thinking maybe you could look after Bonnie. And I'll pick Grandpa up when I'm done with work. No more Bright Beginnings for you two."

Grandpa opened his mouth like he wanted to add something, but his eyes were shiny, and he just nodded his head and smiled so wide without saying a word.

"Oh, Mom. Oh, yes," Bonnie said, letting go of my arm for the first time in two days so she could hug Grandpa.

I swallowed that big lump in my throat and felt proud and scared and surprised all at once, suddenly thinking about how Harriet the Spy had said, *"Life is very strange."*

I didn't really understand what that meant when I read it the first time.

I did now, though.

60

JESSA

Over the past two days in the hospital, some of the feeling had come back to my forearms and hands.

If I really made the effort, I could lift the blue-lidded hospital water jug with a straw stuck in it to my lips for a sip. But so far, I couldn't feel much below my belly button. I couldn't pee on my own. I couldn't move my legs or feet more than an inch. I'd taken the worst of the impact from the heavy, wet dirt—and what turned out to be a massive battery—that had crashed down through the opening in the plywood. I was still too afraid to look at my own body beneath the hospital sheets, looking away whenever the nurse came to change my bandages.

The impact had fractured my L1 vertebra, *"A critical junction between the thoracic and lumbar regions,"* the specialist had told me, which meant nothing to me. I only remembered it because Lisa wrote it down, and I knew she was planning to Google the shit out of it as soon as she got home. "We'll figure this out, Jess," she had said more than a dozen times.

I remembered her saying almost the exact same thing right before my pre-trial hearing. That might have annoyed me before—my sister trying to be optimistic and swooping in to save me from the fallout in my life once again. But instead, I just felt grateful. And loved. And like this time, things would be different.

Yesterday when she came to visit, she told me that Sophie had asked lots of questions about what happened to me and the kids on the bus. She'd also asked whether I would be okay.

I decided to let myself feel loved for that small but significant gesture, too.

The doctor said there was a reasonably good chance I'd regain sensation and movement, once the swelling in my lower spine subsided and the damaged nerves healed. She talked about something called "spinal shock," a temporary paralysis due to the trauma of the injury. It was a waiting game at this point.

Instead of reading into the dark possibilities between her carefully worded optimism, I let myself feel the hope of it, imagining myself feeling a tingle in the soles of my feet again, gripping the rubber handles of a walker to drag myself around for physical therapy, taking steps again on my own.

When I wasn't closing my eyes trying to project my hopes into the future, I was fully giving in to less healthy uses of my time—scrolling on my phone with clumsy fingers. The police had been gracious enough to return it to me from evidence since it wouldn't be needed for the investigation, once they'd verified that I had nothing to do with the kidnapping. To be fair though, I didn't have much else to do.

At first, I just wanted to make sure all of the kids were okay. And they were. Every single child had survived, with only minor injuries, dehydration, and exhaustion. A few of them were still in this same hospital with me right now.

Everyone's blood-oxygen level had been dangerously low when the FBI and police finally broke through to the buried bunker, and there were a lot of headlines screaming about how we'd been minutes from certain death if the puzzle pieces hadn't clicked into place exactly the way they had. I reread those articles again and again, feeling shivers down my spine—that stopped at my damn L1—thinking about Sage's determined digging, Bonnie and the other kids holding the mattresses and that bucket. The way Sage had run for help and told the police everything she knew. The way those police had already been nearby, sent by Sheena Halverson. The way one of the kidnappers had finally found his conscience and pulled the excavator over to dig us most of the way out just in the nick of time.

This morning's headline—published on all the major news sites only twenty minutes earlier—shouted that they'd found and arrested twenty-year-old Andy McQuain. He'd tried to pawn the "Rolex" with a distinctive broken clasp—and faux branding to anyone intimately familiar with expensive watches—at a high-end reseller just outside Boise.

The FBI was already a step ahead, having shared Andy's photo and an example picture of the watch with every reseller, pawn shop owner, and watch broker in the state of Idaho.

The owner called the police the second the guy stepped in the shop. When he tried to run, one of the police dogs tore after him, leading to a chase that had been caught on video. So not only was he now in jail on charges of felony kidnapping, battery, and attempted murder with aggravating circumstances—which could carry the death penalty in Idaho—but the video of his pathetic attempt to escape from the dog outside of the pawn shop had gone viral and was the top-watched video on YouTube.

Big news outlets outside were covering every aspect of the story. And Andy McQuain was now, without a doubt, the most hated man in America. So much so that they'd had to move him into solitary confinement for his own safety the first night he spent in jail.

Reading that was enough to make me smile for a very long time.

It was strange reading about myself in third-person again, too.

There were no secrets about my past anymore. I'd become an internet celebrity overnight in a way that obliterated any press coverage my previous trial had received. And this time, my mug shot and Gary's scathing commentary about my character weren't the focal point of the articles. At least, not the articles hitting the news post-rescue. For a while there, I found out I'd been the prime suspect.

Some people thought I was a saint for keeping the kids calm and safe, given the circumstances. Other people were furious that I'd misled Bright Beginnings, using my maiden name to skirt the out-of-state background check. Still others dug up those old articles about my sentencing and connected them to the recently fired prosecutor back in Utah, and a defense lawyer who had recently lost his license over sketchy closed-door deals and pressuring clients into taking unfair plea deals. That had been my lawyer.

They were saying I never should have gone to prison. That my case of self-defense was more than arguable.

There was a Facebook group that had popped up called "Save Ms. Jessa." I'd already gotten calls from five different attorneys offering to help me overturn my conviction pro-bono.

The attention and the offers of help were a little overwhelming. I hadn't called any of the law firms back yet. However, underneath the overwhelm, I felt those prickles of hope.

Grimacing, I focused my attention on lifting my phone to the bed-side table without dropping it. Then I took a deep breath and grasped the unopened envelope with my name scrawled on the front that had been sitting there since yesterday afternoon.

I already knew who the note was from—the nurse who delivered it to me had told me. Sheena Halverson, Sage and Bonnie's mom. But I was afraid that reading that note would make me feel more vulnerable than seeing my photo and life story and all of the overwhelming comments in the "Save Ms. Jessa" Facebook group.

Before I could chicken out for the umpteenth time, I fumbled with the mercifully unsealed envelope flap, pulled a single folded sheet of paper onto my lap, and started to read.

Dear Jessa,

My daughters have said your name more times in the past two days than I can count.

It's nearly two a.m., and I have written and rewritten this note in my head a dozen times. To tell you how sorry I am that I imagined the worst of you, when all the while you were protecting my babies the best you could. To tell you a story about a toddler in a red hoodie who was swept into the ocean on the Oregon Coast—and the mother who swam toward what looked like self-destruction to try and save her child. And most of all to tell you thank you from the bottom of my heart.

"Knock, knock!" came the muffled voice from outside the door, and I looked up from the letter with a start.

My stiff fingers dropped the note to the floor as I flinched and nudged my chin against my hospital gown to wipe the tears as best I could. "Come in!"

The door opened wide to reveal Lisa's smiling face.

"I'm sorry it's so early," she said. "But somebody wanted to see you before school, and I thought we'd better hustle over here."

A shorter, slighter figure shuffled a few inches forward into the open doorway.

Soph. *My* Soph.

The hospital room melted away, and all I could see was her. My baby, who was no longer a baby. She wore a lacy purple shirt that showed the freckles on her arms. Yellow shorts that looked brand new. Her hair styled into a low ponytail and bangs, with a familiar cowlick. My chin trembled, but I didn't dare blink for fear she'd suddenly disappear like a mirage.

"Hi," she said shyly, her pink cheeks turning pinker as she studied me where I lay in the hospital bed.

"Hi," I managed to reply, terrified that I was going to scare her away by breaking into loud sobs at any moment if I said more.

Sophie took a step toward me. Then another, until she was just a few feet away. She glanced back at Lisa, who was pretending to talk to a nurse at the doorway, her face and shoulders turned slightly away from us. But I could see by the slight shaking of her jacket that she was crying, too.

If this were a movie, she would have called me Mom for the first time in three years, run to me, thrown her arms around my neck and told me she loved me.

Then I would have told her how she was all I'd hoped to see again when I was down in that bunker.

Instead, carefully, like I was trying not to startle a baby bird, I pointed to the chair beside my hospital bed with a trembling hand. "You can sit there if you want?"

And, like watching a tiny miracle unfold before my very eyes, the corners of her lips turned up and she nodded, then sat down beside me.

And it was more than enough.

Psst! **If you scan the QR code below, you can read the first chapter of my next book—*Forget You Saw Her*. It's a standalone prequel to my bestseller *Ask for Andrea*!**

AUTHOR'S NOTE

Like many of my other novels, *Such Quiet Girls* was inspired by actual events: The Chowchilla kidnapping in 1976, where three men hijacked a school bus and abducted twenty-six children and their bus driver. The oldest was fourteen. The youngest was only five years old.

Similar to *Such Quiet Girls*, the kidnappers buried the children alive in a truck trailer they'd prepared with mattresses, food, and water. The struggle to escape was harrowing, and fourteen-year-old Michael Marshall worked together with bus driver Ed Ray. Their bravery and grit meant that all twenty-six children escaped and were reunited with their families. In Chowchilla, February 26th, Ed Ray's birthday, is still celebrated as Edward Ray Day.

If you want to learn more about the real story that inspired this book, I strongly recommend the podcast CNN documentary *Chowchilla*. I feel it's important to reiterate that *Such Quiet Girls* is fiction. The very real people who survived the nightmare of Chowchilla, many of whom are alive today, have lived their own stories.

I'd also like to briefly touch on my inclusion of Alzheimer's as part of this story. My grandpa Max (who is the namesake of my youngest son) died from Alzheimer's in 2004. He was a wonderful person, and I have so many memories of him. I didn't know much about this condition before his diagnosis, and so much of what I learned afterward contradicted many of the stereotypes I'd carried. I want to reiterate that, like many medical diagnoses, each situation and individual are unique. Sheena's dad is just one representation of an individual with Alzheimer's, and Sheena is just one representation of an individual whose loved one has Alzheimer's.

Thank you for taking the time to read this book. I am completely unbiased, but I'm pretty sure I have the best readers in the world.

—Noelle

ACKNOWLEDGMENTS

No book worth reading is ever written in isolation, and this one would not exist without the incredible people who have supported, challenged, and inspired me along the way.

First, my deepest gratitude to Deborah J Ledford for her impeccable editing, sharp eye, and unwavering support. Your dedication to making this story the best it could be is nothing short of extraordinary. Patti Geesey, thank you for your keen proofreading skills and your attention to detail—I am endlessly grateful.

To Steph Nelson, Caleb Stephens, and Faith Gardner, my brilliant thriller friends and sounding boards, I can't imagine this journey without you. Your insight, encouragement, and willingness to talk through the dark and twisted with me have been invaluable.

A heartfelt thanks to Jason Pinter at Simon Maverick—your belief in this story and in me as a writer has been a gift. And to Ezra and Ethan Ellenberg, my incredible agents, thank you for being fierce advocates and true believers in my work. Your guidance and support have made all the difference.

To the incredible Bookstagrammers, Booktokers, bloggers, and book lovers who have become not only champions of my novels but also my friends—thank you for your enthusiasm, your kindness, and for spreading the word about stories like this one.

A special thank you to Dan Blewitt, Lisa Regan, Brett Mitchell Kent, Jacob Robarts, Lisa Hunter, and Anna Gamel—early readers, advice givers, cheerleaders, and true friends. Your feedback and encouragement helped shape this story into something I'm proud of.

And finally, to Nate Ihli, my husband, my best friend, and my greatest supporter—none of this would be possible without you. Thank you for always being in my corner, for believing in me when I doubted myself, and for sharing this wild ride with me.

This book is as much yours as it is mine.

With gratitude,

—Noelle

ABOUT THE AUTHOR

Noelle lives in Idaho with her husband, two sons, and two cats. When she's not plotting her next thriller, she's scaring herself with true-crime documentaries or going for a trail ride in the foothills (with her trusty pepper spray).

Such Quiet Girls is Noelle's seventh thriller-suspense novel. You can find her on Instagram @noelleihliauthor

Made in the USA
Coppell, TX
25 May 2025

49793147R00204